A
Seeker
of
Everyday Magic

by

Alex Charlton

Grosvenor House
Publishing Limited

The right of Alex Charlton to be identified as the author of this
work has been asserted in accordance with Section 78
of the Copyright, Designs and Patents Act 1988

The book cover is copyright to Alex Charlton

This book is published by
Grosvenor House Publishing Ltd
Link House
140 The Broadway, Tolworth, Surrey, KT6 7HT.
www.grosvenorhousepublishing.co.uk

This book is a work of fiction. Any resemblance to
people or events, past or present, is purely coincidental.

A CIP record for this book
is available from the British Library

Paperback ISBN 978-1-83615-240-8

To Rosie,
Megan and Molly,
my weavers of
Everyday Magic

XXX

Earlier Books by Alex Charlton

The Carousel of Time

Saving Graces

The Child at the Edge of the World

Foreword

I don't usually write forewords. But this book calls for one.

At its heart, this story believes in everyday magic—the kind that's there if you know where to look. But it also steps into darker territory.

Josh MacDonald, like most of my characters, is someone I like. He's smart, compassionate, and brilliant at what he does. But he also has a deeply disturbing side. To portray him honestly, I've had to use language and situations I wouldn't normally choose. Some of it's uncomfortable. It's meant to be.

The world isn't good or bad—it's both. So are we. And in a time when the cruelty of the world is loud and constant, the question becomes: can faith, hope, or even something miraculous, still break through?

This story is set just before COVID—when X was still Twitter, and the world felt a little less fractured.

Chapter 1

Less than a metre of rough turf lay between Josh and oblivion. As is often the case with a mind driven to the edge of its capacity to cope, he registered a mix of the inconsequential and the agonizing: he noticed how the sea thrift had almost lost its colour in the strength of the salt-laden gales, simultaneously reliving the series of losses which had defined his life so far.

Each one of his aching senses responded to the power of the Atlantic Ocean as the waves crashed on the rocks, hundreds of feet below him. He felt the spray on his cold face; heard the tumult of the waves; tasted the salt; but above all it was the sight of the deep, navy-blue expanse lying at the foot of the cliff that almost fatally drew him in.

Josh's mind replayed at speed memories from long ago, drawing threads from the past into his present life, weaving an uneven, uncomfortable tapestry.

His mother – his wonderful, selfless mother. How long was it since she died? Twenty-eight years? No, thirty, he calculated swiftly. He was fifty-one; and on the eve of his twenty-first birthday – supposed to be the start of his adult life – he had suffered the body-blow of losing her. His mother had expressed a gentle wish – no more – that she would be able to celebrate this milestone birthday with him, and so he had planned to travel to his remote Hebridean home from Edinburgh where he was studying to be a doctor. Bag packed. Assignments up to date. Leave arranged mid-term with his tutor. He was doing some final revision of aortic aneurisms when the phone in his college room rang and he heard his elder brother's voice, hesitant and quiet – lacking its usual strident self-confidence.

'Josh?'

'Hi Hector. You'll be there tomorrow?'

'Josh, I don't know how to begin to say this …'

'Is it Dad? Has he been lost? Has his boat gone down?'

There was silence, a long silence, and then his brother managed to articulate the words that Josh had been dreading to hear for the last few years, as he had watched his mother become thinner and greyer and quieter.

'It's Mum. She … she died last night.'

Minutes passed as Josh tried to form the words that he needed to say. 'How? Why?'

'We don't know yet, Josh. I found her quiet and smiling when I took in her morning tea. She didn't look dead. She looked happy … happier than I've seen her for years. The post-mortem is tomorrow. I'm so sorry.'

Josh pressed the heels of his hands into his eyes – hard – recalling the slight figure of his mother. Mary MacDonald, or Molly as she was known on the island, had worked all her life to support her fisherman husband. Day after day he faced the risks of taking a small boat out onto the turbulent waters off the West Coast of Scotland, but her sons never felt cheated of their father's presence. It was Molly who helped with homework; Molly who played cricket with driftwood stumps and a threadbare tennis ball; Molly who reassured, cared and healed.

Josh had almost expected it when, two years after the loss of his mother, his father finally drank himself to death. Hector left the island of Fragrey soon after. Unaccountably adopting the life of what he termed an 'adventurer', he joined expeditions to South America to search for a quasi-mythical two-headed snake; and hiked across the Tibetan plateau in the face of Chinese restrictions and outright hostility. The sparse, but spotless, home that their mother had cherished became damp and rat-infested, and the once productive patch of garden was an overgrown wasteland. In the absence of his elder brother, the burden of how to maintain the croft fell on Josh's shoulders. Feeling a complete traitor to his mother's memory, he decided to ring Hector in order to decide a way forward. Despite the phone line between Llasa and Edinburgh making meaningful conversation almost impossible, the decision was made to sell. Needless to say, Josh agreed that the pittance that the dilapidated property raised went to fund Hector's further explorations.

Josh's gaze swept over the turbulent stretch of water between the cliff top where he stood and the enigmatic, so-called Holy Island. Farcical that such a man as his brother – someone who had lived on the edge of risk his entire adult life – should have lost it in a pedestrian sailing accident in view of the island where he had been born!

See-sawing between present and past, Josh's mind returned to the time just after he had qualified as a doctor. Feeling utterly alone and without any family identity, Josh found for the first time how complete absorption with work soothed his pain. But absorption soon became complete dedication, some said obsession. He was lauded and held up as an exemplar of the perfect young doctor, grounded in knowledge, active in research, thorough and intuitive in diagnosis. But inside there was an emptiness that nothing could fill.

The next chapter of Josh's life was equally bitter. After qualification, he sailed into the coveted post of junior registrar in a leading Edinburgh hospital. Here, in a subliminal search to re-find family and a home where he could feel rooted once again, he met and married Elspeth, another newly-qualified doctor. Elspeth was personally ambitious; whereas Josh was ambitious for the wellbeing of the people he served. He had already made the decision to establish his general practice on the island of his birth, which he loved with an atavistic passion and, as soon as his two-year contract had ended, he turned down an impassioned plea to continue on a permanent basis and returned to Fragrey to do exactly this. In contrast, Elspeth made it abundantly clear that her career was centred in Edinburgh. She was appointed to the post that Josh had just vacated and explained that, although she would visit the island, her home would remain in the city. Over the brief years of their marriage, she paid summary service to this promise, visiting Fragrey on just a handful of occasions, but before she finally left Josh, somehow, they managed to have two children – two beautiful girls. Their beloved image was with Josh always and, even in the face of the gale on the cliff-edge and the turbulence in his mind, Josh thought of their dark hair, their passionate features.

But these beautiful ones too had now flown: his elder daughter, Molly, was following her father's path and studying medicine at Edinburgh, expecting to qualify in the summer; and Emily, his younger daughter, was teaching in Cambodia. And now … Josh looked at the single gull fighting against the gale that was blowing straight from the States … he was alone with, as ever, his work as his only constant companion.

He glanced down once more at the Ocean moving like a restless animal. Just at that moment, there really didn't seem much point at all in going on – one short step and it would be over.

Hunching his shoulders, Josh thrust his hands deep into his jacket pockets and his fingers closed around a small envelope which he had folded in there at the end of morning surgery. Just then, he had not been able to take yet another burden onboard, and decided that he had to clear his head of the needs of the stream of patients who had entered, sat, spoken, smiled or wept, and left again.

Holding it hard against the battering wind, he gave a bitter smile at the envelope, pink and quite grubby with a picture of a unicorn on the reverse. On the front, written in coloured crayons, he read again:

TO MY BESTIE

He knew that inside was a drawing of the cancer ward where Carrie Logan, one of his youngest patients, had spent the last seven months. Without difficulty he recalled the wording, branded forever into his brain:

Thank you for making me better. Xxx

But he hadn't. Only yesterday he had sat with Jamie Curtis, the paediatric oncologist, hearing the news that the hospital had done everything they could for Carrie, and that everything just wasn't good enough. They had told her that she could go home and she had been overjoyed, thinking that, at last, her time at hospital was ended and she could once again take up the life that she loved – riding her bike, swimming, attending the Primary School, walking her small dog.

'If she has four months, she will be lucky, Josh,' the consultant had sighed, and Josh had gritted his teeth and reached out his square, capable hand to take the envelope that Carrie had left for him. 'I know you've done your best,' he nodded curtly. 'Do her parents know?'

'Not yet. We felt that they should be given a few weeks of joy together before the inevitable decline starts.'

Josh had severe reservations about this decision, but merely nodded and turned up the collar of his black quilted Barbour, trying to smile.

Returning to his evening surgery straight from the hospital, Josh had placed the envelope, reverse side outermost, next to his computer, the white unicorn with the doe eyes and rainbow mane reminding him that somewhere, somehow, magic might exist.

Atypically, Josh's eyes clouded with tears as he struggled to keep his footing against the Atlantic gale. Once again, he opened the card and re-read the carefully-written words:

Thank you for making me better Xxx

'You bloody coward,' he muttered to himself; and setting his shoulders, Josh MacDonald turned his back on the beguiling ocean and the bitter salt rain and walked at his usual brisk pace, past the *Sleeping Guardians* – the row of neolithic barrows which stood against the sky line – back to the stone fisherman's cottage on the quayside that he called home.

Chapter 2

'Dear Lord, I offer you this day,
All that I think, or do, or say.'

The simple child-like prayer floated unbidden into Alex's mind, as she opened her eyes to the faint blush of dawn. Swiftly she shut them again.

Alex Miller was one of those rare people who consistently wake feeling hopeful and full of anticipation about the day ahead. Whatever issues plagued her brain, the faint light of dawn always stirred her and brought a smile to her face. She had the ability to focus on the best, whilst acknowledging the worst, aspects of her life; and this Thursday morning was no exception.

Behind her closed eyelids, she reflected. Where had the last quarter of a century gone? Where were her precious girls now? She remembered their innocence, their flower-like beauty as children, reading haltingly from the small prayer books which had been given for their Christening by the vicar's wife. She flung back the duvet and opened the window onto the still peace of her garden, just wakening to the blackbird's heart-breaking song, the persistent robin, the exalted thrush.

From that tableau of innocence, her mind shifted to the last time she had seen her daughters: the younger bloated and flushed with alcohol; the elder manic, on permanent overdrive through her cocaine habit.

How could the world at that dawn moment appear so perfect, but contain such hurt? Alex shook her head. And today was – ah yes, Thursday – Yoga Day. Her life had gradually become defined by her exercise classes – the opportunities for escape, the positive points of her week. Her quick mind playing with this concept, she began rehearsing how her diary could be re-labelled in line with the routine that she had been forced to adopt to fill her days.

In comparison with the ecstasy of the birdsong; the still beauty of her garden; the pure, remembered words of the prayer; her beautiful children as they were twenty, twenty-five, years ago; what a shallow, lousy, unfulfilling life she now led.

⇥‖⇤

'How does your day look then, Dave?' Alex asked her husband. The mindless shovelling of food into her partner's mouth continued without a flicker or a pause and without the slightest indication that the hopeful gambit she had tried in order to open a conversation – any sort of conversation – had fallen once again without response into the silence of the kitchen. And so, as had increasingly been the case over the past ten years, Alex switched on Breakfast Television to fill the interminable silence.

Alex had sought every reason, made every excuse, for David Miller's lack of response and inertia. Perhaps he was ill? Depressed? Maybe he had early-onset dementia? But his 'condition', if that is the right word, was stable. He neither improved, nor did he worsen. His IT consultancy was flourishing and Alex wondered acidly if he actually talked to his clients or communicated via some sort of coding! Financially they were very comfortable; but in terms of their relationship, their marriage was the least comfortable thing in her life.

Alex was a passionate, impulsive and impetuous person and everyone had said, when she met her husband nearly thirty years earlier, what a good, steadying influence David Miller would be on her chaotic, colourful life as a trainee teacher. Steadying he had certainly been – but good? Alex knew how she had changed from the life-loving, laughing, brilliant student to what she had now become: quieter, much more cautious, following routine. And tellingly, she couldn't remember when she had last just thrown back her head and laughed at something just for the sheer joy of it. Alex had ceased to love her husband years earlier, but she still cared about him, as she cared for all living creatures.

'Do you fancy going out to *The Philosopher* for dinner or a drink tonight?' Alex suggested after another interminable breakfast.

'I have to prepare the Agenda for the Parish Council meeting on Monday.'

'Would you mind if I met with Sarah for a quick drink then, Dave?'

'No, of course not. You go and enjoy yourself, love.'

With gritted teeth, Alex swung her Yoga bag onto her shoulder and gave her husband the lightest brush on the cheek with her lips.

'See you at lunch – about one-thirty I would imagine. I'll stay for a coffee today I think.'

'As I say, just enjoy yourself, Alex.'

It would be easier, she reflected, if she could *hate* her husband – if he was rude, or violent, or did outrageously unacceptable things. She would then have a valid reason for constantly wishing to be out of the house, away from the wall of silence that imprisoned her.

∻)|(∻

'How's Dave?' asked her friend, Sarah, later on that evening. They were curled up on a sofa set at right angles to the log fire in the cosy, crowded village pub. Compared with the sterile silence of her home, the laughter, quiet conversation and the clinking of glasses was bliss!

Alex groaned and let her head flop back onto the deep pile of cushions, crossing her eyes comically. Sarah placed her glass of red wine down carefully on the pine table in front of them.

'Alex, how long can you go on like this? When is the last time you went out anywhere as a couple?'

'I really can't remember.' Alex closed her eyes wearily. 'Anniversary, I think.'

'Well, that's ironic in itself! And what did you talk about?'

'As I recall, whether we could ever move out of the village. Dave reckons we just can't afford to. He says it would cost the best part of thirty thousand – what with agents' fees and stamp duty and removals. He has said he thinks we have "one more move left in us". But where to, for God's sake – an Old Peoples' Home in about twenty years? Or in a private ambulance, when I drop dead through sheer boredom?'

'Alex, if you don't leave him, you will lose your personality – you will lose yourself! Dave battens on you, Alex. His negativity feeds off you. It's really hard to watch. I could jog along with someone like that because, quite frankly, I don't invest the time and passion in relationships that you do.'

'I'm forty-nine in two weeks' time, Sarah! How could I start all over again? I have no savings of my own – a car, yes, but that's all really. I haven't worked properly for years – only sporadic supply teaching. I can't leave!'

'Just hang on a minute. All the children who have had the benefit of being taught by you never forget the experience, and all the parents of those children have nothing but praise for you. You could get a full-time teaching job tomorrow! Young teachers don't seem able to stay the course any more. The stress of meeting targets, of poor mentoring by headteachers who themselves are under too intense a pressure, ill-behaved children. All these factors stack up …'

'You're really selling this to me, Sarah!' Alex laughed. 'Fancy another wine?'

Chapter 3

In the increasing dark of evening, it was a bitterly cold walk back down from the cliff and along the cobbled quayside to his cottage. The divorce settlement hadn't left Josh with much capital, but he had made the two-up two-down terraced fisherman's house neat and snug and a refuge from the wall of disappointment that sometimes seemed to meet him like a tangible enemy when he stepped outside. He hung up his coat, now damp from the drizzle that was sweeping across the landscape, and headed for the tiny galley kitchen at the back of the living space. He could just about make out the pots of herbs, and small table and chairs, which nestled between the kitchen window and the former outside privy. Hardly rolling acres – but his own!

With a swift succession of incisive gestures that was one of his defining physical characteristics, Josh glanced at his watch – five-thirty and just half an hour to go before surgery – switched on the kettle and opened the fridge door. He harangued himself mentally: a sandwich and coffee were all that he had time for because of his maudlin lingering on the cliff.

He took a quick sip of coffee before setting his mug and plate down on the small oak table in front of the window which overlooked the harbour, and drew the thick curtains against the weather. Then, biting into his sandwich, he opened his phone. Innumerable emails came flooding in – these he would look at after surgery – a scattering of Facebook likes and comments, and twenty-five Twitter notifications. These he would certainly save until later. He smiled without any real humour at some of the online names of the women who had messaged him: Violet Monkey, Sylken Sybarite, Pash & Presh. Narrowing his eyes, Josh imagined the sort of words and images that his phone held. There would be outright pornography and images of breasts and thighs taken with surprising artistry. He would see photos that teased, and those that titillated; and there would be outright offers of sex – real and virtual. What had started as a genuine desire to extend his friendship groups and exchange professional opinion had degenerated into a shallow exercise in self-gratification. How he regretted having ever been drawn into such a world. But, like most addiction, it was all too easy to slip into a habit which gave comfort – of a sort.

And so, in the few precious minutes before surgery started, this complex, intense man switched off his phone, pressing both his hands hard onto its screen as if he could subdue by sheer force of will the draw that it exerted over him. Momentarily, he closed his eyes, before opening a battered Penguin Classic.

Vos, o clarissima mundi lumina,
labentem caelo quae ducitis annum...
... You, O bright splendours of the world,
who lead on the rolling year through heaven...

Josh relished the swelling verse of Virgil's Georgics and his lips silently articulated the heavily-accented words. To Josh, History and ancient cultures as they are represented through classical literature, offered the perfect perspective on the shallow, quick-gain, quick-loss mentality of twenty-first century life.

⊰⊱||⊰⊱

'Good evening, Mrs MacKenzie, and what seems to be the problem this evening?'

The slight, stooped elderly lady smiled into Josh's dark grey eyes with her surprisingly bright blue ones.

'Well, I think it could be the rheumatics, doctor,' she answered softly.

'So, where does it hurt and how would you describe the pain?'

'Er, mainly in my arm, and er … sore.'

'Right arm or left?'

'Right.'

Josh's phone rang, shrilling into the sterile silence of his surgery.

'Excuse me, Mrs MacKenzie, this must be urgent or I wouldn't have been disturbed during a consultation.'

The old lady nodded without comment.

'MacDonald.' Josh frowned as he listened to the voice of Morag, his receptionist, secretary, assistant, and complete support. After a couple of minutes, he responded, 'Of course they must come. An evening surgery that lasts ten minutes longer is neither here nor there. But you must go home, Morag, of course you must.'

Josh replaced the receiver and gazed at it without expression for a couple of seconds before smiling rather stiffly and apologising once again for the interruption.

'Just please hold out your arm.'

Mrs McKenzie extended her left arm.

'I thought you said it was your right arm that hurt,' he said gently.

'Oh well, er …'

'How any people have you spoken to today, Jessie,' Josh asked softly.

She shook her head.

'Or this week?'

'No one – apart from the new girl in the grocery store.'

Josh turned his chair until he faced his patient. 'I don't think that rheumatism is the correct diagnosis, Jessie. Will you be in tomorrow?'

'Yes – I am in most days,' she smiled sadly.

'Well, I will schedule a home visit and we'll sort out some really effective treatment for your problem. You take yourself off home now. Keep warm. Perhaps watch some television? How would two-thirty in the afternoon suit you – just after lunch.'

'That would be perfect, doctor,' Jessie MacKenzie smiled broadly, getting slowly to her feet. 'I will make you a nice cup of tea – it'll be the high spot of my week!'

'Another miracle cure, Josh!' Morag Kitchener, his receptionist, grinned. 'Mrs MacKenzie looked about fifty years younger when she came out of your surgery. Was it just your overwhelming charm, or some new and revolutionary treatment that you suggested?'

'Neither Morag – just human company. She's lonely – it's not neuro-surgery. Can you schedule in half an hour for a home visit tomorrow for 2.30 – 3.00 pm.'

'Doctor! You're already out almost without a break between morning and evening surgery. This patient is *lonely,* not terminally ill! Do you have to visit?'

'Yes,' replied Josh curtly. 'I do. And talking about terminal illness, did Mr and Mrs Logan say why they wanted to see me?'

'They are increasingly worried about Carrie. She seems tired and listless.'

'Not surprising since we haven't been able to halt the cancer. Morag, can I have a coffee please? Strong and sweet.'

'Just like you,' his receptionist teased.

Josh threw back his head and laughed. 'Keep your maternal instincts under control – or exercise them on your grandchildren please!'

⊰�») | («⊱

Josh suspected that he had the beginnings of a migraine: the pressure had been steadily building behind his eyes and across his temples since his painful meeting with Mr and Mrs Logan.

'Carrie just seems so tired, doctor,' Mrs Logan sighed, stroking her toddler's hair absent-mindedly. 'She fell asleep in front of the fire after school. My mother is at home now with her, cooking her tea.' The Logans' younger daughter, Lisa, had the same white-blond hair and cornflower-blue eyes as her older sister. 'We thought she would be much more lively after all the treatment she has had.'

Josh cursed silently. Why hadn't the hospital been straight with these down-to-earth people? How could they have peddled false hope? How *could* they?

Without hesitation he leaned across his desk and clasped Mrs Logan's hands in his own.

'There is no easy way to say this, Jeannie …'

'Oh God, she's still got it, hasn't she? She's still got the cancer?'

'She has. And every week, every day, every second that you spend with your lovely daughter needs to count. She may not be with us for too much longer, but now, at this minute, you still have her to love. Hold on to this! She is such a fine wee girl – a complete credit to you and Neil …'

Josh ran out of any remotely comfortable words to give to these grieving parents, who were clinging physically together in the face of losing their eldest child. His emotions, complex as always, ran through wanting to ram the oncologist's head down a toilet, to giving his patient's family false hope. But, as always, honest to a fault – literally – he folded his hands on his desk and said, simply, 'I understand how you must feel. Not because I have lost a child, but because I have lost others whom I loved. I have been honest with you, because this is what you deserve. I am here – always – for you all. If you need me for advice, for anything at all, just ring and I will be there.'

He had sat for a full hour at his desk, sightless, gazing at nothing, before the dragging pain in his head had driven him home in the driving rain to his two-up, two-down sanctuary.

And now, omelette quickly made and eaten, red wine equally quickly downed, he opened his phone once again. Checking into his Twitter account – named after his mother's soubriquet, Molly, or *Star of the Sea*' – he looked at his notifications page. There were 35 likes for various trite tweets concerning coffee, weather and positivity; and then the Direct Messages, including 15 from his favourites. Violet Monkey had surpassed herself.

'Could you do this, Star?' she simpered, attaching a short video which demonstrated extreme and athletic sexual prowess.

He reflected that without doubt he *could* – but not to this botoxed, overblown beauty.

Josh fired off suitable stock photos, which he knew would satisfy the shallow intellects and animal lusts of his 'followers'. He then switched off his phone, poured himself a scotch, which as a doctor he knew was not in the least beneficial, turned off the lights, and went to bed, to listen to the driving rain and the gale gusting around and battering his small, secure place of safety.

Chapter 4

It may have been the moonlight which woke Alex, shining full on her face as she lay restless in the small bedroom which she had made her own some four years previously. Or it may have been the melancholy hooting of the owls on the old pear tree outside her open bedroom window. Whatever the reason, in an instant Alex was awake, with one single thought in her mind: she just could not go on living like this. Sarah had been completely right. Another twenty, thirty, forty years of utter boredom and loneliness, was more than she could contemplate. She would leave her husband. She had to. It had become an absolute imperative.

Alex walked quietly across the thick carpet and rested her hands on the window-seat, gazing out across her lovely garden, monochrome in the wash of the moonlight. Once her garden had been her joy, but that too had gradually become an empty exercise as she realised the futility of gardening – for whom or what exactly? Dave was infinitely more engrossed in his clients or the games on his iPad than by the roses which she used to cultivate with such joy. *Gertrude Jekyll, Olivia Rose Austin, Rambling Rector* ... the names were as evocative as their scents.

She didn't bother turning on the light, but opened her phone and scanned her social media accounts: happy family photos of her friends and their children on Instagram and a scattering of notifications on Twitter – mainly affirming, positive soundbites and a couple of new followers. *Grass is Always Greener* appeared to be a self-help group of quite elderly, vulnerable-looking people. Alex looked hard at her profile photo, taken during a rare afternoon of sunbathing in the garden. She expanded it. Did she look elderly and vulnerable? Is that why this group had approached her? She had thought she looked tanned and relaxed, smiling at her phone as if it was her best friend. Ah well … The other new follower was *Star of the Sea,* and once again Alex questioned why. This man had spare, fine features and spiky dark hair. He was looking directly at the camera, or phone, or whoever had photographed him, without the flicker of a smile and with an unreadable expression in his eyes. The self-help group Alex blocked; but she followed *Star of the Sea.*

⊰⊱

The next morning, after the trial that was breakfast, Alex slipped her laptop into the boot of her car alongside her gym bag. When she had told her husband that she had some shopping to do and that she would be out longer than usual, his imperturbable features didn't indicate whether or not he had registered what she had said. And so, her frustration mounting almost unbearably, she had compressed her lips in order to contain her anger and left him to his computer without further attempt at communication.

She sought to kill every ounce of that frustration through her exercise, stretching her muscles and working them hard to focus on her body, rather than on her emotions. Effortlessly she progressed through the Pilates class and other members of the group noted – with pleasure or with jealousy, depending upon their character – how the years that Alex Miller had devoted to her exercise showed in her slender, fine-muscled body.

None of Alex's close friends were at the gym that day, so she ordered her usual latte and switched on her laptop, going straight to the Times Educational Supplement website. There were an unusually large number of jobs advertised and Alex scanned the web pages with an ambivalent flutter in her belly, which could have been of excitement or fear.

Through most of the previous endless night she had thought through the logistics of leaving Dave: where she should go; how she would live; *where* she would live – in a flat, in a house? Everywhere she looked, there was uncertainty and myriad questions. Just how did one start to prepare to leave a husband of twenty-eight years? Alex took a sip of coffee and shook herself – almost like an animal trying to get rid of something that was uncomfortable or damaging to their health – and refocussed on her computer screen. Her mind was divided between escaping utterly from the South-East and finding somewhere remote to re-invent herself and re-establish her life; and staying within a twenty-mile radius of where she currently lived. If she were on her own, she reasoned that surely she would need her friends, her gym buddies, the shops where she bought her clothes, the hairdresser who had done her hair for the past twenty years – all the subtle support systems that a human being establishes through just being alive.

Eventually she short-listed three positions which evidenced the dichotomy in her mind. The first two jobs were local – one in an academy which stipulated '*utter dedication to the relentless pursuit of excellence in all aspects of the curriculum'*. The second, in stark contrast, stated baldly '*we are seeking a resilient class teacher with limitless personal stamina to take our Year 6 class. The children have a range of diverse and complex needs, but appropriate dedication will achieve its own reward.'*

But she had never seen anything like the third advertisement. It sat within a box at the top centre of which was a coat of arms, composed of a mermaid entwining her arms around the proudly-arching neck of a unicorn. It was headed *'Teacher-in-Charge'* and read: '*Are you a seeker of everyday magic? Can you inspire this wonder and love of learning in the children you teach? Take on the challenge of a lifetime and send for our information pack to the Chair of Governors, Fragrey Independent Endowed School, The Western Isles of Scotland.'*

She re-read her shortlist again and then, for the first time in years, she actually threw back her head and laughed out loud. She deleted the smug advert from the academy where high achievement was prized beyond nurture; and the sad petition from an establishment that was clearly struggling, and started to compose a letter to Fragrey Independent Endowed School.

Chapter 5

'What did you say this place was called?' Sarah asked Alex a week later.

'Fragrey.'

'I just can't get my tongue around it, Alex. Where is it and why on earth is the name so peculiar?'

Alex chuckled. 'I've researched diligently! Apparently, the name means *Beautiful Island* in Old Norse and it's about fifty nautical miles from the west coast of Scotland. The Vikings settled on the island and left their heritage in terms of place names and traditions. The population is just under a thousand, slightly less than some of the other Western Isles, but it has benefitted from being effectively 'ruled' by the same family for the last five centuries – the MacLeods. Lucilla MacLeod, mother of the existing chieftain, Jenna, left a considerable sum in the form of an endowment to found a primary school on the island for as long as there are children to attend it.'

'Why on earth would anyone want to live there?' Sarah asked in astonishment. 'What do they do for a living, for goodness' sake? And are there still sufficient children to make a school viable?'

'The islanders are mainly fishermen or subsistence farmers and yes, surprisingly, there are enough children. They go to the island school until they are eleven and then they travel by ferry to Benbecula to attend secondary school there. There are shops, a doctor and a dentist.'

'You sound like a guide book!'

The hefty pile of paperwork which lay on the table in front of Alex had arrived in the post that morning, after a mis-direction. Lifting it, and plonking it down again heavily, she said, 'It's all in here, Sarah! It's fascinating, like looking into a different world.'

'Won't you miss,' Sarah made a sweeping gesture 'all of this?'

Alex surveyed the cosy club bar with groups of women chatting comfortably over coffee and young people laughing in the swimming pool which was visible through floor-length windows and said, 'Of course I will, Sarah.' But her traitor thoughts couldn't wait to see the curving white sands and black rocks of Fragrey. She longed to climb its highest peak, Ravenstor, and to visit the cosy inn which nestled on the quayside of the major town, Heillstath, the 'place of healing', which 'sheltered six hundred souls'. Whoever had compiled the background information for the post of *Teacher-in-Charge of Fragrey Independent Endowed School* had a talent for writing, combined with a rather old-fashioned turn of phrase. Be that as it may, the mixture of evocative description and anachronistic vocabulary had drawn Alex in until she longed to breathe the scents of the island and to learn more of its culture and legend.

'I'm leaving you, David,' Alex said softly after breakfast the next morning. She had no idea how her husband would receive this news. Sadly, she realised that she had no idea how he would react to *any* news. She had anticipated him shouting, storming out of the house, possibly tears. But what she had not anticipated was the terse response she actually received. 'OK. When are you going?'

Alex flinched. 'Well, I have an interview next week … but I may not get the job …'

'If you want to leave, then go. There's no point in staying.'

'And if I don't get the job?'

'You're going to stay?'

'No … I don't know …'

'I can't give you what you want. You can't give me what I want. Best to go as soon as you can.' And with that bleak statement, David Miller turned to his default position and played the next game on his ipad.

Alex was shaking so much when she reached the shelter of her bedroom that she could hardly pick up her mobile. She breathed deeply, looking for Sarah's number, but then hesitated. What was the point? Strangely enough, however brutal her husband's response had been, he had been right. He had severed the final thread of duty that had kept her here, in his house, longing daily for release. Well now she had it.

She sat quietly on her bed, hands resting on her knees. Practicalities! She had nothing except her car, fairly new and probably worth around £8,000. If she sold that, she could fund rented accommodation of some sort. It was pointless delaying further, whatever the future held for her. So, almost in a daze, Alex packed her clothes, zipped up her laptop, glanced at the fading photographs of her daughters when children, and left the spotless, spacious house which for twenty years she had cleaned and decorated and tried so hard to fill with love.

Chapter 6

Carrie Logan's funeral took place in a thick snowstorm. The icy flakes swept mercilessly into the faces of the people standing around the open grave, which was becoming coated and filled with snow. Josh thought it was just as well that the weather was cloaking the almost palpable sadness: to an onlooker, the wet cheeks of the assembled inhabitants of Heillstath could be due either to the melting snowflakes or to their falling tears. As the tiny white coffin was lowered into the whitening space in the ground, Carrie's mother groaned, cuddled her grizzling toddler to her, and leant closer to her husband. Looking at Carrie's family, his patients, Josh felt the familiar pain of realising that whatever he did, however much he studied and worked, there was one thing that he could never halt – and that was death itself. Carrie's dog, still a puppy, bought for her to care for when she thought she was 'better' and had come home, lay in the snow and edged her way on her belly to the grave edge. To Josh, it was as though she was trying to maintain some sort of closeness to her young owner. This was just too much and turning up his collar, Josh strode quickly away, back to his surgery, which he had closed so that he could attend the funeral.

He had reflected that, since most of the population of Heillstath would be at the Kirk, there was little point in lingering in his consulting room when all he wanted to do was to make his final goodbye to his 'Bestie'.

He knew that everyone would be at *The Inn* – the unimaginatively-named establishment on the harbour-side – for Carrie's wake, and so he decided to catch up with his admin. Josh MacDonald hated the mindless form-filling and endless report-making. He was an intensely active man, loving nothing more than doing his rounds, or holding a busy surgery, performing minor operations or playing football on the island team. Morag, his secretary, fielded the routine approaches from pharmaceutical companies trying to persuade him to try, and buy, new 'wonder' drugs; and entered regional meetings meticulously in his diary, managing his time with care and understanding. But the research aspects of his career, the complex professional decisions that he had to make for the benefit of his patients and his practice, he alone could deal with, and they took up more time than he actually had at his disposal.

Josh opened his Inbox and watched the emails filtering in, inexorably. He never used to feel like this in the face of his work, so why suddenly did everything seem to be a burden? Perhaps he needed a holiday? Perhaps this latest death – of a young girl whose life should have stretched joyfully in front of her – had finally shown him how futile his own efforts were. He breathed deeply, set his shoulders, and scanned the emails, pausing at one which had been sent from the Director of his Regional Health Board. It was headed *Exchange Opportunity with Clinical Practitioner in New York City.* There was a single sentence above the forwarded email: *I strongly recommend that you should seriously consider this Josh. It's for just three months and would refresh your practice.*

Josh was used to reading between lines and to decoding meanings which lay beneath words. This was no suggestion from his Director – it was an instruction. Swallowing down his resentment that the work to which he devoted all his energies should need 'refreshing', he sent off a reply: '*Great idea. Will you take this further, or should I contact direct? Regards MacDonald.*'

⊰∥⊱

Alex had seen the card on the gym noticeboard the same day she had moved into Sarah's spare room. Marge, one of the women who attended her Yoga class, had posted:

Vintage VW Campervan for Sale
Fully renovated and refitted.
Orange
£4000

Well, Alex reflected, she had no home; she couldn't stay at her friend's house indefinitely; she had already risked everything and won – or lost, depending upon one's viewpoint. Why shouldn't she take this next, risky, step and buy something that would provide both transport and a roof over her head?

'Are you feeling OK, Alex?' Sarah asked seriously, toying with her pasta.

'Sorry, what do you mean?' Alex frowned.

'Well, are you menopausal?'

'What? What are you talking about?'

'Alex, within the last week you have left your husband, secured an interview for a teaching post on an island with an unpronounceable name which is thirteen hours by ferry from Oban, and are now thinking of selling your lovely car to buy an ancient Campervan? I think many people would question just one of those decisions, but taken all together, your actions seem just a tad eccentric!'

Alex laughed. 'Do you know, I haven't felt more sane, or more free, for longer than I can remember. I have hardly thought of Dave since I left. How can someone who never communicates be missed? He lives inside his own little hermetically-sealed bubble which excludes everyone else! I can't wait to see the island where history lies behind place names and people still believe in 'everyday magic'. Have *you* ever come across a coat-of-arms which combines a mermaid and a unicorn?'

'That's exactly what I mean ...'

⇒)||(⇐

'This is perfect!' Alex exclaimed, stroking the glowing orange paint.

'We really have loved this old girl,' Marge smiled. 'But with looking after the grandchildren, we just don't have the opportunity to get away as much as we used to. John has renovated her – down to burnishing the last screw! He removed all the fitted cupboards and polished and re-set the doors and panels. We have had new carpet fitted and even found a miniature fridge which sits perfectly in the space next to the sink. The mattress is new and the front seats have been recovered in orange leather and hand-sewn.'

'Are you sure £4000 is enough?' Alex asked, honest to a fault as always.

'Bless you, yes! Gladys is getting on! She was first registered in 1970!'

'Careful, Marge – so was I!'

'Ah, it was meant to be then, Alex,' Marge chuckled.

'Can I pick up, er, Gladys, tomorrow, Marge? I will finalise the deal on my car and come straight round.'

'We'll deliver her to – you're at Sarah's aren't you?' Alex nodded.

'To Sarah's tomorrow. Would 3 o'clock be OK?'

'Perfect,' smiled Alex.

⊰║⊱

Later that evening, Alex, sleep a million miles away, restlessly went into her Twitter account.

One woman with significant past mental health challenges was seeking reassurance concerning an interview for a new job. She had not worked for two years, but Alex was pleased to see that she had taken the media name *Newbeginnings* and hoped that this may be an indicator that she would succeed. *Newbeginnings* had posted photos of her outfit – even a separate one of the shoes that she had bought especially for the occasion. Alex's compassion went into overdrive.

You look lovely! She tweeted. *And I have shoe envy!!!*

Thanks, Alex! X came the reply, then seconds later, *So do I, but I don't think they would fit me!* from Star of the Sea.

Alex tweeted three laughing faces.

Then came another tweet from Star of the Sea, *Be positive! Remember how far you have come – by yourself, through your own efforts. Don't give up! Always believe!*

Always, echoed Alex.

Always, re-echoed Star of the Sea.

Alex re-read the brief exchange. She realised that she was smiling, looking once again at the small, circular profile image of the man who found time to reassure people at the end of their resources. She clicked on it, to see in full the photo of the man with the evocative Twitter name and hundreds of followers, who cared enough to reaffirm and reassure. Then, thoughtfully, Alex stroked the finely-drawn features with her thumb and forefinger, bringing his face nearer, into sharper focus, trying to interpret his closed, enigmatic expression.

Chapter 7

Alex had not realised that Gladys would be quite so physically demanding to drive. She recalled arcane conversations between her father and his friends about their early experiences with cars, double-declutching being a phrase that stayed in her mind. She didn't know whether or not she was double-declutching, but her ankles and calf muscles ached, as did her arms, due to the heavy pedals and lack of power-assisted steering.

She had left a very concerned Sarah early that morning, having sorted her clothes to a minimum and given the rest to a local charity shop. Trying to ignore her friend's worried expression, Alex waved out of the slightly stiff sliding-window of the campervan, feeling an immense sense of freedom. She sailed off optimistically along the M11, wondering just how many people had held the large, old-fashioned steering wheel and depressed the heavy steel pedals. But all too soon she realised just how limiting her transport actually was. 50 mph was the maximum speed that she could coax out of the ancient vehicle and, even in the slow lane, this was *too* slow. The distant era of the 1970's, which started soon after the *Summer of Love* and ended with the *Winter of Discontent,* was a slower time, when people fought for their ideals but had infinitely more compassion. But now, nearly fifty years later, SUV's roared past her, often sounding their horns unnecessarily – a measure of the anger and stress which bubbled too near the surface of society in 2018.

Alex had allowed a full week to travel the length of the United Kingdom and get herself to Fragrey several days in advance of her interview, in order to give herself time to become familiar with the island and its people. She had optimistically hoped to clear the M11 and A14, getting onto the A1 by the end of her first day's driving, but at ten o'clock at night she was only approaching Cambridge. She had run out of devices to keep herself awake, singing loudly being the most recent, as radios or anything more sophisticated had no place in the stark 1970's engineering of her vehicle. Alex realised that she would just have to stop and, with a frisson of excitement that she was actually driving her own home, pulled off the motorway and headed a couple of miles towards Grantchester. Eventually she found the sort of place she was looking for – a stretch of Forestry Commission land with ample parking at its entrance.

Alex swung the ancient vehicle onto the pot-holed parking area and sighed with relief as she switched off the noisy engine. She could still feel the vibrations in her body as she got down from the driver's seat and stretched herself before heading at speed towards the nearest undergrowth – there was no room for the luxury of shower or toilet in her tightly packed campervan.

As quickly as she could – it was distinctly creepy in the dead-dark of the woods – she ran back to Gladys and locked the door against the night, drawing the curtains and blinds across the rectangles of darkness.

She boiled her kettle for washing, then made tea and sat cross-legged on the cushioned bench that would soon become her bed, munching sandwiches and willing her body to relax. If she closed her eyes, she still saw the rear lights of the stream of vehicles in front of her, and those which passed her. She simply had to do something to switch her mind into non-driving mode, and so, as was becoming increasingly the case, she went into Twitter. She noticed that she had a handful of new followers and a new conversation had started, which initially she found quite offensive.

Women were made to please men, one Neanderthal had tweeted.

Depends upon the man ... Came one coy female reply, followed by a scattering of other, similar sexually-charged tweets.

Then, cutting across the innuendo, came the measured comment, *A woman should be affirmed and encouraged by her man.* Star of the Sea was online.

To which Alex replied, *And a man should be supported and completed by his woman.*

Always.

Chapter 8

Alex's dreams were vivid. Her subconscious mind had put aside the monotonous motorway and the aggressive driving. She dreamt that she stood on a high cliff with a wild and foaming sea hundreds of feet below her. At first she was just looking to the horizon, blurred and misted by the driving rain and the sea spray. But then, as is the manner of dreams, she turned and saw that she stood next to a man: dark, intense and silent. He too was gazing out to sea with a frown marring the spare planes of his face. He took a further step towards the cliff edge and Alex dreamed that she stretched out her hands and held him by the arm until he turned towards her. She smelled the sharp scent of him, felt the taut muscles beneath the quilted jacket, traced the unshaven abrasiveness of his face with her fingertips and, finally, met his narrowed, unfathomable glance with her own troubled one. She was breathing deeply, feeling the sort of desire that the restrained emotion of her husband had never roused in her.

The sea was becoming louder, each wave crashing like a blow on the rocks below her feet, and then, gradually, she realised that the sound was that of someone banging on the door of her snug home. She opened the passenger window a mere two inches.

'Sorry, miss, didn't you read the notice? You can't park here overnight!'

Her vivid dream shattered into shards, Alex stood, trying to make sense of where she was and what exactly was happening.

'Erm … who are you?' she managed to croak.

'I'm the forest ranger hereabouts, miss. And, as I said, didn't you see the notice about not parking here overnight? If we don't enforce this, we will be invaded by travellers and then what would that do to our respectable visitors?'

Sleepily, Alex reflected that it wouldn't do anything, but all she said was, 'Sorry, I was so tired. I will get dressed and move on immediately.'

'Right you are, miss, and thank you for your co-operation.'

Alex waited until she heard the Ranger's truck move then, double-checking from behind the curtain, she leapt out of Gladys and headed for the woods.

⊰╫⊱

The only way to describe how Josh felt was 'jaded'. His Director had rubber-stamped with alacrity his request to swop roles with a medical practitioner from New York City – something that worried Josh. As Lead for General Practice in the Western Isles, did he constantly have to prove himself? Constantly have to suggest improvements and rationalisations to medical care in the Outer Hebrides? Not only was he responsible for the standards of medical care in his own practice, but somehow he had to find the energy to quality-assure that of his colleagues.

Morag had booked his flights, unbelievably only three days distant. He would catch the local ferry to Benbecula, fly to Edinburgh, then transfer to a trans-Atlantic flight to the States. Josh looked at the list of names for his morning surgery and ran his hands through his short black hair. He knew his patients well and anticipated what each would be seeking from him – medical diagnosis, emotional reassurance, a kind word and a smile – such a range of complex human needs.

Morag glanced through the door of Josh's surgery, left slightly ajar, and saw the man she respected and constantly worried about sitting motionless, resting his forehead on his hands. She sighed and shook her head, thinking how the pressures of Josh's work were, literally, killing him. Then she coughed softly to let him know that she was there, causing Josh to swiftly raise his head and pretend to look intently at his computer screen.

'Coffee?'

'Black as night…'

'…and as sweet as you.'

'Behave Morag! I don't feel in the slightest bit sweet at the moment! And please show in Mr and Mrs Logan.'

Squaring his shoulders and lifting his chin, Josh stood to greet the recently-bereaved parents with a mask of positivity, 'How good to see you both! How are you? Please do sit down.'

'Hello Doctor MacDonald. How are we? Well, to be honest, each day is a challenge, but we have little Lisa and she is a great comfort to my wife.'

'And what can I do for you today, Mr Logan?'

'Well, it's like this, doctor, we wonder whether the cancer that took Carrie is in any way genetic? Will her little sister be in danger of the disease in years to come? If we had another little one, what would be the situation there? Sorry for so many questions …'

'Never apologise for asking a question, Mr Logan. Carrie's cancer is not hereditary, be assured on that. We are all open to the range of terrible diseases that attack humankind, but the risk of Lisa – or any future children – getting cancer is no greater because of Carrie.'

'Thank you, doctor. We appreciate your honesty.'

Josh stood up and extended his right hand.

'It's the only way I know, Neil.'

'Aye, and we are the better for it.'

Mrs MacKenzie was Josh's next patient.

'And how are those rheumatics of yours, Mrs MacKenzie?' Josh smiled.

'Ah, fine now thank you, doctor. The meetings at the Kirk and the Community Centre seem to have helped them more than I would have expected.'

'So how can I help you this evening, Mrs MacKenzie?'

'Well, it's how I can help you, doctor, at least I hope so! I have a little something for your tea.' The old lady unveiled the object swathed in a tea towel which lay in the depths of her wicker basket. 'Steak and kidney pudding!' she announced proudly.

'Ah that is a fine pudding,' smiled Josh, savouring the fragrance which rose from the tied muslin cloth, 'and I thank you for it.' Then, with one of the spontaneous, warm gestures that made his patients love him, Josh MacDonald smiled and laid his hand lightly on the bird-like arm of the old lady sitting opposite to him. 'And is there anything else at all that I can do for you?'

Mrs MacKenzie looked him straight in the eye and said, 'You just being here. You caring for us as you do – that is more than enough for any of us.'

⊰)||(⊱

The pudding was superb, but it was those simple words that echoed and re-echoed in Josh's head that evening: 'You just being here. You caring for us as you do – that is more than enough for any one of us.'

He was exhausted beyond tired and flipped through sports channels, nodding in and out of sleep. The abrupt sound of his Twitter feed cut across his semi-consciousness.

Never take a selfie with your campervan!

Alex Miller's photograph, showing tangled hair blowing across her tanned and freckled face, leaning against the radiator of an ancient orange VW, shone into the comparative darkness of his lounge. She was so intensely alive! Her clear blue eyes danced with humour at the less-than-perfect shot she had just taken. He enlarged her photo and saw the wide, sensuous mouth, the lines of experience which surrounded her eyes, and the honesty of her expression. What a beautiful woman – a real, naturally-beautiful woman! Compared with the photo-shopped images that flooded into his account daily, she was the archetypal breath of fresh air.

When the selfie is like this – take one daily! Josh tweeted, stroking lightly his screen and breathing more deeply as his body responded to the electronic image in front of him.

Chapter 9

The airbus A380 thundered along the runway and, as always, Josh reached the point where he was uncertain as to whether the massive plane would ever become airborne. He realised with his usual acute clinical detachment that, in terms of his own future, quite honestly, he didn't care whether it did or not.

Possibly to sweeten the almost brutal swiftness with which the Director of Regional Health Services was despatching him to the other side of the Atlantic, Josh was travelling Business Class, for which he was grateful, despite perceiving the guilt that had motivated this act of apparent generosity. He glanced along the plane to where the massed economy class passengers sat crammed too closely together in narrow seats, noting with distaste how in the first row a huge American was overflowing left and right into his fellow passengers' space and was already cramming food into his mouth. Almost as if such raw humanity was too much for the sensibilities of her business-class passengers, the attractive member of the cabin crew whisked the stiff curtain across the aisle, deftly swooping to pick up a tray of prosecco.

'Sir?' She treated Josh to the dazzling white smile that only an expensive American dental plan could produce. In return he gave her a look that, in one, thanked, undressed and challenged her. She blushed, raised her head slightly, gave a second, uncertain smile and moved on. Josh hated himself like this – adopting the persona that he had cultivated for social media: hard, sexually-accomplished and heartless. Gazing mirthlessly into the depths of the glass, he reflected upon how he took refuge in this brutal précis of a man in order to be able to deal with his emotional vulnerabilities, the crushing hurt when one of his patients was terminally ill, the ceaseless battering that life seemed intent upon giving him.

Josh had saved Alex's selfie and looked again at the image that had haunted his dreams the previous night. There was no clue as to where Alex lived, her status, or her profession – nothing. It was so unlikely that their paths would ever cross and Josh wondered just how far he could take their virtual relationship. Could he send her one of his stock pornographic images? How would she react? Would she respond by sending him a similarly sexually explicit photograph?

Impatiently, Josh drained his glass and raised an eyebrow at the woman who was attentively watching her small privileged flock.

'A refill sir?'

'That would be perfect. Thank you.' This time he did smile and could gauge by her slightly open lips and deepened breathing the effect that he was having on her. When she poured him another drink with a slightly shaking hand, he lightly steadied her wrist. The next time she circulated – this time with menus for the evening meal – he saw that she had pencilled her mobile number next to the desert.

⊰⊱

Cambridge to Leeds: 177 hard-won miles. Although Gladys was tough to drive, Alex was relieved to find that she was reliable – covering the distance slowly, but dependably – not overheating, or leaking oil, or giving any cause for concern apart from the fact that, of the week she had given herself to reach Fragrey, only five days now remained.

Although not as evocative or atmospheric as her previous night's stop, Alex pulled into a Holiday Inn, one of a collection of buildings offering cheap everything – accommodation, food, alcohol, lurid toys. She had to have a shower and a hot meal, however crude the ingredients.

Shower taken, surprisingly good steak eaten, Alex stretched full-length on the clean, utilitarian bed and closed her eyes. Her mind was racing and, as on the previous night, was full of the images of moving vehicles, motorway signs and the sweep of her windscreen wipers, as that day's driving had been wet. She shook her head, sat up, crossed her legs and messaged Sarah.

This drive is interminable! Gladys is a beast to drive, but a reliable beast! Hope you are not missing your gym buddy too much ...

She hadn't responded to Josh's tweet the previous night, but saw that he had posted a photo of himself standing thoughtfully at Ground Zero in front of the ambivalent monument that has been likened both to a dove of peace and an aircraft crash-landing. His face was pale and Alex sensed, as clearly as if there had been a caption, the empathy of the man with the tragedy that had been enacted in that place nearly twenty years earlier.

Terrible, but strangely beautiful, the way that humankind has somehow triumphed in that place of brutality and tragedy, she tweeted.

Almost instantly, as if the three thousand odd miles didn't exist, she read Star of the Sea's response, *Every man's death diminishes me, For I am involved in mankind.*

The words were so heavy, so bleak, that Alex just stared at them, then back at the image of the man who had quoted them. She bit her lip. Should she apologise? Should she try to lighten the tone of the exchange? She was completely unable to decide what to do, so pragmatically she switched off her phone, turned out the light and slept.

⇥❧⇤

'So, what do you do, Josh?'

'Seduce lovely women like you.'

Aimée, the attentive cabin attendant, coloured slightly and traced the rim of her cocktail glass with a pale pink fingernail.

'Sorry, I shouldn't tease you like that. I'm a doctor.'

'Seriously?'

'Yes. Totally serious now.' Josh pulled a wry face and sipped his scotch. 'Don't say you are going to seek my professional opinion on your ongoing medical concerns?'

Aimée blushed more deeply this time and instantly Josh's professional instinct picked up that his attractive companion did, actually, have a medical issue of some sort.

'Sorry again. This time profoundly. I think I hit a raw nerve, Aimée, didn't I?'

'There is something, Josh. But I can't explain it here. Perhaps later. Perhaps not.'

'Another drink?'

'That would be wonderful – thank you. I'm here for three days, so there is time for – well – downtime!'

Mid-evening moved to late evening, then the early hours of the day on which Josh was scheduled to take up his new role. Jet-lag had scrambled his biorhythms so, after his third scotch of the evening, Josh leant over the glass table and touched Aimée's hand lightly.

'As they say, your place or mine?'

She dipped her eyes for a few seconds and then lifted her gaze to his. 'Since mine is a hostel, maybe yours? And maybe we could talk some more?'

In keeping with the luxury of his Atlantic flight, Josh's hotel was the best that he had ever experienced.

'What seems to be the problem?' he smiled. 'Always the most comforting opening gambit I have found.

'Josh … you will find me disappointing.'

'Sorry?'

'I've … I've never had orgasm. I don't know how! My girl friends describe it as ecstasy, as losing a sense of one's own being. I've just never experienced this sort of thing. Is there a medical reason? Am I lacking in something – a hormone or … or …'

'You've never had the right man, Aimée,' Josh said softly.

In the next three hours, Aimée Jonson was led down pathways that she had never suspected, and was lulled and roused and lulled again until she had entirely lost herself to the sexual experience and skills of the man who explored her, again and again.

An hour before he was expected at the hospital, Josh got up, and showered long and vigorously.

'Thank you, Aimée.' He kissed her forehead.

'What? You can't go now?'

'I'm starting a new job in precisely fifty-nine minutes. I *have* to go.' Josh steeled himself for what he knew was coming next.

'How could you, Josh! How could you lead me on like that and then just go!'

Thoughtfully looking at the aroused, naked woman in his bed, Josh simply said, 'Let's just call it therapy, shall we?'

Fifty-eight minutes later he stood opposite his clinical director, his face still stinging from the hard slap he had received from Aimée Jonson.

Chapter 10

The following night, after an interminable drive, Alex was almost catatonic. She had been determined to cross the Scottish border as the interview time-clock was ticking in her brain – four days to go. She pulled into a camp site, switched off the engine, and lay full-length on the floor of her vehicle for a full ten minutes. Her back ached, her shoulders ached and so did her eyes. As she lay immobile, Alex vowed that, after her epic odyssey north, Gladys would be for short trips only. She also decided that if she didn't do well in the interview, she would take some time to just relish being free and explore the Highlands in small stages before deciding what on earth she should do next. Eventually she creaked to her feet, lit the stove and boiled the kettle for tea.

She had bought cooked chicken, salad and a bottle of wine for her dinner and a couple of hours later she sat at her table, her vehicle being rocked by the rising wind. Mellow, to say the least, Alex laughed out loud, looking around her at her meagre possessions and realising that it had been decades since she had been so completely happy – mistress of all she could see, but nothing more. Perhaps ninety-five out of a hundred people would have worried about this, but after the barren years of her marriage, Alex rejoiced that finally she was in charge of her own destiny.

Her meal and the washing up of one plate, knife and fork, one glass and a single tea cup finished, Alex went into Twitter. During the day she had considered how best to respond to Star of the Sea's bleak words and decided to message him direct.

I feel that I upset you by what I said last night. Clearly you were deeply moved by what you saw at Ground Zero. I am so sorry for my clumsy words.

On her Home screen, scrolling through innuendos, photos of the countryside and cliquey chit-chat, Alex was conscious that Star of the Sea was not in his immediate response mode. Eventually, she turned off her phone, washed summarily and went to sleep.

⊰⊱

'And so, Joshua, what research project have you decided to undertake at our hospital over the next three months?'

Apparently unmoved by the question for which he had been totally unprepared, Josh recoiled inwardly – what the??? – but replied, apparently without a flicker, 'the impact of loneliness on the health of the population – cross-cutting, and collecting data from individuals and focus groups from mid-teen to advanced age.'

Brad Jackson nodded. 'Great. I approve. So much impact on physical health from apparently non-clinical factors. We are moving further and further into uncovering the links between psychological and physiological health. My mom always used to quote "Healthy mind in healthy body, Bradley" and as always, Mom was right. Let me have the written proposal for your research by Thursday, Joshua. Good to have you on board.'

And that was that. Apart from having being shown his glass-walled office, and being introduced to Chloe, the Executive Assistant who serviced the clinical research staff, Josh had been left entirely to his own devices. He sat at his spotless glass desk, gazing into the blank eye of a blue Apple Mac, and reflected upon just how weird a position he found himself in. Back in Fragrey he seldom had a minute to himself. If he were not involved in seeing his patients in surgery, he was visiting old and frail people who couldn't get out of their homes to see him, dropping in to community centres to mention the name of someone who needed support, or catching ferries to work with, or quality-assure, the scattering of general practices across the Western Isles. Now he had time to sit, time to stare at a blank screen, time to return to an academic proposal for research. Three months was a life sentence.

⊰⊱⊰⊱

Ach, there is so much negativity in the world, Alex. And Ground Zero was the end of an era and the start of a worse one. You didn't upset me, but bless you for saying that. Have a fabulous day, Alex. Like my new office?

She swirled the coffee bag around in her mug, watching the message appear, swiftly followed by a photo of a sterile glass space. It was cold and soulless.

Tbh I don't like it ... can I call you Star? I really like your Twitter name

There was a pause of several minutes and then the closed envelope of a Private Message showed up on her account. She clicked on it, but there was still a wait until she realised that Star of the Sea had sent her a video. She saw the view from the new office and, as Josh had panned from left to right, he had incorporated a voice message.

I don't like it either, Alex. Too sterile for my taste. I like individuality and a bit of human clutter! And of course you can call me Star – I've been called plenty worse ... You are using your real name, aren't you?

Josh's voice was neither dark nor light and was full of expression. Alex looked at her hands, which were shaking slightly, and decided to reply in kind, speaking across a video of her current outlook.

Not quite so exotic as your view, Star! But this is mine – Gladys, the ancient VW campervan – at once my home and my transport!

Her short video took in the scattered toast crumbs across the red-spotted table cloth, her mug with its inscription *I'd rather be in the Caribbean,* her tumbled bedclothes, and finally came to the mirror which reflected her image, complete with penguin-patterned pyjamas.

Josh MacDonald listened to the soft, clear voice and smiled at the images of comfortable chaos which surrounded Alex. When the video came to rest on the mirror, so did he, expanding his screen once again, trying to capture more intimate details of the woman who had started to fascinate him. Clearly educated, attractive, spontaneous and honest, why would such a person be living in a campervan? She looked relaxed and natural – happy with herself, just being herself – and Josh felt his desire for her rising.

Have you just got out of bed, Alex?
Yes – exhausted from a too-long drive yesterday.
If I was with you and not in this goldfish bowl of an office, we would be back in that inviting, rumpled bed, Alex.

Reading the unambiguous words, Alex immediately switched off her phone, her heart beating more quickly. How on earth was she supposed to respond to this? During her marriage to Dave, she had ceased to feel remotely feminine, or attractive. She fulfilled her part of her marriage automatically and without any pleasure. Pressing her thumb on her phone to open it once more, she looked more closely at Star of the Sea's image. He was undeniably attractive, every feature finely-drawn. His profile picture showed him wearing sunglasses and so it was impossible to see the colour of his eyes, but every other aspect that she could see roused her interest and her long-forgotten sexual desire. And this man would like to go to bed with her?

Never had Alex felt so out of touch with the current world and its protocols. Should she flirt back? Ignore the message? Say she didn't intend to accept sexual innuendos?

She stood up quickly and put the kettle back on the stove for more coffee. Then, blushing as she remembered the words of the message she had just received, she shook her duvet and stowed it away under the seat, sliding the wooden panels firmly shut on her bedlinen. Energetically, she washed, brushed her teeth and hair and dressed, whisked back the curtains and sat to drink her coffee before embarking on the next stage of her seemingly interminable journey. Her phone sounded.

I'm sorry if I offended you. But you are a very desirable woman.

I'm not sure how to respond. You hear so much about false identities on social media. How do I know you are who you say you are?

Refreshing honesty! I'll send you a photo of me now, here, in this hospital.

I don't even know the colour of your eyes – I can't see them behind your sunglasses…

You can see them now…

Josh's image flashed onto her phone, standing in his clinical whites in front of the glass wall which separated him from the eight and a half million people who lived and worked, loved and died in the pulsating, complex city which surrounded him. He was frowning slightly, but his compressed lips were lifted in a slight smile which reached the deep grey-blue of his eyes.

You're lovely, Star…

But he was gone.

Chapter 11

Alex reached Oban three days before her interview. She sat in the bar on the CalMac Ferry drinking tea and thinking that as soon as she reached Fragrey, she would spend at least one day sleeping! The last three days' driving had been hard, but she smiled quietly at her achievement. She had done it! The small victories of surviving brutal Pilates, challenging Yoga and remembering the 88 form in Tai chi were as nothing compared with the quiet satisfaction of having coaxed, cajoled and loved Gladys along motorways; up hills, when she had longed for a lower gear; and through rainstorms. But Gladys was as stalwart as her owner and both had supported each other in the long trek north. Alex almost laughed as she felt an impulse to check on the car deck to see that her vehicle was all right.

Her Twitter feed showed a private message.

How's Gladys?

You must be psychic! I was just debating whether or not to check on her wellbeing! Better than I am: we're the same age, but I haven't had my engine replaced!

How's the goldfish bowl?

Fishy! I'm not quite sure what they want of me here – too much spare time!

To think of me?

To think of you.

Oh no! She had tried levity, but it had been brought back to seriousness. She changed tack.

So how does your day look, Star?

Pretty boring tbh. I love action, not words – that's why I became a doctor! Got a meeting with my clinical director to review my research proposal in – erm – exactly ninety seconds. Must go xx

Looking at the message, Alex blushed and instantly criticised herself for behaving like a teenager. For God's sake, she was a forty-eight-year-old woman with two children – alienated though they may be. But the two kisses and the frankness and everyday nature of the message warmed her heart.

⇴⇇

'Joshua, this is *good* ...' drawled Brad Jackson.

Josh said nothing, but just sat with his ankles crossed wishing he was back in his impossibly busy surgery on the island he loved.

'To be truthful, I was worried when Clive approached me re this secondment.'

Josh raised an eyebrow.

'He didn't say anything specific, but gave me to understand that he thought you were in the process of burnout. But how you present yourself, and this ...'

Brad gestured to the five-page proposal 'paint a very different picture. Can I be honest with you, Joshua?'

'Of course. Personally, I can't be anything else,' Josh replied tersely.

'I think you have been sold for thirty pieces of silver.'

'Sorry?'

'I think Clive wants rid of you.' The big man walked slowly to his window and looked out at the neat enclosed gardens at the centre of the hospital – a green oasis. Without turning around to look at Josh, he continued, 'Did you know that Clive Saunders visited us last year?'

'No, I did not.'

'Well he spent four months observing our practice over here. And he was very hands-on – some said too hands-on.'

'I'd appreciate clarification, Brad,' Josh exclaimed impatiently.

'Clive became particularly friendly with a final-year medical student called Maitland Morgan. He mentored her, supported her …'

'Do you mean they had an affair? I can't be doing with hints and half-truths, Brad. Please do me the courtesy of being honest with me.'

'I believe so, yes.' The clinical director turned and met Josh's gaze without flinching. 'And it was Maitland that he particularly asked to be your exchange partner.'

'So you mean that I have been sacrificed on the altar of his unfaithfulness?' Josh paced to and fro, arms folded. 'And is this woman a good doctor? When did she qualify?'

'Six months ago – and she is promising, although she has the arrogance of inexperience.'

'And this arrogant, inexperienced doctor has been placed in my practice, with care of my patients?'

'Yes Josh, she has. I can't be less than frank with you. I believe that Clive hoped that he would wrong-foot you by dropping you into a situation for which you had not been prepared – a research post, not a practical clinical one.'

Josh threw back his head and laughed bitterly.

'By God, you're acute! You picked up that I was thrown when you asked me what research project I was planning to undertake?'

'Yes, Josh, I did. And that is why I'm saying to you now that if you want to repay treachery with treachery, I am offering you a job with us here in NYC. You're smart, you're experienced, thorough, honest – my kind of junior clinician.'

Josh stood up and extended his right hand.

'Thanks, Brad. That means a lot, but I need time to process all this. I'll think carefully about your proposition and see you bright and early tomorrow.'

'Sure, Josh.'

Back in his luxury apartment, Josh showered, letting the stream of water soothe and wash away his anger. What Brad Jackson had said made complete sense: the sudden suggestion that he should make this exchange; the speed with which the arrangements had been made; the sops of business-class travel and luxury accommodation – it all stacked up.

Towelling vigorously, he asked himself the central hard question: could he settle to the sort of life that he would live in New York? He knew it would be a life of superficialities – not where his work was concerned, never that, but in terms of how he lived his personal life. Self-analytical to the point of self-harm, Josh was only too aware of the darker side of his character, which sought to find release in sexual pleasure from the intense world of suffering and death with which he was involved.

Josh recalled a conversation with his mother, following the discovery of an injured seagull on his school playground. He had grabbed a cardboard box and folded his rugby shirt inside to make as comfortable a resting place for the animal as he could, and had run home with it. To his horror, when he undid the box, he saw that the bird was tearing at the wound on its wing as if that itself was the cause of its pain. Tears came to Molly MacDonald's eyes as she placed a gauze pad over the damaged wing.

'You're like this poor bird, Joshie, tearing away at the hurt in you to make it go away. But trying to banish pain with more pain can never work. It will destroy you. Be kind to yourself, my son.

But he never had been kind to himself, and "trying to banish pain with more pain" had almost become a synopsis of his life.

Glancing at the pristine bed, he remembered his first night in the city – entertaining and being entertained by Aimée Jonson. He recalled her eager beauty and the intensity of the experiences they had shared. He also remembered that the night had been one of raw sensuality as far as he was concerned, with no depth of feeling – and he hated himself for it. Feeling angry because he had been banished from the island and the people that he loved so much, he had, he knew only too well, simply used Aimée – "trying to banish pain with more pain."

Dusk was spreading over the top storeys of the skyscrapers which surrounded him, and the streets far below were already dark. But as Josh stared out of the windows of his apartment, he saw none of this dramatic shadow-show. He saw the resigned face of Mrs MacKenzie; the pale wistfulness of Carrie Logan handing him the card carefully inscribed: *To my Bestie;* the agonised faces of her parents; the concerned and capable features of Morag, his secretary. On and on his mind ran, thinking of the respect and care which he felt for his patients and which they returned to him with open hearts. In leaving them he would be rejecting the best aspects of his character for what? Revenge?

His phone sounded.

I could almost believe that this is a mermaid!

Alex had sent him a photo of a choppy sea with the tail of a dolphin disappearing into a white-caped wave. Josh smiled and felt himself relaxing. The myriad mundane, undramatic events which are the stuff of life were taken by this woman and made beautiful, funny, magical. So often an amusing emoticon, exclamation marks, and her silly selfies made him laugh and relax. And in doing so, he was able briefly to touch base once again with the sensitive, thoughtful adolescent he had been before bitter experience had created out of him someone that his mother, his own 'Star of the Sea' would never have recognised.

Takes one to know one, Alex! he replied, appending a string of blond mermaids.

Chapter 12

Alex had never imagined how beautiful Fragrey would be.

At last the ferry moored at the jetty and she was reunited with Gladys, who had not moved one centimetre as far as Alex could see, as her heavy sub-frame had been manufactured when strength in a vehicle was prized before speed. Slowly Alex manoeuvred her campervan around the bulkhead of the ferry, up the ramp and onto dry land again. And what a land!

It was a perfect morning in early March and the machair – that magical territory between the beach and the countryside – was studded with the golds and blues and reds of countless early flowers. As soon as Alex cleared the port, she stopped, switched off Gladys's engine, and stepped out onto one of the rarest habitats in the world – a unique mixture of grass, flowers, shells and sand found only in the Western Isles and Ireland. Silence was total, apart from the sounds of the natural world: the sea, the wild desolate call of gulls, and the sighing wind in the sedge. Alex just stood and tried to absorb the peace and the delicate palate of colours. Blue in all its shades was paramount in this landscape – the cold navy-blue which was the expanse of the Atlantic; the ice-blue of the clear sky; the burning blue of viper's bugloss at her feet. The sand was shockingly white against the black rocks, themselves splashed with the vivid orange seaweed that clung to them. Ahead of her a wide bay curved to sheer black cliffs at the foot of which the ocean churned and surged. Along the margin of the bay straggled a haphazard cluster of houses, the homes of crofters who grazed their sheep on the machair and fished, mainly to feed their own families.

The application pack had contained a map of the island showing the route from the ferry-landing to Heillstath, so Alex knew that she had to follow the road which skirted the long crescent of the bay, then snaked over the ridge of hills which ended abruptly in the sheer cliffs to her right. But, filled with an indefinable joy, before she embarked on the last, short leg of her journey, Alex tilted her head to the cold sunshine and took the deepest breath of the fragrant, ozone-laden air.

Gladys chugged comfortably past the scattered crofts: low, whitewashed houses, most of which had identical extensions to their rear – which Alex was later to learn were bathrooms, funded by government grants back in the late 1960's. The old campervan seemed in her element here, in this slower, calmer world with few vehicles and none of the anger and aggression Alex had encountered on the mainland. Small dark-fleeced sheep grazed incuriously along the road, cropping grass and flowers. Even the steep climb up the hilly ridge didn't seem to worry Gladys, making Alex smile and pat the dashboard affectionately. When they had reached the highest point, she pulled into a lay-by that seemed as if it may have been put there for the sole purpose of resting weary vehicles, or animals.

Once again, Alex switched off the engine and eagerly stepped out to look at what she imagined must be the settlement of Heillstath, the 'place of healing', which lay below her. Behind her on the cliff line was a line of long-barrows, swelling from the close-cropped heather and telling of times past when warriors were buried to overlook the sea they had crossed to reach the land where they had settled.

Heillstath nestled in a river valley which meandered down to the sea. Here it ended in a neat, horse-shoe shaped quay, crowded with stone terraced houses and sheltered from the full force of the Atlantic storms by the high headland and a short jetty. Once again, the houses were mainly single-storied, but there was a greater variety of buildings here in the town than she had encountered on the island so far. Alex noticed that the terraced cottages which lined the quay were two storied, and she made out the high, pointed gable end of a small church or chapel and a scattering of shops. A neat T-shaped building was set a little way out of town, on the lower slopes of the hills; and her heart beat faster as she made out the tarmacked playground and small playing field of the school. Above the school, a turreted Manor House was set apart from the other buildings in elaborate, tapestry-like gardens.

The application pack had made it clear that Heillstath was not geared to tourism and that only *The Inn* could provide accommodation. Fortunately, Alex had not booked a room before she left Kent – if she had she would have been four days overdue. But she had telephoned the previous evening, booking their sole ensuite bedroom for the next three days. Taking a deep breath, she pointed Gladys down the series of bends which would finally take her to her destination.

'Brad, you will never know how much I appreciated your honesty, but I cannot accept your offer.'

Brad Jackson stood silent, eyeballing Josh.

'It sounds corny to say I love my patients – but I do. The world is a thankless place for children with cancer, for parents who don't have enough to provide for their families, for old people who are unwanted and unloved and for whom loneliness becomes a disease that will kill them. I have no option but to return to my home.'

Some seconds passed, during which Brad paced the floor whilst, controlled as always, Josh stood watching him.

'I completely accept this Josh. I didn't think for one nanosecond that you would accept my offer. But perhaps you will accept my advice?'

Josh said nothing.

'You are a brilliant medic and your skills are matched by your compassion. But I can also see that you are unhappy. Cut yourself some slack! Congratulate yourself on how you are making use of the skills and talents that you have for the benefit of humankind.'

'So you're not going to drop me like a pariah?'

'Why should I? I've met a man with principles like my own. Senior or junior clinician – does it matter? We are both men. If your research matches your proposal, I will give you a reference that *dreams are made of.*

You will have no cause for bitterness because of me.'

⊰⊱⊰⊱

It was midnight and Josh was restless.

After his surprising conversation with Brad, he had dropped into the gym in the basement of his apartment block and had worked out hard for an hour and a half. At least that was one consolation for living in this impersonal place, he reflected ironically: he had a gym on site. Consequently he could enjoy the luxury of warm, dry exercise, rather than running for miles along uneven roads and tracks, fighting blustery winds or freezing rain, as he did in Fragrey. After a supper of salmon and salad, Josh had worked on the introduction to his proposed research, and had started to plot the individuals and groups that he would talk to. The list was long. Outpatients were one obvious source of information, but there were the junior doctors of both genders whose long hours of work precluded most social interactions. The elderly concierge who seemed glued to his chair in the vestibule of the apartment block; the newspaper vendors in the streets; the florist always on her own outside the local subway station; the managers of the crèche facilities provided for the range of clinics in the hospital – all seemed to be lone-workers, potentially subject to the insidious impact of loneliness.

By the time he stopped work for the evening, he had scoped out the detail of his research project. The next steps were to timetable interviews and allow sufficient time for data analysis in order to reach some sort of meaningful conclusion. He had been in the States for a little over a week, and the time that remained of his secondment should be ample to complete the project.

But now he was restless as he stood and stretched his arms and shoulders, rolling his neck to ease out some of the stiffness. The city moved below him as if it were at the height of its activity – the city that never sleeps – the man that never sleeps, he thought wryly.

I'm going to sleep forever! Zzzzz!!!

Alex's message instantly made him smile.

Now it's you who's psychic! Just thinking about sleep myself...xx
Bet my view is better than yours!

Alex had taken a photo of the view from her bedroom window at *The Inn.* Not much was visible, just the broken pattern of the moonlight on the waves that flowed into the harbour at Heillstath and the black line of the breakwater against the sky. It could have been any harbour, anywhere in the Western Isles or remote coastal region in the UK – there was nothing particularly individual to identify it – but to Josh's subconscious mind it was familiar and secure, and these feelings were subliminally transferred to Alex – familiarity and security.

Very scenic! Sleep tight, Alex xx
Sleep tight, Star xx

Chapter 13

'Do you know when Dr MacDonald is coming back, Rory?'

Rory Cameron, the landlord of *The Inn,* poured a whisky thoughtfully.

'To be honest, Alan, I don't – but it can't be a day too soon for me! I went to see the new American doctor for my regular blood test, and all she did was examine her long pink nails for a moment, before saying that I would have to catch the ferry to Benbecula and "attend the diabetes clinic there, because they have the latest techniques at their fingertips." Dr McDonald has been monitoring me for the last five years and I'm stable, thanks to his care. No wonder Dr Maitland Morgan referred me, I don't think she understood what to do! It doesn't look as if she has anything of use whatsoever at *her* pointed fingertips.'

Alex sipped her red wine and attacked the venison casserole that she had ordered. It was the end of her first full day on Fragrey and she was starving. Warm, relishing food that hadn't been cooked on her barely-adequate Calor Gas stove, and letting the conversation flow over her gently, she reviewed her day.

She had slept until mid-afternoon, having put the battered *Do Not Disturb* sign on her bedroom door, and she awoke refreshed and full of anticipation. Yawning, she wandered over to the window, which overlooked the harbour where all was now quiet – it was nearly ten hours since the morning fishing boats had left and probably another six until they returned. The calm in this place was palpable: there was no traffic, and a scattering of folk just went quietly about their business. She stood under the shower for far longer than necessary, relishing the luxury of abundant hot water pouring over her. Refreshed and warm, she left the empty pub and made for the headland which she had seen – from its opposite side – on her arrival the previous day. Passing the snug stone cottages which huddled together along the quayside, Alex smiled as the thought struck her that they actually seemed to be physically supporting each other. All were neat with polished windows, and here and there a pot of herbs or a shrub softened the harshness of the stone.

Soon Alex had left the cobbled quayside behind and started the climb up the steep headland. The weather was perfect for a walk – clear and cool – and she rejoiced that the challenging drive was behind her and that tomorrow she could explore her surroundings at leisure before her interview on the following day.

The more she saw of this island, the more she was drawn by it. Everything seemed understated, but had its own powerful beauty. There was nothing garish, nothing obvious, to attract the tourist – just the authenticity of a small, remote community that sought to make a living in a tough land surrounded by a deep, inimical ocean. Surely to live here one's character would have to be tough too: capable, and with deep personal resources. She had met only a small handful of people since she had parked Gladys the previous day: the landlady, Catriona Cameron, pleasant but quite reserved; her husband, Rory, outgoing and extrovert; and a couple of locals who watched, smiling good-naturedly, as she hauled her bags out of the campervan and made her way towards *The Inn.* Compared to the often-false bonhomie of the south-east, this straightforward integrity delighted her.

At the top of the headland Alex left the track and walked across the thrift-strewn grass to the cliff edge, to the spot where Josh had stood with such bleak thoughts several weeks earlier. But Alex's mindset couldn't have been more different. Where Josh had seen only futility and darkness, Alex saw the future, stretching bright and clear. Glancing out to sea, she noticed for the first time a small, vividly-green island, shaped like a tear-drop with a slender crescent of white sand on its nearest shore. She made a mental note that she would ask Rory Cameron what it was called – it looked at once inviting, but unbelievably remote.

She turned and surveyed the town, which she fervently hoped would become her home, before turning up the collar of her quilted jacket and heading straight for the school. She walked briskly and had descended the headland, crossed the narrow settlement of Heillstath and covered the gentle rise from the town to the school in twenty minutes. A blue and gold board proudly proclaimed that this was *Fragrey Independent Endowed School* and the coat of arms which had intrigued her on the original *TES* advertisement was replicated here, larger, bolder and in full colour. The unicorn was a startling white, with a rainbow-coloured mane; and the mermaid, who had vivid auburn hair, had flesh of a vibrant pink. Alex laughed as she attributed this to the sub-zero temperature of the Atlantic Ocean for most of the year.

'Do you find our school name-board amusing?'

Alex spun round to see an elegant, tweed-clad woman standing several paces behind her. She was holding a basket full of cleaning materials and a large bunch of roses.

'On the contrary, I laughed with delight at the way in which the school embraces the magic at the heart of life. If children can't find magic here, they will find it nowhere.'

The set of the woman's shoulders relaxed a little. 'I haven't seen you before,' she continued in a cultured voice, 'Would you like to see around our school?'

'Thank you! But I must tell you that I am here to be interviewed for the post of teacher-in-charge of the school. I would love a guided tour, but I might be infringing selection protocol if I do. What do you think?'

'I think you are probably right. Isn't it dreadful that our lives are directed by petty rules and regulations? Jenna MacLeod, Chair of Governors and daughter of the founder. Pleased to meet you.' And the current chieftain of the Clan MacLeod extended a green-gloved hand.

⊰∥⊱

Finishing the last morsels of her venison casserole, Alex recollected the cool and appraising look from

Jenna MacLeod's eyes, which were the exact green of her gloves and the tweed which skimmed her slender figure. Beyond a shadow of a doubt, this self-contained individual would be one of the panel interviewing her and she recalled the maxim that a person was successful – or otherwise – in being appointed to a new role within the first thirty seconds of entering a room. What instant impression had she given to the Chair of Governors of the school? She had hardly looked professional, being dressed in jeans, boots and quilted jacket … no make-up … hair wind-blown. Ah well! She could do nothing about that now. What would be would be.

⊰⊱

'Another Merlot please, Rory.'

'And will you be wanting any pudding at all, Mrs Miller?'

'Yes please! What are you offering tonight?'

'Jam roly-poly – with custard or cream.'

'Would it be possible to have both?'

The landlord smiled broadly. 'Aye, it's a pleasure to see a woman enjoying her food, rather than fretting over her figure.'

Drinking deeply from the glass set in front of her, Alex thought about her forthcoming interview. Every hour she spent on this island made her long more keenly for the job of teacher-in-charge of the island school. Would her impromptu meeting with its Chair of Governors lessen her chances of success? She honestly hadn't a clue, but decided that, in a way, her encounter would help her to relax and be herself during the interview process – and that must be good.

Chapter 14

'Some of us are going downtown after clinic this evening, Josh. It's Friday and it would be a great opportunity for you to meet more of the team. Would you care to join us?'

Brad Jackson smiled across his desk and the computer screen on which he had been reading Josh's research proposal

'That would be good, Brad. About seven?'

'Perfect.'

※

The group of eight colleagues was diverse: another senior clinician who directly supervised outpatients, and five junior doctors. It struck Josh – not for the first time – how polished the appearance of American professionals was: hair and teeth of both genders were perfect; their figures were well-toned and they appeared quietly confident of their abilities and their role in society. As was happening more and more, Josh's mind flipped to the profile of the patients that he loved. Most were crofters struggling on the breadline – even in 2018 – sacrificed upon some empty political altar;

many cut their own hair, many hadn't had the opportunity or the income to visit a dentist in years. But all were *real*: individuals formed by the harshest of existences. Raking the group in which he sat with his eyes, Josh reflected that it was like sitting in a privileged club which admitted only the intelligent, the successful and wealthy. Josh was increasingly home-sick and longed for the raw and exhausting role that he had carved for himself on the remote island that, almost certainly, his urbane companions would never have heard of. But, closing his eyes briefly to collect his thoughts, he turned to the woman on his right.

'Josh MacDonald. Good to meet you.'

'Parvati Patel. I've seen you around, Josh. Hope you are settling in to the most vibrant city in the world?'

There was so much else that Josh could have responded here, but he merely smiled and nodded.

'So glad you could come out tonight, Josh,' Parvati continued, her eyes subtly assessing her companion. 'We have so little opportunity to socialise in the hospital. It's good to have downtime to get to know colleagues better … perhaps supper at my place later?'

'I would like that, Parvati.'

The evening continued with social chit-chat, discussions about partners, career choices, leisure pursuits – all the usual limited topics of conversation that were within the remit of occasions such as this. People started to drift away around eight-thirty and Parvati turned to Josh with a radiant smile, 'Let's get a cab, Josh. See you tomorrow, guys.' And, linking her arm through his, they left Brad and Simon Schuster, the other senior clinician, alone in the bar.

'What do you make of MacDonald, Brad?' asked Simon.

'First-class brain. Brilliant diagnostician. But depths of unhappiness. I don't know what is going on in the UK, but he has been let down badly by the system and by his line-manager. He told me that he has supervisory responsibility for General Practice in the Western Isles of Scotland, a somewhat challenging remit! Have you seen the infrastructure – or lack of it – over there? Mainly ferries or planes. And, on top of that, he runs his own practice single-handed on Fragrey.'

'What was that name again?'

Brad repeated it. 'It's Viking for *Beautiful Island* according to Josh. He's genuinely devoted to the community of subsistence farmers and fishermen who live there.'

'No Mrs Josh?'

'There was apparently, but she left years ago "because of an unfortunate combination of over-work and unfaithfulness". But I sense there may be more to that story than these simple headlines.'

⊰)|(⊱

Walking out of the high-end bar, Josh believed that he could almost write the script for the coming evening with Parvati. But in practice he was light years away from what actually happened.

'Is cheese paneer all right for you, Josh?' she had asked when she had poured them both large glasses of wine.

'Are you a vegetarian, Parvati?'

'I am a Hindu and eating vegetables seems the most natural way of living to me,' she had smiled.

The food was delicious, as was the company. Parvati told Josh that she had worked with Brad Jackson for five years and had found him the best manager she had ever had.

'He's kind, genuinely kind. He's also perceptive and supportive. In fact, if you think of all the positive attributes of a good manager, he has them in spades. He's also a world lead in neurological surgery – did you know that?'

'I had no idea. I think that's one of the most attractive aspects of Brad's character: he doesn't advertise his own skills.'

'I agree. Whilst you are here, you really ought to try to observe some of his practice. Patients are brought to him from all over the world for the most delicate brain surgery. He is a master – and I admire men who know exactly what they are doing in their own sphere.'

'Do you, Parvati?' The momentary silence was loaded. 'And will you stay here, do you think?'

'I want to return to my home city of Jaipur. There is so much work to do there and so few qualified people. I also want children and my parents would be broken-hearted if I didn't marry someone from my home country.'

'So Western men are not to your taste,' Josh said softly, tracing with his eyes the line of her long neck to her collar-bones and lightly following the curve of her small breasts.

Parvati breathed more deeply and moved closer to Josh.

'Western men are very much to my taste, but not for serious relationships. Just … for … fun…' and with each word she undid Josh's shirt buttons.

Later on, it was Josh who lay exhausted on the dark blue silk sheets of her bed. Parvati had introduced him to sexual practices that – even in his extensive experience – he had only heard of. Parvati was an experienced and skilful lover, but relentless in her demands. Again and again Josh met her, until he felt that, literally, he had nothing more to give. Lying on his back, looking at the asymmetrical scattering of inset spotlights above him, Josh saw the humour of the situation. How many times had a woman – Aimée Jonson being the last – been left exhausted and breathless by his greater experience? And now it was his turn to feel used, out of his depth, less than successful, by a woman who could have written the Karma Sutra herself! For probably the first time since the early years of his marriage, Josh started thinking about just how important love is. He wryly reflected how sex alone, which undeniably brings sexual release, is such an empty mechanical act; whereas sex underpinned and informed by love – well such an experience is nothing short of transcendent.

'Want a protein shake, Josh?' Parvati called from her neat, galley kitchen.

'Make that two!' he replied, laughing.

Josh made it back to his apartment by four, and watched dawn lighting the grey sky imperceptibly.

Not heard from you for a bit. Hope you are OK? Think of me – I'm off for an interview…

Oh Alex, I'm sorry! Combination of work and socialising … It must be – quick mental calculation – nine o'clock with you?

Yes – and good for you! As my grandmother used to say "All work and no play…dims your starlight" No she didn't say that – that's a version from me. Do you like my outfit?

Alex's selfie showed her dressed formally in a navy dress with fuschia detailing along hem and cuffs, navy shoes and hair straightened within a centimetre of perfection. The taut profile of her figure was vividly apparent. She wore minimal make-up, but a smile that lifted Josh's heart.

You look lovely, Alex! But I prefer your penguin pyjamas! 😄😄😄 *xx*
TY. I'd love to see another photo of you, Star... xx
Later xx

Chapter 15

Alex decided that she was going to drive Gladys to her interview. Rain was sweeping horizontally across the island and if she had not seen for herself during the previous two days the spectacular views from almost anywhere on Fragrey she would have thought that her environment was grey, featureless and dull.

'Good luck, Mrs Miller,' Rory Cameron had smiled at her over breakfast. 'Would you care for an extra sausage this morning? I know how you enjoy your food.'

'Thank you, Rory, but I feel as if this dress is quite a lot tighter than the last time I wore it! Mrs Cameron's cooking is fabulous – but not for my waistline!'

Gladys chugged into the school playground and Alex noticed the other cars parked there: a black Golf, two Land Rovers and a Fiat 500. Taking a deep breath Alex entered the school. In front of her was a small reception space with, on the right, a window into the school secretary's office. Straight ahead was the school hall, brightly lit against the gloom of the day. Alex shook off her waterproof and hung it on a coat stand near to the entrance door. She entered the hall and saw a group of people helping themselves to coffee.

'Good morning!' she announced clearly. 'Alex Miller. Good to meet you all.'

Five faces turned and regarded her with a range of expressions.

'Alex – good to see you again!' The cool green eyes of Jenna MacLeod looked straight into her own. 'Let me introduce you: Mike Whitfield, our ex officio governor and the rector of the church here in Heillstath; Agnes Muirhead – how would you introduce yourself, Agnes?'

'Oh, something simple and understated, like "the wise woman of Fragrey" smiled the tall, ageless woman who stood regarding Alex with an appraising gaze.

'I will be guided by you, Agnes. Alex, may I introduce the wise woman of Fragrey? And the final member of the governing body represented here today, someone you know already I believe: Rory Cameron.

'Rory! I had no idea! Isn't it illegal or inappropriate or something that I should be staying at your inn and we know each other to a certain extent?'

'No' pronounced Jenna firmly. 'Rory is our community governor and is incorruptible! Our interview panel should have one further member – Dr MacDonald – but he is on a sabbatical in the States at the moment.' Used to decoding emotions in the children she taught through the slightest change in expression or gesture, Alex couldn't help noticing the faint flush on Jenna's high, aristocratic cheekbones as she mentioned the name of the missing governor.

'And this is?' asked Alex uncertainly as she looked at the small, dark-suited figure sitting, sipping water, to one side of the table bearing the refreshments.

'Jeanne O'Hara, the other candidate for the position.'

'Pleased to meet you, Jeanne,' Alex smiled, extending her hand.

'Indeed,' came the quiet reply.

⋙‖⋘

Half an hour later, coffee had been drunk and the buffet food eaten. Alex had been invited to go to interview first and Jeanne had made her way from the hall to the room set aside for the candidates.

'Alex, why did you want to apply for this position?' Jenna rocked back on her chair and looked intensely at Alex.

'I was attracted by the wording of your advertisement: *Are you a seeker of everyday magic? Can you inspire this wonder and love of learning in the children you teach?* That is what drew me in. I deplore the way in which the creativity and imagination of children has been strangled by the narrow expectations of the current government. I *am* a seeker after everyday magic, because I believe that just to be alive is magic, but to find a way for children to unlock that bottomless potential within themselves is beyond magic.'

'What resources within our church would you use to build upon the ethos of the trust?' asked the rector, his eyes looking earnestly at her from behind rimless glasses.

'If you can't find magic, miracles, within the Christian faith, then you may as well go to Mars,' Alex replied.

'Would you like to say more, Alex?'

'Well yes, I would. Thank you. People dismiss the stuff of the New Testament, but if you look at myths and legends which people here, and in other rural situations, believe in fervently, then why is Christianity so denigrated? I believe that "magic" has a deep and broad interpretation. It is to embrace "magic" to believe that Jesus worked His miracles and changed – and is still changing – lives. It is also accepting "magic" to believe that unicorns and mermaids can embrace. But why is that less believable than the Bible? Sorry, can I go on?'

'Of course, Mrs Miller,' Rory Cameron nodded vigorously.

'I believe that magic is the stuff of childhood. It is soon snuffed out, soon drowned in pragmatism. I have been in Fragrey for two and a half days and already I love it. Around every corner is beauty and history, learning and magic, and to deny that is to deny their inheritance to the children who live and are being educated here.'

There was complete hush in the school hall. Alex knew that she had flushed deeply and flicked her gaze around the assembled interview panel members. All had their eyes downcast and all were making notes, apart from Agnes Muirhead who, once again, was eyeballing Alex.

After a long pause, Jenna looked up. 'How would you integrate the government's emphasis on literacy and numeracy within an island-based curriculum?'

'There are opportunities for both disciplines everywhere we look on Fragrey. Research has proved the link between oracy – talking freely and articulately – in younger children with later excellence in writing. We could role-play on the beach, in historic buildings, in church. Older children could write guide books for visitors to the island; could create their own myths and legends based upon the culture here. Everywhere are opportunities for data collection and analysis. The list is endless.'

For the first time since Alex had encountered Jenna Macleod, she smiled – a warm, open and completely genuine smile.

'Thank you, Mrs Miller.'

Alex walked briskly back to the small staff room which had been made a base for the candidates during the interview process. She passed a Religious Education display, above which was a mirror with the caption *Look in the Mirror to see something infinitely precious to God.* As is usually the case when a human being sees the direction 'to look' Alex did, and saw her reflection: flushed, her eyes bright, looking more alive and excited than she had felt for years. Reading the simple words, her eyes filled with tears – partly at the magic that she had herself lost over the years as she had been gradually changed and subsumed by the crushing boredom of marriage with David; partly because she was surprised at her intense longing to be given the privilege of weaving an irresistibly attractive curriculum for the children of the island.

Jeanne O'Hara sat quietly, hands folded in her lap, in the same attitude that she had adopted earlier in the school hall. After-shock hit Alex and she sat heavily down in one of the three dilapidated chairs and leant her head back.

'Was it gruelling?' asked Jeanne quietly.

'Yes, no – I don't really know. I just said what was in my heart to say. I honestly don't know how I did!'

'I'm sure you did as well as you could. I can see the effort that you put into the interview just by looking at you.'

Alex sat up straight, unsure of how to react to such ambivalent words. 'I'm sure you have nothing to be concerned about, Jeanne. You look so composed! What's your background?'

'I was Headteacher of a small school in Berkshire for ten years. I then moved on to become Executive Head of an Academy Trust near Faversham in Kent.'

'I see. So, what brought you here?'

'Oh – personal stuff ...'

Alex sensed that this was a no-go area, so swiftly changed tack. 'If you have a pedigree like that, I may as well just go back to Gladys and head for the mainland!'

'Gladys?'

'Sorry – yes, my campervan.'

Jeanne smiled, then started to laugh, which transformed her delicate, dark features. From being almost invisible in repose she became vibrantly attractive.

'Ms O'Hara? Would you like to come through please?'

'Good luck, Jeanne,' Alex smiled – and meant it.

Chapter 16

How did it go, Alex?

It was wonderful! But I'm by no means sure I've got the job, Star…

Why? Didn't they tell you?

They said they needed twenty-four hours to decide. The other candidate was an ex-Headteacher … I'm sure her experience will count for more than my enthusiasm!

You are a teacher then?

I am – for my sins…

Well I don't feel too enthusiastic tonight myself…

???

Oh just met an exhausting colleague last night… I've not been able to focus as I usually do today.

I'm sorry to hear that, Star. I am an expert in cuddles and have won prizes for them!!! Huge cuddles down the computer wires or whatever – through the ether…

You're lovely, Alex xx

So are you, Star xx

On opposite sides of the Atlantic, Josh and Alex re-read their conversation.

Josh hadn't just been physically exhausted after his marathon with Parvati, he had felt emotionally troubled and profoundly guilty that he had caused quite a few – if not exactly countless – women to feel disappointed, used and useless, just as he had felt all those things. Reading those gentle, comforting words from a woman had both soothed and added to his guilt. For as long as he could remember, Josh had used sex as an analgesic for the tide of despair and powerlessness that he felt in the face of death and disease. As with everything he did, Josh tried to give pleasure to the women with whom he slept, and no complaints were ever made about the care and sensitivity he showed to all his sexual partners. But Josh knew that for him sex had become soulless – an act which was an end in itself, not the ultimate expression of loving a person; and his cool scientific mind assessed his prowess as a lover at the same time as deprecating it. Brushing his teeth, he glanced in the mirror. He looked the same as ever – a look that he had cultivated over the years – closed, self-contained, with none of the less-worthy aspects of his character visible on his face. He decided that just at the moment he really didn't like himself very much.

Compared to Josh's dark and intense self-analysis, Alex's reflections were much more straightforward. She smiled as she thought how easy her friendship with *Star of the Sea* was. She could be frank, funny and say pretty well whatever she wanted; and his responses stimulated her and made her smile. For the first time she thought about how that friendship might change if they were to meet in real life, rather than virtually, and felt in her belly a frisson of expectation – excitement – desire? Difficult to identify the emotion precisely.

Josh had an early night, but couldn't get Alex out of his mind. *I am an expert in cuddles and have won prizes for them!!! Huge cuddles down the computer wires or whatever – through the ether...*

He pressed his phone into life and went to Alex's home page. He gazed at her selfies and expanded the photos to show her smiling mouth and the laughter lines at the corners of her clear eyes. Despite the experiences of the night before, he felt his desire for her rising and, on a whim, messaged, *I want to be inside you, Alex xx.* It was three am in the UK, and the last thing he expected was a response, but almost immediately he had one:

And I want you there xx

⊰⊱

Alex's phone rang. She had hardly slept at all the previous night – stemming from a combination of the adrenalin-fuelled interview day, the unexpected message from *Star of the Sea* and her even more unexpected spontaneous response to him.

'Mrs Miller, could you come along to the school this morning please?'

'Of course,' Alex managed to croak, her throat constricted with nerves. 'What time would you like me there?'

'Shall we say ten-thirty?'

'Will Jeanne – Ms O'Hara – be there?'

'Sadly, no. She had to return to the mainland after the interview due to the lack of accommodation on the island.'

Did this mean that she had got the job? Alex frowned. Usually things were much more straightforward than this and involved a telephone call on the evening of interview to confirm success or failure. More likely she had *not* been successful and this was the kindest way in which the Governors could let her know. Ah well, whatever the outcome, she had to attend.

⊰◈⊱

'Mrs Miller – Alex – we find ourselves in a unique position.' It was a replay of the previous day, and the Governors who had interviewed her sat once again at the end of the hall, their chairs arranged in a semi-circle, facing her. Jenna MacLeod, dressed this morning in a softly-draped dress in her favourite shade of green, slender ankles crossed, sat directly opposite Alex, who said nothing and clasped her hands hard to stop them from shaking.

'We have been most impressed with both you and Ms O'Hara and it has been very difficult for us to reach a decision ...'

Alex's hands were clasped so tightly that her nails started to dig into her palms. She had been unsuccessful! How could she compete with an ex-Headteacher?

'Jeanne O'Hara's academic credentials are striking. She took her first school from Special Measures to Outstanding in five years. The attainment of her children was in the top ten per cent in England. She is experienced in school leadership and highly competent in administration.'

'She really is most impressive, Jenna. Thank you for being so kind and asking me to come here in person to explain, but I quite understand your decision.' Alex jumped to her feet and started to move towards the door. 'I would just like to say how much I appreciate being invited here for interview to your wonderful island. I will never forget …'

'But Alex, please sit down again! We want to offer *both* of you positions here in Fragrey Independent Endowed School!'

'What? Really?'

'We had never heard such a passionate declaration – utterly in tune with our own ethos and educational philosophy. But you have never actually *led* a school. Jeanne has.'

Rory Cameron smiled warmly at Alex. 'As chair of the finance committee I have advised our governing body that we are in the fortunate position of being able to employ an administrative head – Jeanne O'Hara – as well as teacher-in-charge – yourself. Our children will, we are convinced, flourish in your hands, and we feel sure that the administrative burden of the school will be dealt with in an exemplary manner by Jeanne. Grace Meredith, the present senior teacher, will be retiring at Easter and this will give both you and Jeanne the entire summer term to get to know the children and plan for next school year. Alex sat completely silent for several seconds, then she said quite simply, 'Thank you all from the bottom of my heart. I will never let you down.'

Chapter 17

Alex's first impulse was to return to *The Inn* and message *Star of the Sea* with her news, but his last message and her response to it seemed to stand in the way of the funny and frank chats they had had to date. Instead, she rang Sarah, 'Guess what?'

'You have turned into a mermaid!'

'No.'

'You have met a real live unicorn?'

'No – I've got the job!'

'On the island with the unpronounceable name?

'Fragrey.'

'That's the one! Seriously, well done, Alex. I'm so pleased for you. But isn't it bleak and unstimulating up there?

'No – it's … well, it's just magical! How's things in darkest Kent?'

'Ah, you know – hysterectomies and haemorrhoids …'

'Nothing changes then?'

Sarah paused. 'Well, some things have changed and there is one thing that you should know about really.'

'David's having an affair with the post woman? I saw him ogling her long brown legs in those fetching Post Office shorts!'

Alex expected a soft laugh from her friend, but again there was a loaded silence. 'Your Diana has come home. She's living with David.'

Alex froze and felt that tightness in her stomach that she always experienced when either of her daughters was mentioned. It was a sort of panic – that despite the years of nurture and love, her girls had turned out as they had. She would never stop loving them, but she couldn't condone their way of life. She gritted her teeth as she thought how, when one or other of them had done something which she, Alex, considered immoral, or dishonest, or hurtful, and she was mustering all her energies to tell them how unacceptable she had found their behaviour, they would send a message to her mobile. 'I love you, Mum.' 'I miss you, Mum.' This seeking for an expression of unconditional love seemed to be concomitant with the action that Alex had found so alien to her own values. Maybe it was, maybe it wasn't – but it tied her emotions in knots that could never be untangled. Gripping her mobile, she closed her eyes and remembered the last time she had seen her younger daughter – unconscious on a friend's sofa. 'A girly evening' had turned, almost inevitably, into a heavy drinking session. It was as if Diana had no off-switch: one drink led to another and another until she passed out or threw up – or both. On this memorable occasion, the friend had tried to wake her without success and had telephoned Alex – at two o'clock in the morning. 'Can you come and take your daughter home please, Mrs Miller? My parents would go spare if they found her like this, and Dad's got to get up for an early shift.' Alex had shrugged on jeans and jumper and had hefted her daughter into the back of her car. David had slept through the phone call and the noise of their return when she had half-carried, half-dragged their daughter into the sitting room and dumped her unceremoniously on the sofa. With a complex mixture of concern and disgust she had looked down at the clammy, bloated face of her once lovely daughter – and turned out the light.

These crowding memories took split seconds to replay, and were as vivid as if they were happening in front of her at that very moment.

'Why's she come back, Sarah? Do you know?'

'I dropped round to see David a couple of days ago. I've tried to keep an eye on him, to make sure he is all right. Apparently, she's lost her job ...'

'Again ...'

'And has come home to "regroup". She was trawling through the internet, and said with complete confidence that there were several jobs that she was going to apply for. Although she believes she is "overqualified", she's certain that they will snap her up. You OK, Alex?'

'Oh, I suppose so! I'm just tired to death of the same story playing and replaying itself. How many times has this happened now? Five? Six? Each time she starts off with such promise but then things unravel in exactly the same way – absence, "illness" for which read being insensible or ill through drink, then dismissal. She's twenty-seven for God's sake, not thirteen.'

'Do you want me to tell her where you are?'

'No, Sarah, I don't. For the first time in decades, I feel free to be myself again. No inert relationship; no emotional blackmail; no regret or self-analysis as to how I could possibly have been such a lousy mother. I'm ... well I'm happy!'

'I'm pleased to hear that, pleased for you, Alex. Everyone deserves to be happy. I wish I could say that David seemed so, but he doesn't ...'

'I'm sad to hear that. But, do you know what, Sarah? It's just not my concern any more. He had twenty-eight years to make our marriage work, and ignored every suggestion, every idea I had.'

'Do you want me to give him your regards?'

'Not really. You may think I'm heartless and cold, but I have drawn a line under my life in Kent and I'm not erasing it.'

'I don't think I could do that, Alex, in your place.'

'But you're not in my place, Sarah. Remember the Native American Indian saying that you have to walk a mile in someone else's moccasins before you can really understand them?'

Alex heard her friend sigh. 'OK. Take care.'

'Bye, Sarah.'

'Bye, Alex.'

⊰∦⊱

Josh had scheduled the first of his focus groups into his timetable for the day that lay in front of him. But insidiously, the last message that Alex had sent kept drifting into his mind … *I want you there* …

With that message – and more significantly, with the one he had sent, which had engendered this response – their fun and easy relationship had changed. And once he had registered this change, he realised how far he had been drawn into her world. He hadn't a clue whereabouts her interview had taken place, but he cared about the outcome – for her. He wondered about her ancient campervan. Was it still roadworthy? Where would she live? Surely not in that ancient vehicle. For the twentieth time he checked his Twitter account – nothing.

Somehow he got through the day, switching to professional mode without any apparent difficulty, but he still checked for messages from Alex.

He worked out in the gym, ate an omelette and drank half a bottle of chardonnay, started the analysis of the data he had gleaned from his discussions, then slammed his notebook down on the granite counter surface of the immaculate kitchen.

Alex! Would you like a photo? xx

And almost without the pause came the reply, *I would love to see one! Yes, thank you. xx*

Hesitating for only a nanosecond, *Star of the Sea* selected one of his stock pornographic images of himself and sent it to Alex. He felt better after that. At least he had taken decisive action to further the relationship that he wanted to forge with her. He would shower and then see how she responded – perhaps with the sort of reciprocally erotic photo that other online female followers had sent.

Midnight, and Josh was ready to sleep, thinking with anticipation of Alex's response. He went into his Twitter account, his Direct Messages – nothing. Then he messaged Alex, reverting to the open exchanges they had established.

Really hope you got that job! xx

But the only response he received was:

Alex Miller 247 blocked you.

Chapter 18

There were just four weeks to go before the retirement of Grace Meredith, the present teacher-in-charge, and Alex decided that she would use that time to help in class in order to become familiar with the daily routines, and to get to know the parents, but most importantly, the children.

Jenna MacLeod strolled alongside Alex as they went into the school playground. It was the end of break time and the children had just disappeared inside for the rest of morning lessons.

'When can Jeanne start?' asked Alex. 'I expect that she will have to give a considerable length of notice in her position.

'Actually, she is not currently in post,' replied Jenna, 'so she will be able to start at the same time as you – the beginning of the Summer Term.

Alex knew better than to press Jenna on this point, but it was very unusual for a Headteacher not to be in employment and she was puzzled. Perhaps she had been ill? Maybe her school had closed? Anyway, Alex thought, she would know soon enough. The gentle babble of voices came from the school hall, which doubled as a classroom for the older children; and singing came from the infant classroom which was smaller, brighter and more snug. Singing was what had brought Alex into teaching in the first instance. She remembered how years earlier she had been walking back to her car from a hair appointment in Tunbridge Wells when she had passed a tall, brick-built Victorian school. All the windows had been open to let in the balmy summer air and she had literally been stopped in her tracks by the sound of children singing. It was pure, innocent and beautiful and at that moment she had decided on her future.

Alex shrugged off her waterproof – it was raining again – and she tried to leave her thoughts about Star of the Sea on the peg with her waterproof as she made her way towards the infant classroom. She had been shocked by the photo which Josh had sent her – not because she was innocent of male anatomy, but because she had believed that a wholesome friendship had been developing between them. Alex had picked up that Josh was a highly intelligent, witty man and the photo had seemed too crude, too obvious. She even suspected that someone may have hacked his account. Blocking him had been a knee-jerk reaction and she had wondered ever since whether this had been the right thing to do.

Grace Meredith sat on the floor, entirely at home with the five, six and seven-year-olds that surrounded her. The children adored her and copied her hand movements as she tapped different parts of her body according to the rhythm of the song that she and the children were singing. She jumped up and shook Alex's hand warmly. 'So good to meet you, Mrs Miller! The children have been so excited that they were going to meet their new teacher today. Make a space for Mrs Miller please! She is going to join in our welcome song.'

Fiona Black, Fiona Black, where are you?
Here I am, here I am, how do you do.
Jamie Stuart, Jamie Stuart, where are you?
Here I am, here I am, how do you do.

Through question and response, each child introduced the next until the circle of eighteen had been completed and the last child before Alex sang,

Mrs Miller, Mrs Miller, where are you?

And Alex replied,

Here I am, here I am, how do you do.

The rest of the day passed more quickly than Alex could have expected. She was pleased to be asked to take the junior class after lunch and launched into a session that she had prepared which combined literacy and art.

'When I was just a little younger than you, my mother used to read me stories about a family of little pigs who lived with a badger as their guardian in a cottage close to the woods. These books were full of magic – the magic that lies just beneath the surface of the world, just waiting to be discovered if we keep our eyes and minds open. Let me read a little bit from one of those stories about a dragon discovered by one of the pigs, called Sam, when he revisits a place where he had once seen a rock move.

There were the finest blackberries on a bank where the trees were scarce, and the rocks broke through the earth. He picked the juicy fruit and filled the little

basket, and ate a good few himself. Then he put the
basket under a tree and wandered on with the fiddle
under his chin, playing a tune as he walked. The wood
seemed to listen, the birds cocked their heads and sang
in reply, the trees waved their branches in slow lazy
rhythm, and Sam Pig felt happy and carefree. He saw
the rock which had once moved and there it was, solid
as the earth, weather-worn and black with rain, yet
when he stared at it, he thought it was somehow
different. He could trace a kind of shape about it, a
bulging forehead, heavy brows, and even eyelids, long
slits cut deep in the rock, half covered with bright
moss... the bracken began to wave, the earth quivered
and shook, and the rock was slowly uplifted. It was a
scaly dark head, very large and long, with half-shut
eyes concealing a glimmer of light like stars in a
cloud... '

Hands shot up.

'I've seen a rock shaped just like that, Miss! I can
take you there if you wish and you can see for yourself.'

'Is it that one behind the kirk, Geordie?'

'Yes.'

'So you see,' interjected Alex, 'you have already
started to discover the magic in your island.'

'And dragons, Miss, they come in lots of different
colours and shapes you know!'

All the children – especially the boys – were buzzing
with excitement.

'Can we start, Miss?'

'When you know exactly what I would like you to
do today, yes of course you can start. But first, please
listen carefully.'

Alex crossed the hall and switched off the lights. 'This is so you can see with your imagination! I would like you to think of one place on your island which you find especially magical. Then think about what sort of mythological beast could live there. It could be a dragon of course, disguised as rock or stone. But it could be a phoenix, hidden in the long grass of the machair; or a mermaid whose hair you see spread out upon a rock. Perhaps a unicorn lives with horses that you know on someone's croft – are you sure that you have looked right into the depths of the stables? Sometimes, is there not a long, pointed single horn just disappearing out of sight?

'When you have identified your mythological animal, I would like you to write your story – not too long, but dealing with why the animal is found where it is found. Then and only then can you create a picture of your creature and its environment.'

'Can we draw it first, please Miss?'

'I am going to say no, because as you write you will find you add more detail about how your beast looks and how it acts and this will make your painting or drawing more powerful and detailed.'

Alex glanced up to check the time and saw Jenna standing just outside the hall door, smiling broadly. 'Ah, a true seeker of everyday magic! I knew you were an inspired appointment, Alex.'

Chapter 19

Josh MacDonald was furious with himself. As his feet pounded on the treadmill, he asked himself for the hundredth time what the hell he had been thinking of sending that photo to Alex. It was obvious she was expecting something that would give further insight into his life – possibly a photo of him in clinic or further ones of New York – not the sort of thing that sent too many of his followers into ecstasies and caused flurries of erotic responses. One of the things that he had found so overwhelmingly attractive about Alex was her naivety: her selfie of herself next to Gladys; her penguin pyjamas; her open sharing of tiny aspects of her life; and her warm spontaneous messages that showed she actually did care about a man she had never met who sent her dubious, totally unsolicited, messages.

On he ran. What was the matter with him? Why had he let his life veer between extremes, swinging from intense focus on his medical practice to sexual release through pornography. He thought back to his marriage to Elspeth. They had the girls within the first five years of marriage and from then on there had been a gradual disintegration of everything that he thought they shared together. He knew that she was frequently unfaithful, but the evening when she told him that she was pregnant by someone else had, he thought at the time, been the worst evening of his life. He realised that he had been wrong when, a week later, she had an abortion – an act that went against everything that he, and he thought she, believed. His love for her had finally died when she had come home from the abortion clinic pale but unrepentant. He had started divorce proceedings the following day. From then on, Josh realised, he had distrusted all women, apart from the memory of his mother Molly, his Star of the Sea.

He showered, towelled himself vigorously, and checked his Twitter account in the remote hope that Alex had unblocked him. She hadn't and he hurled his phone against the plush leather sofa in sheer frustration. Then he sat, for a full ten minutes, just gazing at the lights and lives pulsating outside his apartment window. There was nothing for it – he would just have to carry on as if he had never met Alex Miller. A month earlier he had never heard of her; and in a month's time, he told himself brutally, he would probably have forgotten her.

⊰⊪⊱

In sharp contrast, Alex returned to *The Inn* feeling happier and more fulfilled than she could ever remember. Rory Cameron grinned broadly at her.

'I don't have to ask if you have had a good day, Mrs Miller!'

'Please can you start to call me Alex? I feel like my mother-in-law when you address me like that!'

'I'd be delighted to! Shepherd's pie all right for supper tonight, Alex?'

'Perfect,' sighed Alex, circling her thumb and index finger. I'll go and have a quick shower and be down as soon as I can – I'm starving!'

Rory shook his head fondly as he watched Alex's retreating figure, bounding up the steep wooden staircase to the only guest room *The Inn* could boast. He, along with all his fellow Governors, couldn't believe the quality of the interview that Alex had given and he knew that his own grandchildren and the children and grandchildren of the other islanders would be in the very best of hands. The appointment of Ms O'Hara had been a much more difficult decision and it was this that had taken the governing body so long to discuss. Jenna MacLeod had been adamant that the demographic trend over the next five years was such that there should be a substantial increase in the number of children attending the island school. But the range of factors to take into consideration was so complex that they had to be sure of their ground and Rory was still not one hundred percent certain that this second appointment should have been made.

❧‖❦

Showered, relaxed and happy, Alex took one last look at her Twitter account. A few desultory tweets had filtered in, but there was nothing remotely meaningful any more, now that the heart-warming process of getting to know Star of the Sea had been terminated. Decisively, she switched off any further Twitter notifications and went down to her supper.

Placing a large dish of apple crumble in front of Alex, Rory asked, 'Will you continue to live here, do you think?'

Alex paused, frowning slightly. 'I'm not sure, Rory. I can't live here permanently and I *do* have Gladys. Perhaps you could find me a little field or something close by so that I can continue to banquet like a queen and take showers so that I don't smell too awful!'

'Bless you – of course. You can drive Gladys around the back of *The Inn* – the ground is solid rock there and the rising land to the north provides good shelter. We also have outside privies which are not luxurious, but served my parents perfectly well when they were landlords of this place.

'Why did you ask, Rory?'

'Well, to be honest, Jenna wants Jeanne O'Hara to live here. We aren't the Ritz and I don't think Madame O'Hara would care to bunk down in the snug!'

'When is she coming back?'

'A week before term starts, I believe. She won't have any curriculum planning to do – that will be down to you.'

'So that's … in three weeks. When do you want to evict me, Rory?'

'Well, to be honest, never – but let's say three weeks minus one day, shall we?'

'You're a darling!'

'If I wasn't a taciturn Scot, I would say "You too!"'

Chapter 20

Rory watched the two women in his bar attentively and thought that they could not have been more different. Alex, smiling and spontaneous, was unashamedly enjoying the steak which Catriona Cameron had cooked to perfection for this landmark dinner. In contrast, Jeanne almost toyed with her food, leaving half of the sirloin untouched on her plate.

'Is the meal not to your liking Ms O'Hara?' Rory asked in genuine concern.

'No, it was fine. I just don't eat a lot, Mr Cameron.'

Or drink a lot either, reflected Rory, eyeing her glass of water before saying, 'Another Merlot, Alex?'

'Yes please, Rory. Just the one more, though – we have work to do tomorrow.'

'What brought you to Fragrey, Alex?' Jeanne asked as she sipped her decaffeinated coffee.

Alex laughed and answered honestly, 'The magic of the advertisement!'

Jeanne stirred her coffee with the small spoon, sitting silently and saying nothing more. Alex was slightly irritated that her companion felt she could ask such a direct question, but then simply close the conversation, so she said, 'And you?'

Jeanne looked up with an unreadable expression. 'Personal reasons.'

It didn't often happen, but this answer really irritated Alex. 'In that case, Jeanne, I will bid you goodnight. See you at 8.30 tomorrow morning at school.'

Rory watched as Alex flushed, stood up and left the bar for Gladys. He saw that Jeanne watched her from lowered lids and, as the door was closed – rather too firmly – he felt a distinct chill as Jeanne gave one of her rare smiles.

⊰╬⊱

'Our first two priorities are to have a look at the attainment tables for the school to make decisions about how we group the children, possibly whether we should stream them; and to make an inventory of equipment and supplies so that we can budget appropriately for what we shall need during the coming academic year.'

This was the sort of sterile stuff that Alex hated, so she nodded and smiled non-committedly. She was hoping that Jeanne would become immersed in data and leave her to look at the children's current work, to assess where they were in terms of their learning, and decide what the next steps needed to be. Above all she was looking forward to gaining precious insights into their lives and personalities through what they wrote and recorded.

She was right. Initially, Jeanne verbalised her thoughts: 'Fiona – clearly a bright girl, but underachieving. David – mm … possible dyslexia from his attempts at phonics and letter reversal …' But soon, her intense, bird-like stare excluded Alex and she went systematically through the well-tabulated records and test results for the children, making notes on her laptop.

Alex quietly walked away and went into the junior classroom. It was quiet and tidy, but with that indefinable scent of healthy young children that never fails to raise anticipation in a teacher. She pulled six of the eighteen drawers out of their storage units and sat down on the carpet with them in front of her.

Elizabeth Currie, aged eight, was a neat and tidy little girl, from farming stock. She was a careful but unimaginative writer, with sound phonic knowledge and could write reasonably complex sentences. Fiona Campbell was, clearly, very bright. Aged nine, her free-writing books were overflowing with lengthy, imaginative stories. Alex rejoiced to see that her current teacher, Grace Meredith, had only amended her work according to an agreed focus, and had not littered with dreaded red pen marks the rambling, untidy writing with its generous scattering of spelling mistakes. She knew from her years of teaching how easily the imagination of a bright child could be stultified by over-correction.

Alex, through her observations, journeyed through the lives and imaginations of the children who were going to be her responsibility in a few short days. As always, she was fascinated by the ways in which the learners threaded their own young experience through their writing and art work. Glancing through the open door to the school office, where Jeanne was still poring over data, she shook her head imperceptibly, thinking how barren an approach to education her colleague represented. Pale, her attitude rigid and tense, Jeanne O'Hara was recording her recommendations for streaming the children which Jenna MacDonald had asked her to make.

'Shall we stop for lunch?' Alex asked.

'I don't usually stop work in the middle of the day,' came the quiet reply. 'And I have about an hour's work left before I finish.'

'OK. I'm off back to the comforts of Gladys, soup and my camping stove.'

The neatly groomed dark head remained bent over Grace's files.

Alex returned to school at two-thirty and found Jeanne O'Hara waiting for her, virtually on the threshold. 'How long do you normally take for lunch, Alex?'

'Quite honestly, when I am working in my own time, within school holidays, just as long as I like,' Alex replied, looking levelly at Jeanne. Once again, she found herself surprisingly irritated by the attitude and tone of the woman almost blocking her entrance into the school reception area. For a long moment the women stood looking at each other in silence, until eventually Jeanne stepped aside. 'Can we discuss my cognitive assessment of the junior children when you're ready?'

'I'm ready right now, Jeanne! And we can compare notes, my findings with yours.'

'Have you found further data files, then?'

'No. I've found the information from the children's work itself, where their passions, opinions and life-context, as well as the quality of their work, give a 360 degree view of their achievement.'

For once, Jeanne O'Hara seemed caught off-guard. 'Can you come into the office then, please, Alex.'

'Actually, Jeanne, I think it's more sensible if you come into the classroom. All the files are laid out there and we can verify your findings through reference to the children's work.' Alex turned and headed directly for the classroom where she had left the last of the drawers neatly-stacked on the carpet. She was unsure whether Jeanne would follow her, but after a few minutes, she came into the classroom, carrying her laptop. It struck Alex just how out of place she looked. She wore a plain black jumper and pencil skirt and a single rope of pearls, whereas Alex had put on her usual non-school-day outfit of jeans and sweater, thick socks and suede ankle boots. 'Why don't you join me down here?' she asked her colleague, patting the carpet.

'If you don't mind, Alex, I'll work at a desk.'

Alex couldn't help smiling as she realised that, dressed as Jeanne was, sitting on the carpet would be virtually impossible. And at the end of the afternoon, Alex was still smiling as she strode back to *The Inn,* shaking her hair free in the cool breeze which always seemed to be blowing across the island. She felt that the afternoon had been crucial in establishing the parameters within which she and Jeanne O'Hara would be working. Jeanne's supposition had clearly been that she would be the figure of authority within the school and that Alex would do her bidding. But, remembering the terms upon which her appointment and that of the other woman had been made, Alex was certain that the Governors had intended that the responsibility for the education of the children of Fragrey should be shared between them. She was '*teacher*-in-charge' of the school, whereas Jeanne was '*administrative* head'.

Lighting the Calor Gas stove and plonking her battered kettle on the flame, Alex lay full-length on her sofa-bed and closed her eyes. Her mind was racing and she was tired. Like most people, she hated confrontation and felt that that day had held little else. She was fulfilled, she couldn't wait to start teaching the children, but she was also lonely. Alex had spent far too much time trying to keep alive a barren marriage to make friends, apart from Sarah, who was now approximately six hundred miles away by boat and road. That was one of the reasons she had enjoyed her chats with Star of the Sea and she realised, once again, how much she missed their funny, warm exchanges.

She hesitated for some time, then sat up, opened her phone and went into Twitter. Swiftly, she unblocked Star of the Sea and then sent a direct message:

Blocking you was a daft thing to do – I've missed our friendship xx

Seconds later a message came on her screen

Star of the Sea blocked you. You are blocked from following @Starofthesea and viewing @Starofthesea's Tweets.

Chapter 21

The following day passed in an almost identical fashion, the only difference being that Jeanne didn't constantly try to establish her authority. Alex felt that she no longer had to account for her actions, or the length of time she took for lunch. But still the undercurrent of tension between the two women was there, and Alex was disappointed.

Jeanne's analysis of the infant class's attainment levels and Alex's understanding of their strengths and areas for development was finished around two o'clock.

'Would you like to come for a walk?' Alex asked tentatively.

'I have paperwork to catch up on and a couple of articles to finish reading, so I'm sorry but I can't.'

Alex reflected that Jeanne's expression didn't show regret, but rather smugness that she would still be involved in educational matters in her own time. She shrugged, knowing that she had done her best, and actually felt quite relieved that she would be free to explore further on her own. Jeanne made for *The Inn* and the quasi-office that she had established in her room; whilst Alex headed for the high headland, where the changing beauty of the view never failed to delight her.

Today Alex felt as if she wanted to celebrate and so she stretched her arms wide and took deep measured breaths of the cold, salt-laden air. Then, smiling into the sun, she raised her arms and started the flowing movements of the sun salute, feeling the springy turf under her limbs as they stretched and extended in one of her favourite Yoga practices.

'Do you practise Yoga regularly?'

The soft, gentle voice hardly disturbed Alex. It seemed as one with the wind sighing through the gorse and short, sheep-cropped grass.

'Agnes! Yes, I do … and do you practise your wise-woman spontaneously-appearing act regularly?'

The self-styled 'wise-woman of Fragrey' smiled warmly at Alex.

'My wise-woman habits are a part of my life, Alex.'

'As Yoga is part of mine.'

'Where is your colleague? I had hoped that you would spend time together before the children return to school, getting to know each other.'

'We have been working in school today and yesterday, Agnes, but Jeanne had to return to her room to work.'

'Mm! What do you think of her?'

'Professional, thorough, obviously with an outstanding track record …'

'But what do you *really* think of her, Alex.'

'Really? Well, I echo your wish that we should spend time together, getting to know each other as women and as educators. But she seems too absorbed in results and data, rather than wanting to understand each child in our care. If a child's father is a fisherman, his or her learning and social context will be quite different to a child whose father is a crofter, or a doctor. Unless we tap into this context, our teaching will never be as effective as it could be. I'm sorry, I've probably said too much.'

Agnes Muirhead looked seriously at Alex. 'As a matter of fact, I totally agree with you.'

'Rory explained that the school budget is healthy and will sustain two positions – but what was the real reason behind the Governors' decision to appoint Jeanne as well as myself? It seems, well, extravagant, to be honest.'

Agnes paused thoughtfully for a time, before asking softly, 'You know that Jenna MacLeod is Clan chieftain?'

Alex nodded.

'The MacLeods have huge influence in Fragrey and its neighbouring islands and, in honour of her mother's memory and with a nod to her own status, it's a dream of Jenna's that our school will take an educational lead in this western outpost of the so-called United Kingdom. Our doctor – our real doctor, Josh MacDonald – holds a pivotal role in overseeing standards of General Practice in the islands, and Jenna's wish is that her role should match his.'

'Is there another connection between Jenna and Dr MacDonald? It seems rather a random aim.'

'How astute you are, Alex – a student of human character and motivation indeed! Yes, they were "an item" for quite a time, shortly after Josh divorced his wife.'

'She's a very lovely woman. I'm surprised that she's single.'

'I think *she* is surprised that she's still single! She made such a play for Josh. As my mother would have said, "They made a perfect couple." Both striking and charismatic, intelligent and cultured.'

'So what went wrong?'

Agnes threw back her head and laughed. 'Who can ever really explain? Two people seem perfectly suited in every regard, but there is a factor missing – let's call it factor X. Wise-women through the ages have made fortunes trying to replicate it through love-potions and spells, but I prefer to let nature take its course. Do you fancy an adventure?'

'Yes – always!'

'Can you swim?'

'I can and have several life-saver medals awarded during my school days to prove it!'

'I'd like to take you to Haligrey.'

'Where or what – or even who – is Haligrey, Agnes?'

The older woman laid her arm across Alex's shoulders and pointed to the vivid-green island a short distance to the west. 'There it is, Holy Island.'

'There must be a story behind this,' Alex smiled.

'Oh there is. I will tell you during our journey over there!'

Chapter 22

Agnes was an accomplished oarswoman: her lithe body swung in an easy rhythm as she manoeuvred her small rowing boat out of the harbour.

'Why did you call your boat Frigg?'

'Ha! Because I am Viking to the core. Where do you think I inherited my height and hair colour from? Frigg is the most powerful of the Norse goddesses and I have claimed her protection for years as I make my way about these islands. The ocean is kind today, but make no mistake, it can become a roaring beast at the drop of a hat, or the dip of an oar. But all traces of the old gods have been banished from where we are going today.'

'Is it part of the Job Description of a wise-woman to be obscure?' laughed Alex.

'Of course, my dear.'

Agnes pulled strongly towards the island, and although there was only a gentle swell, the small vessel rose and dipped dramatically between the waves. Alex could see why Agnes had checked on her ability to swim, and had insisted that she should wear a life-jacket.

'You promised me that you would tell me the story behind the island's name,' she reminded Agnes lightly.

'Do you still start story-telling for your children with that wonderful old phrase "Once upon a Time"?'

'I do when the story is traditional, yes.'

'Right, well, *Once upon a Time*, a very long time ago, there was a monk called Aelfric. He was the son of a nobleman who held great sway in the north of Ireland and he served at a friary that had been established to the east of the Giant's Causeway. In those days, early Christianity embraced paganism and pagan sites and sought to divert its followers to the way of salvation. Aelfric had a vision that Jesus Christ was calling him to leave his home shores and to take the faith to another country. He knew that St Columba had, only a few years earlier, left Ireland and had settled on Iona, which, as I am sure you know, is an island off the west coast of Scotland. Travellers who sheltered at his monastery told how Iona Abbey had become a centre of learning and place of miracles.

'In his vision, Aelfric was told to build a boat with the wood of an ash tree that grew near a holy well by the friary and to cover it with the cured skins of the sheep that grazed the sacred ground. This he did and he set sail in his tiny, frail craft. His brother friars watched and prayed as the tiny vessel bobbed and turned and was then caught in a powerful current which bore it away to the north-east, far beyond their straining sight. Shaking their heads in doubt, they returned to their home and place of worship and celebrated mass to petition for the safety of Aelfric.

'Day after day the coracle circled its way towards these islands. All Aelfric had to sustain him was a skin of water from the holy well and some bread and goats' cheese. On the very day when he had consumed the last morsel of bread and sipped the last drop of water, his coracle was washed gently ashore on the beach that we see ahead of us now, Alex. We call it *the beach of homecoming*. In true saintly fashion, where Aelfric bent to kiss the earth that he now stood upon, a spring of pure water appeared.'

'Is this a legend, or history?' Alex asked. In common with most ancient stories, the tale had a satisfying simplicity, but whether this was due to fact or skilful storytelling, Alex was unsure.

'The facts are true,' Agnes smiled. 'Aelfric was a scholar and wrote prolifically. His detailed annals were preserved in the Abbey of Iona for centuries, and are now in the British Library. But, as with all good storytellers, I have embellished the detail!'

Agnes jumped lightly out of the boat and pulled it on to the bright white sand of the *beach of homecoming*.

The boat crossing had taken less than half an hour but, looking back at Fragrey, Alex felt that she had arrived in a different world. Often, when standing in an ancient place of worship, she felt as if the very stones, the atmosphere of the place itself, had been sanctified by lives well-lived and by prayer. It was the same here. The colours of the island seemed brighter and purer than those on the surrounding islands and the air was sweet, almost fragranced. Alex and Agnes stood side by side, without speaking, simply absorbing the beauty and peace of the place.

It was some time before Alex turned to her companion and asked, 'Where did the monk, Aelfric, live?'

'Up this gentle rise, past the holy well. Follow me.'

A path led from the right-hand side of the white crescent of beach towards the centre of the island, which they reached in a few minutes. Here there was a hollow with grassy, flower-studded sides, sheltering a tiny stone building. Its door, if ever it had had one, had long since disappeared and there was a single window-opening facing the track along which they had just walked. The turf roof remained, making the building look like part of the living, breathing land which surrounded it and from which it had been formed. The silence was absolute and Alex felt an almost insurmountable desire to kneel and worship: God; the beauty of this small island; the happiness which she had found back in Fragrey; perhaps just being alive and able to appreciate such things. All these factors filled her with an unexpected joy. She enjoyed the quiet fellowship of her companion and realised that an unspoken understanding had developed between her and Agnes, who, empathetically, had walked back to the track, leaving Alex alone in the quiet, cupped hollow.

She just couldn't help it. She sank softly to her knees in the damp, springy turf and pressed her palms into its surface. It was almost as if she was absorbing the energies of the place and a cool, tingling sensation started at her fingertips and flowed gently up her arms to her shoulders and then spread throughout her body. Alex had an absolute conviction that this was a moment she would remember forever and, when eventually she moved her hands, she exclaimed involuntarily as she saw the outline of a crude Celtic cross impressed into her palm. The atmosphere of Haligrey was such that, by now, Alex fully believed that it was entirely possible for miracles to happen here, and that, somehow, the shape had appeared on her hand through supernatural means. But when she looked closely at where her palm had rested, she saw a carved stone Celtic cross embedded in the ground. It was an easy task to prize the tiny artefact out from its resting place, so she slipped it into her pocket before taking a final long look at the stone building and following the track back to the beach.

Passing the holy well, Alex paused and smiled at the steady, sparkling stream of water which was pouring from the limestone scarp into a roughly-shaped trough, covered with moss. She squatted down, cupping her hands under the cold, clear water, murmuring, whether to herself or the spirit of the monk, who had lived here so long ago, she was unsure. 'Did you shape this stone trough? Did you strike the rock and cause the water to flow?' Almost dazed by the beauty of the day and of the island and the sensuous feel of the soft damp moss, Alex drank deeply.

'I see that the island has touched you, Alex,' Agnes murmured softly.

'Yes. Look what I found.'

'Ah, it has not just touched you, it has captured you! Look at the gift I was given, when I first visited.' Agnes extended her palm on which rested a tiny exquisite chalice, carved with a pattern of dolphins and seaweed swaying in a sea-current. 'I warn you, Alex, that once you have tasted the magic of this place, your life will never be the same.'

Chapter 23

'She's not right, doctor.' Neil Logan hugged his daughter Lisa even closer to him as he looked intently at Maitland Morgan.

'In what way "Not right", Mr Logan?'

'She's unsettled, feverish and keeps complaining of a stiff neck.'

'How old is your daughter?'

'She will be four in a week's time.'

'Does she have all her teeth yet?' drawled the doctor, glancing across her surgery into a mirror which was hung directly opposite her desk.

'All her *teeth!*', exclaimed the blunt fisherman. 'Why do you need to know about her teeth?'

'Well, in my experience, young children often have fever and restlessness associated with teething. Rather than jumping to extreme conclusions, it is always sensible to start with the most obvious cause. Do you have any other children, Mr Logan?'

'Yes. Carrie.'

'And did you not experience similar symptoms with her when she was Lisa's age?'

'Yes we did. And she died two years later of lympho-sarcoma.' Neil Logan got to his feet slowly, his arms folded around his daughter protectively. 'And could I suggest that in future you should read your patients' notes carefully before trying to advise them? Lisa and Carrie's mother is beside herself with worry. We have lived this tragedy before, and do you know what? Our doctor – our *real* doctor, Dr Macdonald – lived through the tragedy with us. Sometimes he looked as ill as Carrie was, through worrying, through research, through battling on our behalf with the medical powers that be. He never had a mirror in *his* surgery.' Neil gestured with barely controlled anger to the expensive stainless-steel mirror, which had replaced the table of tide times in Josh's consulting room. 'He never looked at himself – but always at others. He is a great doctor – and a great man – and I just cannot *wait* for him to come back to us. Look at your patients Dr Morgan, not at yourself! This is the best advice I can give you!' And, turning on his heel, Neil Logan walked swiftly out of the room and slammed the door.

For a few brief seconds, Mailtland Morgan looked out of the consulting room window at the wet rock and bleached grass which swept from the exterior wall of the surgery to the summit of one of the sheltering hills which surrounded Heillstath. Then she raised her eyes, got slowly to her feet and started her Pilates stretch routine. Eventually, after twenty or more minutes, she rang through to Morag who was trying to keep order in the packed and restive surgery. 'Next patient please, receptionist.'

Morag Kitchener, having seen the ravaged face of Neil Logan as he left the consulting room, made a decision.

'Brad, I've got to go home.' Josh was pacing the senior clinician's room, lacing and re-lacing his fingers as he thought through the email he had received last night from Morag.

'But you are only three-quarters through your project, Josh.'

'What the hell am I supposed to do when my so-called replacement ignores the clinical background of my – her – patients and their emotional wellbeing?'

'Only yesterday Clive emailed me saying how well she had settled down.'

'For fuck's sake, Brad! She dismissed the concerns of one of my most vulnerable families as a child's teething troubles, when it could be a recurrence of cancer in a younger sibling. And after all you told me, do you think that Clive's opinion is an honest reflection of her impact on my practice?'

Brad Jackson frowned and turned his back slowly on Josh.

Long seconds passed – a trial of strength of character to both men. Josh was beyond angry and, although he realised that he had probably jeopardised the best reference he was ever likely to get, should he wish to progress his career, he couldn't have cared less. All he could think about was the agonised face of Jeannie Logan, and Carrie's careful, childish writing as she dedicated her drawing to her 'bestie'. He took a deep breath.

'Brad, you have been the best line-manager I have ever had – your integrity is beyond reproach, but, man, *so is mine!* Whatever you think about Maitlin Morgan …'

'Maitland,' the senior clinician corrected gently as he turned to face the agitated man opposite him.

'Whatever – I cannot tolerate this. Write the worst report ever to my clinical director. Quite simply, I just do not care! I cannot live against my own conscience, Brad. I can't.'

'Josh, sit down. Drink?'

'It's half eleven!'

'Boring to repeat myself ...'

Josh took two brisk steps towards a cream leather sofa, set at right angles to the plate glass wall overlooking the memorial gardens which fronted the hospital, and beyond these the endless structures which denoted the city. Quickly, he ran his hands over his face and through his hair, before raising his eyes to the concerned steely-blue gaze of Brad Jackson.

'Scotch?'

Josh nodded wearily.

Carefully, the older man poured out a deep measure of whisky for both Josh and himself, then sat down without a word and swirled the amber liquid around the heavy-bottomed glass. Still he said nothing, until Josh exploded. 'Is this some sort of new management technique? Death by a thousand silent inferences?'

'I don't know what to say to you. I can't fathom where to start to apologise.'

As was often the case with his interactions with Brad Jackson, Josh was wrong-footed.

'I thought ...' he began.

'You thought that you had cooked the proverbial thanksgiving goose? Josh, I would be beyond grateful if you could just postpone the finalisation of your research project here, rather than abandon it. You must return home – of course you must. And as for me,' the older man got heavily to his feet, 'the imperative is to tighten mentoring of my newly-qualified staff.' Brad

Jackson got to his feet and looked levelly at Josh, before extending his hand and saying briefly, 'It's been a privilege to work with you. I have learnt more over the past weeks than I have in years.'

Josh returned the proffered handshake. 'Thank you, Brad. And just for the record, you have restored my faith in professional integrity.'

The two men looked at each other, acknowledging that over the past few months they had each given and received something infinitely unexpected and entirely precious.

Chapter 24

'Who knows where Haligrey is?'

A forest of hands shot up.

'Yes, Miss, it's that green island which sometimes looks really close, but sometimes seems a long way away! It's got a kind of magic of its own, my granny says.'

'And I think that your granny is right1 I have felt exactly the same since I arrived on Fragrey. Well, once upon a time, long, long ago, a monk called Aelfric lived on our own magical island.'

'Alfred, Miss?'

'Aelfr*ic*, Rory, an old-fashioned name which means 'Elf ruler'. People tend not to believe in elves and fairies these days and so the name has dropped out of use.' Alex paused briefly, before saying to the class in general, 'Would it be a good idea, do you think, if we saved questions until the story is ended? We can use our notebooks to jot down questions that come into our minds and then we will have a Q & A session after playtime. Just like grown-ups do. What you think?'

There was a wave of head-nodding and a ripple of serious expressions as the children opened their rough notebooks.

'Aelfric travelled from his home country, Ireland, in a little round boat called a coracle, and the sea carried him directly to Haligrey. As soon as he landed on the bright, white beach, called *the beach of homecoming,* that we can sometimes see from our own cliff tops, Aelfric knew that the beautiful island would become his home.

'There are two things that I would like you to do this morning: first of all, try hard to think of everything that the monk would have needed to live there – things to make his body healthy, his mind occupied and his thoughts fresh and exciting. Please can you then make a list of these things. Secondly, I would like you to write your own story about the sort of life you think he would have led, living alone on a tiny island. You can make that story factual and refer back to the list you have just made; or if you prefer, you can create your own myth or legend involving Aelfric and Haligrey.'

Alex glanced at the clock at the back of the junior classroom and said, 'Remember, we will have our Q & A session when you come in after break. Perhaps you would like to decide during your free time on whether you think you might like to write a realistic story, or create a legend of your own; and think too of the questions that we can discuss which would help to make your writing more authentic. Off you go – gently Archie, please don't push.'

Mike Whitfield, who had volunteered to help Alex in class that morning scratched his head thoughtfully, 'I must be very dim, Alex, but I don't quite see how the children will be learning about Religious Education and Geography if they are considering how an Anglo-Saxon monk would have lived on a remote island a thousand years ago…'

Alex grinned at him. 'When we were children, Mike, we were taught facts directly – at the time they likened it to 'filling up an empty vessel'; but over the years educational research has shown that children engage better with facts and remember them if their creative imagination is involved. The children will have to think about what the monk would have needed spiritually, as well as physically, for survival and in doing this they will have to revisit or explore their understanding of Christianity. And so, both RE and the settlement aspects of Geography will become involved in their thinking. If children choose to write a myth or legend, then they will have to consider how to write about things we cannot see, or touch or hear – in other words, how to represent the world of faith.'

'Why are you only a classroom teacher?' Mike asked, shaking his head in admiration. 'Have you never wanted to progress in your career?'

'*Only* a classroom teacher!' Alex laughed. 'It's the most privileged job in the world. You can keep your admin and strategic planning! Just give me the children to educate. One of the things which struck me in my training was that the word 'education' is based upon the Latin for "to lead out from". From what, exactly, is down to one's own interpretation. Mine is from not knowing, to knowing; from ignorance to understanding. What could be more important than that?'

Jenna MacLeod had timetabled herself in to support the session after break and she arrived at the classroom door, positively glowing. 'Guess what, Mike? Josh is coming back to Fragrey on Friday!'

'Josh?' echoed Alex blankly.

'Ah sorry, Alex, I forgot you haven't yet met our doctor, my friend Josh MacDonald. He is such an important part of our community – everyone has missed him.'

Alex reflected to herself that it was pretty obvious from Jenna's heightened colour and shining eyes that her Chair of Governors was number one on the list!

⊰)||(⊱

Josh stood at the front of the ferry like a grim figurehead. Dashing the spray and drizzle out of his eyes, his gaze devoured every well-known rock and promontory of the island as the ferry turned slowly to dock alongside the quay. He could make out all the things that meant so much to him: his cottage on the quayside, waiting closed and quiet for him to return; the surgery, neat and orderly with red geraniums in pots outside the entrance – bless Morag. He scanned across the valley to the school, where he struggled to fulfil his governor duties due to the myriad other calls on his time and energy; and the ornate gothic Manor House which belonged to the head of the Clan MacLeod. He gripped the rail on the boat until his knuckles were white, forcing himself to remain composed and civilised before joining the short queue of passengers now waiting to disembark, rather than pushing past them in his haste to stand once again on his beloved island.

It was late Friday afternoon and Josh was grateful that his first surgery would be Monday morning. The trip from the States had seemed interminable, and he was tired. But so keen was he on taking up again the hard life he loved – even though at times he found it unbearable – that he had not considered practicalities at all. The shops on the island would now be closed and heaven only knew what – if anything – he had in his small freezer. Ah well, he reflected philosophically, he could always go to *The Inn* and take pot luck with whatever Catriona Cameron had produced for supper.

Walking along the cobbled quay, Josh inhaled deeply. It was so good – no, not just good, it was joyous – to be back! He felt his step lighten and quicken as he walked past the familiar fishing boats, *The Lively Lass, Dolphin's Touch, The Road to the Isles.*

'Good to see you back, Dr MacDonald!'

'Hector! How's the old trouble?'

'Much the same, Josh – but I was damned if I was going to let the American woman lay her talons on *that* part of my anatomy!'

'Open for business on Monday, Hector!'

'Aye – I'm relieved to hear that,' grinned the sailor.

Josh looked down momentarily as he flung open the blue-painted door of his cottage. Used all his life to disappointments, he dreaded seeing damp, mould, mouse-droppings. But when he had shut the door behind him and lifted his gaze, what he did see was bread, milk, fruit, cheese and eggs, with a note propped up against the milk container: *Bet you hadn't thought of the practical stuff and I know you favour omelettes! Can't wait to have you back in the surgery, Your devoted slave, Morag x*

Laughing, Josh threw his head back speaking out loud as if his receptionist and right-hand woman were beside him: 'the only thing you have missed out, Morag, is a bottle of red wine. But not to worry we have Scotch substitute!' And turning on his heel, Josh headed for the dark oak, battered corner cupboard which was built to one side of the open fireplace. Glancing down he saw that he had trodden on a cream envelope that had clearly been pushed under the door by hand. Gritting his teeth as he recognised the handwriting, and the coat of arms on the reverse of the envelope, Josh took out his penknife and slit open the envelope.

So glad you are back, Josh. The School – and I – have missed you. Supper at my place tonight? xx

Oh God, thought Josh. Would she never give up? Wearily he whipped out his phone and texted:

I'm knackered, Jenna. Wouldn't be much use to you tonight! Catch up during the week. Josh.

⊰∥⊱

Metres from where Josh stood frowning at his phone, Alex lay on her bed gazing at Gladys' orange roof. She remembered the intent looks on the faces of the children, who had clearly felt so grown-up during their Q & A session, studiously trying to make notes, listen and talk at the same time. Their work had been outstanding. The gifted Fiona Campbell had written a fascinating fable, which involved Aelfric talking to the dolphins which visited the seas around Haligrey. He had learnt to interpret their language and was kept from becoming lonely by listening to the dolphins' stories of the far-off places they had visited and the beautiful sights they had seen. Archie had produced a story above and beyond the usual range of his imagination in which the monk had found a coconut which had been washed up on the beach and had used it as a football to keep himself fit. But it was Gemma Blisset who had excelled herself. Up until that afternoon, Alex had not been able to get the measure of the dreamy, quiet little girl, who often seemed to be daydreaming as she looked out of the classroom window rather than getting on with her work. But today Gemma had written a moving account of how difficult Aelfric had found his solitude at first. How he had missed his fellow Irish monks and had turned increasingly towards prayer and talking to God. Through this, he had become ever more devout and resilient. The story had moved both Alex and Mike Whitfield to tears.

Jenna MacLeod had been very abstracted during the period between break and lunchtime. Alex noticed that she consulted her watch approximately every five minutes, frequently tapping it and checking with the wall clock to ensure that it was keeping accurate time. She tried her best to support the group of children with whom she was working, but it was painfully obvious that her mind was elsewhere – Alex suspected with the island doctor. When the bell rang for lunch, Jenna almost shot out of her seat, but did have the presence of mind to compliment Alex on the morning's teaching and learning.

'You could have been made specifically for your role in our school, Alex,' she smiled, one hand on the classroom door. '"Everyday magic" could be an accurate description of what you are offering our children.'

'And the school could have been specifically made to suit my mindset, Jenna! I love my work. I consider every day here a complete privilege.'

Alex stood up and stretched as far as she could within the confined spaces of Gladys, taking the two small steps towards her Calor Gas stove to put on the kettle for her final hot drink of the day. There was only one blot on her cloudless horizon and that was Jeanne O'Hara. Thankfully, she saw very little of her cool and detached colleague, and frequently wondered exactly what she did behind the closed door of her office. Occasionally, Jeanne would drift silently into Alex's classroom and sit to watch a lesson, making notes in a hard-backed notebook. Occasionally, she would observe the children playing, but never did she interact with them, and only once since the start of term had Alex met formally with her.

'Could you come to my office after school today please, Alex?' she had asked one Friday lunchtime. Alex, maintaining her determination to be treated as an equal, responded without a flicker, 'Actually, Jeanne, I have the week's assessments to do. It would be much easier if you could come to my classroom, please.' Jeanne O'Hara had flushed slightly, but had acquiesced.

Alex poured the boiling water onto the tea bag nestling in a mug with a sheep emblazoned on its front and stirred the contents thoughtfully. Her first Governors' meeting since she had taken up the post of teacher-in-charge was on the following Thursday evening and she was interested in seeing whether Jeanne would be treated on the same footing as she would be, or whether there would be some subtle differences. Wickedly, she couldn't help but smile as she anticipated the charged interactions between the Chair of Governors, Jenna MacLeod, and the newly-returned island doctor.

Sleep felt a million miles away and Alex opened Gladys' stable door, resting her arms on the bottom section as she gazed at the fathomless milky way. Skies were dark in Fragrey, and even with the faint glow from the windows of *The Inn*, she soon lost herself in the depths of the night skies. She felt restless and for the thousandth time thought of Star of the Sea. But this was ridiculous, she reminded herself: how could someone she had known only virtually have such an impact on her life? Breathing in and exhaling slowly several times, Alex brought herself back to the present moment: the planning for teaching on the following day; the preparation for the Governors' meeting later in the week. All this had to be done and she should turn on her laptop. But what she actually did was to activate her iphone and access her Twitter account. She still hoped that Star might have unblocked her, but all access to his communications were still barred. Wearily, she scanned the vacuous tweets that had filtered in, sardonically registering that she was shedding followers like a dog sheds its coat, because she had seldom engaged in social media since she had blocked Star of the Sea. Then, with a decisive action, she switched off her phone, accepted the inevitable, and went to her computer.

Chapter 25

'My god, Josh, but I'm glad to see you!' Morag Kitchener exclaimed as Josh walked into the sunlit surgery on Monday morning. She was busy polishing every surface of the already immaculate reception area. 'I know you'll hate this, but I will just have to give you a hug.'

Josh pretended to feint away from her, grinning, but returned her hug with affection. 'You have no idea how very good it is to be back, Morag!'

'It's a wonder you have any patients left, doctor,' she continued, 'That woman was useless! She just didn't care, Josh. She kept people waiting for no good reason. Once I entered her consulting room more quickly than usual after knocking and she was doing some weird sort of contortions on the floor!'

'Pilates perhaps – or Yoga?'

'Well whatever it was, it was utterly out of place. The waiting room was full to bursting. Children were crying, people were getting impatient …'

'Well that's all over now, Morag. You won't find me tying my limbs into knots – I might never untangle them again! Running – preferably in a straight line – is much more down my street.'

'And the other thing was that the Clinical Director for the Highlands and Islands was never off the phone! If only he gave *you* the sort of attention he gave to that woman!'

Not trusting himself to speak, Josh simply held up his mug and inclined his head.

'I'll get that coffee for you, doctor,' Morag smiled. 'Strong and sweet …'

⨅

'Hey, Lisa, that's a pretty dress you're wearing today.' Josh sat, smiling, despite the knot of fear in his belly at the fragile appearance of the little girl as she sat on her father's knee.

'Yes, new … from mummy.'

'And do you play out in such a pretty dress, Lisa?'

'Don't want to play out,' the little girl murmured.

'It's lovely weather. If I wasn't here in my office, I would be playing out,' Josh said gently.

'Tired,' murmured the little girl.

'You're going to have to be a big brave girl, Lisa. I need to make a prick in your arm and take some blood, so that we can see if we can make you less tired. Can you do that do you think?'

'Course I can. Just like my big sister Carrie!' smiled the child.

Tears came into Neil Logan's eyes – and into Josh's, but he swiftly turned away, pulled out a drawer and took out a white, toy rabbit, which he gave to his small patient.

'This rabbit comes out only for the bravest girls!' Josh told her. 'How about telling her a story, whilst I'm getting this ready?' Josh gestured to the syringe in his hand, as he had always followed the axiom of explaining exactly what he was doing to his patients, however young.

'What do you think, Josh?' Morag asked at the end of the packed morning surgery.

Josh levelled his steely-blue gaze at his receptionist's homely features. 'Beyond any probability that I anticipated, I think Lisa has the same cancer.'

Morag shook her neat, permed head. 'This will finish off Jeannie Logan for sure … maybe Neil too. For all he's big and bluff, he adores his family. Why is there such pain in the world, Josh?'

Josh took both Morag's hands in his and held them tight. 'That's a question I have asked myself for as long as I can remember, Morag. And I'm still no nearer to finding the answer. Sometimes it drives me to despair … but at the moment I have no time for this sort of bleak reflection! See you at four this afternoon? Same place?'

'It's a date.'

Although he would never breathe a word to anyone on the island – it would be far too unprofessional – Josh was seething at the damage that the American locum had done. When he thought about the backstory to her appointment, he knew that he would have to do something about this, but exactly what he was not, at this point, certain. People's ailments had been brushed aside as 'minor'; the psychological impact of anxiety, or of loneliness, had been ignored; but most damagingly, some of the long-term prescriptions for the control or stabilization of conditions had been cancelled or changed, due to 'excessive cost'. Josh had asked Morag to review the notes of all patients and note those in the latter category and he gritted his teeth as he anticipated the extra work that this would involve – both for his faithful assistant and for himself. With an exclamation of sheer exasperation, he jumped into his car and started on his home visits for the day.

Chapter 26

By Thursday evening, Josh felt as if he had done a month's work in four days and the thought of attending a Governors' meeting that evening after surgery actually made him groan. The main purpose, as far as he could make out from the Agenda which Jenna had circulated earlier in the week, was to welcome the two new members of staff to the school and to discuss arrangements for the Leavers' Service which was to take place on the last day of the summer term. Growling at Morag for coffee, he had told her in no uncertain terms that he would much rather have an enema than attend! But here he was, striding impatiently along the quayside, listening to the gulls' desolate cries as they swooped and landed in the wake of a fishing boat returning to harbour with its catch.

It was a perfect spring evening and the sea was ablaze with the gold and purple of the setting sun. The fragrant peace and the beauty of the island, as always, started to soothe his exhausted mind and he smiled as he anticipated the appearance of the women – he had at least been told their gender, although he hadn't been given their names – whom he would be meeting in a few minutes. Female Primary School teachers in his experience were intense, dowdy and inevitably wore home-knitted cardigans, and he hoped that he would be able to stay awake, as the merits of *The Sound of Music* or *Les Misérables* as a suitable send-off for the Year 6 children, were discussed.

It took only twenty minutes for Josh to reach the school. He knew that already most of the Governors were there, since the well-known array of vehicles were parked haphazardly in the school car park. He noted, however, the addition of a black Golf and a vintage orange camper van. Josh squared his shoulders, took a deep breath, and walked briskly into the school hall.

'Josh, welcome back!' Jenna cried, kissing him on both cheeks. 'You've been away far too long. I've set out wine and some light refreshments just over there, so do please help yourself. I bet you haven't eaten, have you?'

'A tad difficult since surgery ended only half an hour ago and my walk over here took twenty minutes!' Josh retorted acerbically.

'I would have cooked you supper,' Jenna rebuked him, adding in a much softer voice, 'I still can.' When Josh almost imperceptibly shook his head, she briskly returned to the business of the evening. 'But anyway, let me introduce our new members of staff. Well one at least – I'm not sure where the other is!' She glanced at her watch before gesturing to where a dark-haired woman, astonishingly suited and booted, was talking quietly to the vicar. 'Jeanne, this is Dr Josh MacDonald, recently returned from secondment in the States; Josh, Jeanne O'Hara is the newly-appointed Administrative Head of our school.'

'Delighted to meet you,' Jeanne said with a radiant smile, 'Your reputation goes before you.' Seamlessly she turned her attention, and conversation, from Mike Whitfield. 'How did you find the States – New York I believe?'

Josh reflected that Jeanne would be more suited to a home-counties setting than to an isolated island school. And so much for the vision of a knitted cardigan and limited conversation. This woman was a sophisticated socialite – and a very attractive one at that. But there was something Josh felt almost repulsive about her. There was a closed personality behind the dark eyes and the cool appraising glance.

'Where's Alex?' asked Jenna impatiently.

'Sorry, Jenna, I haven't the first idea,' Jeanne responded.

'I'm *so sorry,* Jenna!' Alex bounded into the hall, face flushed and hair windblown. 'Archie had quite a bad nosebleed and I had to sit with him until it had stopped. You know how his granny frets about him! Losing his father in that lifeboat disaster has made her over-protective and I didn't want to alarm her. I …' Alex's glance swept apologetically around the assembled Governors and came to rest on Josh.

There are just a handful of occasions in life when time literally appears to stop and the brain seems incapable of directing thought, or speech, or movement. For both Alex and Josh, this was such a moment.

'Well you are here *now,* Alex,' Jenna said. 'Do help yourself to a glass of wine before our meeting. And can I introduce Dr Josh MacDonald?'

Alex and Josh merely nodded to each other as, for the moment, speech or action was just impossible. Their online relationship stood like something tangible between them and they hadn't the faintest idea how they could get through the next two hours. Then, embarrassingly, both made a move towards the refreshment table at the very same instant, but stopped simultaneously. Taking a deep breath, Josh made a monumental effort and asked stiffly, 'Red or white?'

'Red, please.'

His hand shaking slightly, Josh poured wine for himself and Alex and handed it to her, forcing himself to meet her glance. He had prepared to meet resentment or anger, but what he saw shook him: Alex was fighting tears. Although he had been attracted to the virtual Alex, nothing could have prepared him for the combination of innocence and maturity he saw now, standing opposite the living, breathing woman. Experience was written on her face, but her eyes were guileless and her gaze open and entirely honest. He cringed mentally at the memory of his glib, sexually-specific comment that he had wanted to be inside her, and shame washed over him at the spontaneous answer that this lovely woman had given to him: 'I want you there.'

His mind in turmoil, Josh sat down, positioning himself as far from Alex as he could. He barely followed the direction of the meeting, as he played and replayed the exchanges that they had had on Twitter – and again and again, with crushing embarrassment, he recalled the final pornographic image that had caused Alex to block him. What was really exercising him was how on earth they could continue to live together in the same small settlement, let alone maintain a teacher/governor relationship. Various courses of action suggested themselves to him. Should he ignore what had gone before? Should he deny that he was *Star of the Sea?* Could he apologise? What, for God's sake, if she needed medical attention? He must have crossed some unethical threshold in his too-frank relationship with her. Round and round ran his thoughts like a hamster in a treadmill, and he was no nearer to finding a resolution as Jenna ground through the Agenda: introductions; consideration of various unsuitable ideas for end of Year 6 productions. Would it never end?

The comparative merits of *The Lion King* and *Frozen* were being discussed in such detail that Josh honestly thought that he would have to escape by saying that he had a medical emergency to attend to, when the interminable circling stopped and Alex spoke.

'Why are we discussing dramas set in Africa and Norway? Surely our children would be more comfortable enacting a story, or legend, which took place here on their own island? I have only been in Fragrey for a few short months, but I have been blown away by the richness of history here.'

Agnes Muirhead smiled softly. 'You're right Alex. There's a whole raft of tradition and history in and surrounding our island. The children's lives have been spun from it and woven into it. Could we create a pageant, based on the island wildlife, perhaps? Or weave that into the story of the monk, Aelfric, who settled on our beautiful holy island. What could be more meaningful and dramatic than that?'

'How about telling the story behind the boat burial that we re-enact in January?' suggested Rory, warming to the subject. 'We symbolically burn the old year at the start of the new, and maybe we could find a parallel with the end of the children's time at our island school and the start of their time at the High School – a type of new year for them.'

Josh was shaken by Alex's soft laugh. This woman appealed to all his senses.

'Aelfric I've been introduced to – but the boat burial?' Her quick sense of humour kicked in despite the excruciating situation in which she found herself. 'Do you select a member of the community to sacrifice each New Year? Or is it entirely random?'

Josh also found himself responding to the humour of the situation. 'Rest assured, the islanders don't ask me for recommendations, Mrs Miller.'

'But I'm certain you could find a victim if they did,' came the swift response, which plunged Josh back into silence.

Jenna firmly took back control, wresting the meeting away from the banter and swift exchange between Alex and Josh. 'Alex has the right approach, I think. Perhaps she can research with the children exactly what they would best like to do and report back to us in, say, one month? I would hope that the remaining eight weeks of term would give you a long enough time to rehearse the production with your children?'

Alex nodded thoughtfully. 'That should be fine.'

'Do you have anything to add, Jeanne?' continued the Chair of Governors.

'On this subject, no. But I do wish to table an item under Any Other Business, if the Chair will permit?'

Jenna acquiesced graciously and nodded approval as Jeanne sat up even straighter and arranged her notes on a small table which she had placed to her right.

'In order to develop the already very good standing that the island school holds within the Western Isles, I have, since my arrival on the island, researched a range of fairly local Multi-Academy Trusts which we could join. If the Governors wish, I can summarise my findings, but, in short, there is nothing remotely suitable for the ambitious vision that we all have for our children and our school here. I would like to propose to the Governing Body that we should establish our own Multi-Academy Trust – let's abbreviate that to MAT – and put ourselves in a position to lead and support other island schools.'

Rory frowned and ventured, 'I for one would need much more information on exactly what that means, Jeanne.'

'I have prepared a briefing paper which, if the Chair allows, I would like to circulate. I am proposing that we should ourselves establish a MAT with three founder members – Jenna, Mike and myself. We could drive through the measures for improvement that are necessary in the 21st century and create for ourselves a name that resonates through the Western Isles.'

Josh watched the interactions of his fellow Governors closely. Jenna was positively glowing. Jeanne, he was sure, was her appointment. Mike looked, quite simply, besotted, and gazed at the composed and articulate woman as if she were an object of religious fervour. Agnes and Rory were sceptical. But reluctantly, it was on Alex that he let his eyes rest. Eyes downcast, face flushed, she looked uncomfortable at best, miserable at worst.

As far as he himself was concerned he was deeply worried that this speech smacked of self-aggrandizement, not seeking the best for the school. Women like Jeanne disturbed him deeply: there seemed to be dark, opaque thoughts that he could not follow, swirling deep in their minds. Looking at Jeanne's almost reptilian stare, Josh marvelled at the speed and complex memory recall of the human brain, as he called to mind the first time he had suffered one of his crushing migraines. His mother had tucked him up in bed and announced that she was going to read to him. Since he was hardly able to see, let alone focus, he didn't have the energy to object, and so Molly MacDonald had read from one of *her* favourite authors, Rosemary Sutcliffe. And here, in stories of ancient Greece, Josh encountered for the first time the concept of the dark and secret female psyche which stood in contrast to the more straightforward open male mind. If Apollo was the male god of the sun, and ruled over all that was bright and evident in the natural world, then Artemis was his female opposite; goddess of the dark and hidden secrets of night.

Lost in his thoughts, Josh did not respond as he was offered a copy of Jeanne's 'briefing paper'. 'Dr MacDonald?' Half-rebuking, half-ridiculing him, Jeanne gave the paper in her hand a little admonitory shake, which made up Josh's mind.

'Sorry, colleagues,' he declared, going through the motion of checking his phone, 'I am needed. Please excuse me.' And without a backward glance he strode from the hall, closing the door firmly behind him and leaving the briefing paper untouched on the chair that he had vacated.

Chapter 27

The meeting had ended very soon after Josh's abrupt exit and Alex left without speaking another word. As she climbed into Gladys, she was fighting back tears of frustration that the life she had thought perfect had suddenly come under threat. She sighed with relief at finally being in her own company, and leant against the campervan door as if to shut out the world.

Behind her closed eyes, instead of seeing the welcome dark, all she could recall was the aspect, voice and gestures of Josh MacDonald. She had thought him attractive online, but his virtual image was nothing compared with the impact of the man himself. It hadn't shown the decisiveness and energy of his movements, or his range of expressions: usually controlled, but sometimes becoming passionate, impulsive, articulate – bespeaking the essence of the man. She hadn't fully appreciated the quickness of his intellect, or the quality of his melodious, expressive voice. His eyes she had explored – expanding the screen of her iphone until she felt that she could see into their very depths. But the range of emotion which they expressed, their deepening colour when he was moved, or angry, those things she hadn't seen.

Automatically, Alex put her kettle on the Calor Gas stove, but before it had started to boil, impatiently she switched off the heat: she would go mad if she remained in the tight confines of her campervan, however cherished a home it had become. For a fleeting moment, she considered going into *The Inn* and getting systematically plastered, but she decided that facing the tight-lipped supercilious attitude of Jeanne as she sipped her inevitable glass of water was more than she could face.

Dusk was falling and she glanced across the courtyard to see Rory switching on the lights in the bar and the dining room. It looked beguilingly cosy, and ambiguously she longed for company, yet knew that she needed solitude to untangle her thoughts. So double-checking that she had switched off the stove, she walked out into quiet expanse of the night.

Alex moved quickly and almost soundlessly along the quay, passing within three metres of where, behind closed curtains, Josh sat, striving unsuccessfully to immerse himself in one of his best-loved Latin texts. Quickly she left the small town behind and climbed the steep track across the heather to the cliff where she had stood weeks earlier in the bright sunshine, marvelling at the beauty and scale of the scene which lay before her.

Allowing Nature to quieten her, Alex let the faint sounds of the still evening wash over her. The full moon was bright and transformed the sea into a sheet of polished silver. Hanging like a slipped halo over Haligrey, the holy island, was the unfathomable milky way.

To Alex, Yoga was a way of linking her own bodily rhythm to the power and cycles of the natural world and, just as on her previous visit she had saluted the sun, now she went through the more powerful and darker movements of the moon salutation. Again and again, her lithe body folded and bent backwards, exposing her heart to the moon's cold light. Gradually the heat in her mind cooled and settled, and her thoughts flowed clear and incisive once again. So utterly focussed was Alex that she didn't see the shadowy figure halt soundlessly as it crossed the springy heather. She was completely oblivious of the fact that her every move, her every aspect were being closely observed; and when she completed the salutation with a strong backbend, extending her arms as if in worship, she was unaware that the figure slipped silently away to disappear once again below the steep curve of the hill.

Shortly after Alex had passed his cottage earlier, Josh had given up on Virgil and placed the treasured, leather-bound book firmly down on the arm of his battered leather armchair. Restless beyond endurance, he grabbed his Barbour from the cupboard under the stairs and slammed his front door shut behind him. Without making any conscious decision as to which direction he should take, he left the quayside and followed the track to the high cliff which protected the small town. Josh walked lightly and swiftly in any event, but the springy heather cushioned his footfall even further and he moved like a shadow. The moon was lighting up the treacherous sea with which he had such an ambiguous relationship. He thought how its light silvered the landscape and made it beautiful, almost magical. And thinking of that word – magic – his mind flitted to the advertisement that the governing body of the school had been at such pains to put together. They had hunted for a 'seeker of everyday magic' – the words had been his own – and they had found Alex.

Rounding a large boulder he stopped, as if he himself had suddenly been bewitched and turned to stone. There in front of him, silhouetted against the moon's disc, the stars and the untidy sprawl of the milky way, he saw Alex following the beautiful sequence of moves through which she was quietening her mind. He felt as if he was watching pure energy – unearthly and monotone – as if she were an intrinsic part of the moonlit night that wiped all colour from the landscape. Finally, as the beautiful figure finished her flowing sequence and extended her arms, Josh started to awake from the enchantment, realising that he had to regain the power of movement or be discovered. As if he still moved and breathed in a dream, he found his silent way back down the track once again to the security of his cottage. Panting, not just from the speed of his descent but from the intensity of the experience, he mirrored Alex's earlier action: he shut the door and leant his back against it. Even with closed eyes he couldn't rid his mind of the image of the lovely woman whose lone presence on the cliff top had moved him as few things had ever done before. Round and round like a rat in a trap his thoughts circled – how the hell was he going to resolve this one!

Chapter 28

'When was the last time Mrs MacKenzie came into the surgery, Morag?' Josh was scanning the notes that his secretary had placed on his desk first thing the next morning.

Morag scowled. 'A casualty of Maitland Morgan's patient care, doctor!'

Josh raised an eyebrow questioningly.

'About a week after you had left for the States she came in, mainly for company as she always does, but she was in your consulting room for less than five minutes and came out close to tears. "Come and take some tea with me," I suggested, but she shook her head. "I need to find something useful to do, Morag" she whispered. "I mustn't waste NHS time."'

'You don't have to be a bloody Einstein to reconstruct the consultation, do you?' Josh jumped up and pressed his hands hard onto the surface of his desk, almost dislodging the vase of daffodils that his secretary had placed there.

'That woman …' murmured Morag softly.

'I'll visit Jessie after my morning rounds,' Josh affirmed through gritted teeth. 'And I may be some time with her.'

As patient after familiar patient knocked and entered his consulting room during that bright Spring morning, Josh reflected that perhaps the break away from his island practice had actually reinvigorated him, although the motivation behind it disgusted him. Some wished to seek advice on a new ailment; some sought reassurance. On that particular day, none were seriously ill. But for all who crossed his threshold, Josh had a warm smile and a firm handshake and gave them his undivided attention and the benefit of his formidable intellect for the ten to fifteen-minute appointment. And to all, he extended his love and care.

'You don't mind if I take Jessie this bunch of daffodils, do you, Morag?' Josh asked when his morning surgery was ended.

'Why should I mind that now, doctor? I wondered whether you would like to take this as well – I made it for you, but Jessie MacKenzie would probably appreciate it just as well.'

'I'm none too sure of that,' Josh smiled, as Morag held out a small Dundee cake, homemade with love, and wrapped in greaseproof paper.

⇥║╟⇤

'Jessie!' Josh rapped on the door sharply, but there was no sound from the tiny stone cottage. Tucked away in a terrace at right angles to the quayside, *Pleasant Row* could not have been more inappropriately named. The houses, crowded together in a narrow maze of dark alleyways, consisted of a single front-room, tiny scullery and shower-room downstairs, and upstairs a front bedroom and box-room. Josh was as familiar with the layout of Fragrey as he was with his own back garden, and so after looking through the front window for any sign of life, he walked a few steps further and followed a passageway between the two central terraced houses, which led to the row of cobbled back yards and former privies. In less than two minutes he had reached the neat area behind Jessie's house, number six, and, shading his eyes, he looked through the back window into the scullery. Nothing. He was touched to see that Jessie had tried to brighten the dark, confined space through grouping pots of bright daffodils and delicate tulips under her windows and by the back door. She was a gentle old lady who never wanted to be a nuisance to anyone and he was utterly horrified that she had had such inappropriate treatment from his practice whilst he had been away.

It was at that moment that he decided that Maitland Morgan would have to account for her unprofessionalism, whatever the consequences for himself.

'Afternoon, Doctor MacDonald.' A bright-faced, elderly woman greeted him warmly from the back door of number seven. 'You're looking for Jessie now, are you?'

'I am indeed, Ginny. Is she away shopping, or visiting, do you know?'

'I haven't seen her for about ten days, doctor. I thought she might be away from the island visiting her brother Roddy in Lochboisdale. To be honest with you, doctor, I did go and check to see that she hadn't collapsed or anything. Jessie and I keep keys to each other's houses. She isn't indoors.'

'Thank you, Ginny. You're a good neighbour. I've been away myself, as you know …'

'Aye, and thank the good Lord you are now back! The island was going through seven kinds of hell in your absence. That woman was terrible!'

Josh flushed despite himself – partly through anger, and partly through embarrassment. 'Thank you, Ginny, once again. And now I must be on my way. I'll ring Roddy MacKenzie tonight – he's Jessie's next of kin. Take care of yourself.'

⊰⧉⊱

Josh pushed away the untasted Dundee cake which he had brought back to his cottage for lunch and re-read the bleak email from the laboratory in Edinburgh.

Blood tests for Lisa Logan indicate that she has lympho-sarcoma. Please contact the paediatric oncology department to arrange for admission of the child for further tests.

He had known it: of all the damned things to happen to that lovely family… It was at times like this when the sheer impotence of the mighty body of medical knowledge horrified him. Why train for years, when all he could say to the Logans was that he could do nothing to make their little girl well again? He ran his hands through his thick black hair and stood up wearily. How old was he? Fifty-one? At that moment he felt like an old man, jaded and disillusioned. What on earth was the point of going on when he constantly lost the battle to keep the islanders he loved safe and well? Going through the motions of getting his jacket and bag for afternoon surgery, he felt the black shroud of depression closing him in, blocking out the light, extinguishing hope. At times like this, whatever the weather or time of day, it was the bleakest, darkest night for Josh.

Taking a deep breath, and trying to settle his mind for what had to be done that afternoon – advising, prescribing, smiling, speaking to the Logans – he picked up the daffodils again to take them back to his surgery and opened his front door onto the quayside.

There were a hundred things that he could have expected to see when he ventured out once again into the familiar world of Heillstath, but Alex Miller was not one of them. She stood, quiet and composed, on the other side of his threshold and she was holding a long piece of red ribbon to which a small, woolly-coated dog was attached. Josh had no idea how long they stared at each other, but it seemed an eternity. Eventually, Alex spoke: 'Can I speak to you please, er, Doctor MacDonald?'

Without answering, Josh held the door open wider and then shut it on the outside world once again.

'Alex…'

'Star…'

They started to speak at exactly the same moment.

'I don't know how to begin to apologise to you,' Josh said. 'I just don't have the words …'

'I was very upset the other night. Not just at you, but at me too.' Alex bent to stroke the dog to hide her confusion. 'I, too, have no words. But I knew that I had to see you. What are we going to do, Star?'

'Well, the first thing is for you to stop calling me Star,' Josh smiled grimly. 'The second thing is that we will have to talk properly about this, but not now. I should be in my surgery and will face the wrath of Morag if I don't arrive there within the next five minutes. The third thing is a question: Why do you have Bonnie tied to a piece of red ribbon?'

'Ah, so that's her name?'

'She's the Logans' wee dog. They got her for their little girl Carrie.'

'We don't have a Carrie Logan at school.'

'She died, back in the winter time.'

Alex frowned at what Josh had just told her. 'Ah, I found her, Bonnie, wandering about behind the school, following some sort of trail, rabbits perhaps. She's a loving little thing.' As if to prove the point, Bonnie started to wag her small tail and licked Alex's hand.

'Look – Alex – I need to speak to the Logans this afternoon. Should I take Bonnie to my Surgery?'

'I can keep her, St... er, Doctor MacDonald, er...'

'For all our sakes, could you call me Josh, please? And surely it is as inappropriate for you to have a dog in school, as it is for me to have one in my medical practice.'

Alex nodded, but then a radiant smile lit up her face. 'We can do observational drawing! And Bonnie can be our live model! You speak to her owners, Josh. I'll look after the dog.'

'I really must go. But can we meet this evening?' Josh asked.

'In *The Inn*?'

'No, here. I will cook.'

'That would be good, I think. But just one thing ...'

'I *must go,* Alex!'

'I'm not keen on lobster – or caviar.'

'Thank God for that! Eight o'clock?'

'Eight o'clock.'

Chapter 29

Josh jogged along the quayside. How could a brief conversation have so quickly dispersed the darkness and brought the sun into his life again? He thought of Alex's mobile and expressive features; the beautiful arch of her eyebrows above her clear blue eyes, her sensuous mouth and her slender body – and he smiled.

'Afternoon, Morag,' Josh announced cheerfully as he erupted into the surgery, brandishing the daffodils.

Morag silently pressed her index finger against her lips. 'Doctor, Mr and Mrs Logan and Lisa are waiting to see you.'

'Ah right. Please see that we're not disturbed for at least half an hour, Morag.'

The next thirty minutes were some of the most excruciating of his life. Lisa's parents were beside themselves and he had nothing to say that would really calm their worries.

'So what's the point, doctor, having children? Those long months of waiting and feeling your baby growing inside you; the pain of giving birth; and then the utter joy of looking at the little face that you have been longing to see for nearly a year … what's the point of all the love and sleepless nights and … everything. What's the point of *anything*?'

'Jeannie, it may seem like this to you now, but …'

'Doesn't *seem*, doctor, it *is*! Whatever am I going to do? I couldn't believe that we would lose Carrie – she was at the beginning of her life – but we did. I just don't have faith anymore. I don't have faith in anything.'

Josh pushed his chair back impatiently and knelt in front of the distraught woman, taking her cold hands in both of his. 'Jeannie, if I didn't believe in what I was doing, you know I couldn't continue being a doctor, don't you? It's just not in me to do something which I have no faith in. At the moment, things seem bleak, but this is Lisa, not Carrie. We are dealing with Lisa's immune system, not Carrie's.' His throat tightened as he continued, 'My mother, Molly, had a hard and difficult life. Father was away at sea most of the time, scratching together a living for the four of us, and she bore the brunt of everything – childhood illnesses and tantrums, misbehaviour, all the things that normal, healthy children get up to. I remember, time after time, when my brother or I took to her the thousand desperate worries of childhood, she would stroke our hair and say in her quiet lilting voice, "Ah but Josh, where there's life, there's hope," And there *is* Jeannie – there must be.'

Choking back her tears, Mrs Logan stood to her feet and said bleakly, 'Is your mother still alive then, Doctor MacDonald?' Josh silently shook his head. 'So where is that hope now?' she whispered.

'Jeannie,' Neil Logan admonished her, 'The doctor was just trying to say something positive to soothe you.'

'But your wife's right, Neil.' Josh got wearily to his feet and resumed his position opposite the Logans.

'So when shall we try to arrange for Lisa to travel to Edinburgh?'

'We'll have to plan to buy ferry crossings or train or air travel, Josh,' Neil muttered.

'None of that, man. You tell me when; I'll arrange the transport.'

'Not out of your own pocket, you won't, doctor!'

'Don't worry on that score, there is funding available for this sort of thing,' Josh lied. 'Shall we say one day next week?'

'We'll leave that to you, doctor,' Lisa's father said quietly. 'Just please let us know.'

'I will,' Josh affirmed. 'But one good piece of news before you go: don't worry about Bonnie. She was found behind the school running about chasing rabbits and is safe with one of the teachers. When would you like to have her back, Neil?'

Jeannie looked bleakly at her husband and then back at Josh. 'I just don't seem to have the energy to look after the wee thing any more,' she sighed. 'I hadn't even realised that she had gone! We are going to have to find a new home for her. Every time I look at her, I see her creeping towards Carrie's open grave on her belly, trying to follow her. I've run out of energy for caring, doctor.'

'Leave it to me, Jeannie. If necessary, I'll take in Bonnie myself.'

⊰╫╢⊱

One of the ways in which Josh de-stressed was through precise focus on detail, in a kind of practical mindfulness. After the longest day he could remember, he left his surgery at half past six and walked briskly along the quayside, making a brief stop at the local independent store which sold everything from mousetraps and fishing lines to the pate and puff pastry he needed to pick up that evening.

Once home, he showered, finally turning the cold tap full on for a good thirty seconds in a brutal attempt to clear his head of the emotional load of the day. At seven-twenty, consciously slowing his movements, he relished the soft touch of a thick cream cotton shirt, the freshly-washed smell of his black jeans and the gentle massage as his razor moved across the dark stubble that had grown again since that morning.

Maintaining his deliberate, quiet movements, Josh unwrapped the puff pastry and cut it carefully into two equal rectangles, which he meticulously spread with pate. He prepared the mixture of finely-chopped mushroom, onion and herbs, seared the fillet steak, and made up two neat parcels which he slipped in the ancient Rayburn chugging away at the back of his living room. Seven forty-five. He opened a bottle of Côtes de Rhone and placed it centrally on the simply-laid table, together with a bowl of dressed salad. Cheese lay in the fridge for desert; savoury biscuits on a plate in the larder.

Despite his tried and tested routine for taking control of a situation and dealing with panic, or depression, Josh was deeply agitated. Since the end of afternoon surgery, he had tried to rehearse a form of words that would combine apology with the desire to continue to get to know Alex, but every phrase he could think of seemed insultingly trite. He had met her in the flesh less than twenty-four hours previously, but already she hovered like a promise on the periphery of his mind. How would she act when she arrived in … five minutes time? Brittle? Cool? Distant? Ironically, he didn't know her well enough to anticipate her behaviour. Over the years of his medical practice, Josh had trained himself to keep a tight control on his physical reactions, but such was his state of mind that he jumped convulsively at the light tap on his front door. Taking a deep breath and muttering an obscure invocation to whatever gods might be listening, he lifted the latch.

'You don't mind my bringing Bonnie, do you?' Alex was flushed and slightly breathless. 'I thought she'd be lonely by herself. I've just taken her for a walk and she's done what a dog's got to do … so I don't think your carpet is in danger!'

So, after all his anxiety, all his wondering, here was the object of his thoughts: lovely, spontaneous and open as always. In sheer relief, he threw back his head and laughed, deciding to be as honest with Alex as she always seemed to be with him. 'I just didn't know what to expect, Alex. I didn't know where to begin …'

'Look, Josh. What has happened to us has been, to say the least, odd! From an anonymous virtual reality, we have both been placed in a small, closely inter-related society where each of us holds a public role. On social media we can live in a fantasy world where the rules of everyday society just don't operate. You acted as you did within that context. If you acted like that now, it would be unacceptable.' Then, realising what she had said, she flushed a deeper pink. 'Mm! Not the most tactful thing to say – but you know what I mean.'

'I do. And I am more grateful than you realise. It will never happen again!'

'I should hope not!'

And now it was Josh's turn to flush.

Chapter 30

'That can't be the dawn chorus – surely?' Alex looked around the living room sleepily, trying to find a clock.

Josh glanced at his watch. 'It's five o'clock Alex – and I can't think what else it could be, unless of course the birds have lost count of time, as we have.'

The evening had been at the same time easier, but more frustrating, than either Alex or Josh had anticipated. Alex was at peace with the decision she had reached at the end of her moonlit Yoga practice: to let the past go and to do everything she could to live in harmony with the man who had so deeply stirred her senses and her mind. When Josh had invited her to dinner, she had welcomed the opportunity to put this decision into practice. But she had underestimated the impact of Josh's quiet intensity: his rare smile; the unspoken thoughts behind the changing expression of his eyes; his spare and economical movements and gestures. And all these things drew her irresistibly.

For Josh, the evening had been exquisite torture. He longed to be able to react towards Alex as he would in more usual circumstances. Life had taught him that if he wanted a woman – almost any woman – she was his for the taking. But he had set himself the strictest parameters for the evening with Alex, and could only observe at a distance the changing, dynamic loveliness of the woman who laughed, talked and responded so warmly. To go further, to attempt to possess, this he had forbidden himself.

But despite the resolve of each to maintain complete constraint and distance, one hour had slipped into the next, and conversation flowed more easily than either could have anticipated.

'Where shall I park Bonnie?' Alex had laughingly asked, before she sat down at the precisely-laid dinner table.

'Perhaps let her park herself? And whilst she finds a suitable space, tell me about yourself,' Josh said, pouring Alex a glass of wine.

'Married, but separated. Two daughters that I have effectively lost because their ways of life are so alien to mine that they may as well live on the moon. I love my profession. And against all the odds, I love this island. My life in a nutshell! And you?'

'Divorced – for fifteen years. Two girls, both absorbed in themselves rather than their crabby, bachelor father. I love my profession too. And I was born and bred on this impossibly beautiful and frustrating island.'

'Why frustrating? And this beef wellington is awesome! Where did you learn to cook like this?'

'To answer your second question first – necessity; and frustrating because I try to look after the islanders, but they still seem determined to fall off cliffs when they are really too old to climb them; to eat food that is less than fresh because their income is derisory; and to drink too much because they try to forget the harshness of their everyday lives.'

'It's like when a child has a special educational need. One pummels one's brains – I don't suppose that's a medical possibility, but it feels like that – to find a way in, to teach them a concept. But a teacher's ingenuity can only go so far, just like a doctor's skill, I suppose.'

'Exactly. You don't stop caring because they have done something unacceptable, or something that is not good for them. But,' the lines of tension at the corners of Josh's eyes tightened, 'every time, every single time you lose someone, it's like a punch in the guts.' Josh ran his fingers hard through his hair, as if to get rid of the black thoughts that were crowding his mind. Rather awkwardly, he changed the subject.

'Would you like some cheese, Alex?'

'Love some.'

'What really brought you here?' asked Josh, neatly stacking the plates in the sink.

'Magic – everyday magic. I had decided to leave my husband – our life together was a living death. Every day was mere existence. Each morning when I woke I thought of the people and places in the world that I would never see, never meet, because I was trapped in a sterile existence which was extinguishing every spark of spontaneity and joy in me.'

'Ah, so the advertisement drew you in?'

'Yes – completely. There is magic everywhere, Star. Ah no! – will I ever stop using your beautiful Twitter name?'

'For both our sakes, I hope so,' smiled Josh grimly, gripping the cheeseboard so tightly that the edges left lines across his fingers. He had never met a woman so naturally passionate and outspoken and it left him, literally, breathless.

'How did you and the other Governors decide on the wording?'

'Do you want the truth, or an abridged version of it?'

'What do you think?'

'We had been working for hours on the person specification for the post you now hold. It was a Friday evening and, as usual, I was exhausted. In sheer desperation, I suggested that we didn't need a conventional teacher, but someone who could tap into the earth magic of this place – the history, the pre-history, the legends and the impact that the rock, the machair, the heather, the very stones of the island have on the children that are born and raised here. So Jenna, the Chair of Governors, leapt at the idea and this became the core of the advertisement.'

'I bet she did,' laughed Alex. 'It strikes me that she would support anything you suggested, Josh.'

Josh's laughter mingled with Alex's. 'You're astute!'

'Call it female intuition. What's the story there?'

'It's a part of my history that I'm not particularly proud of. I will explain to you sometime, but not now – please. It's too late and I've had too pleasant an evening.'

'Sorry,' blushed Alex.

'Ach, don't apologise. I'll reveal all one day!'

The evening flowed on, punctuated by comfortable pauses, when Josh stoked the woodburning stove, or poured more wine, or later whisky. It was one of those occasions that stand out of time. When two human beings are getting to know each other and the assimilation of that knowledge ebbs and flows between the parties. Sometimes understanding leaps forward, sometimes it circles and eddies, but at the end of the period of time the relationship between the two people involved is changed forever.

⊰⊱

'I'd better go,' yawned Alex, getting slowly to her feet. 'Ooh, I'm stiff! Yoga practice required I think …'

Josh saw again in his mind's eye the supple figure bending and stretching in the moonlight and impulsively reached out both his hands to the lovely woman who stood before him.

'Thank you, Alex. Thank you for everything. I think we are both comfortable going forward now. We've established our relationship within the real world, wouldn't you say?'

Quietly, Alex took Josh's cold hands in her warm ones and did what he had longed to do all evening: she kissed him lightly on the lips. 'And thank you, Josh. And yes, I think we have established our relationship within the real world.'

Silently, he opened his front door onto the bracing early morning of an island spring day. Alex slipped out and as he watched her moving away from him, Josh's whole body felt more alive than it had since he was a young man. Every part of him seemed to exist as pure sensation: his mind was clear; his muscles flexible and ready to walk or run; his heart rate and breathing faster than usual; and every atom of him longed to possess the woman with whom he had, unbelievably, spent the night in conversation.

Seagulls circled, witnessing Alex's swift, light steps along the quayside and back to Gladys, as did Jeanne

O'Hara, gazing out of her bedroom window at the sunrise. As she watched her colleague return to her campervan, her expression was unreadable. The only sign of life in her impassive face was a cold flame that flickered behind her dark eyes.

Chapter 31

'Come on, Bonnie – good girl!' Alex had slept for only a couple of hours, but the sun was bright and she was up by eight o'clock, walking the small dog that she seemed to have temporarily acquired by default, up along the cliff top and past the barrows that faced out to Haligrey, like a line of dominoes. A swift mental calculation told Alex that their direction lay east/west: one end facing the new day, welcoming a new life; the other, in shadow, marking the end of that day and of earthly existence. She noticed that almost all the barrows were still sealed and had a vivid mental image of the ages-old skeletons within, maybe laid in a dignified supine position; or possibly in a crouched foetal curl. Alex found great comfort in reflecting upon the layers of history and the lives and the deaths of which it was comprised. Other people may have been disturbed by the thought of human remains so close by, but Alex was affirmed that other people had lived and died, loved and suffered as she had and she rejoiced to be part of the panoply of history. She passed a couple of barrows where the eastern end was open and the stone structure under the turf walling and roofing was visible. She bent to look inside the first: it was dark and almost warm, womb-like. She smiled and walked on, watching the ramblings of Bonnie with joy.

Alex was unsure exactly what breed of dog Bonnie was: she was medium-sized with a curly, amber-coloured coat and a short fluffy tail which wagged ceaselessly. Alex loved the quiet companionship of the animal. David had never let her have a pet and now she rejoiced in the way that her consciousness seemed to extend from herself into the intense sensory experiences of the small dog: the exploratory snuffling, the delicate scenting along tall blades of grass or shrubby bushes, the way she raised her nose to drink in huge lungfuls of the clear, salt-laden air.

Bonnie seemed to have picked up a trail of some sort and was zig-zagging randomly across the short-cropped grass and heather. She stopped, as if to evaluate the data that her acute sensory information system was feeding her; then she was off at double her former speed, heading towards the next barrow, at the top of a gentle rise. Alex called her, but in vain. So strong must the scent be that nothing could stop Bonnie now and so Alex, ever pragmatic, ran after her as fast as she could.

Panting, Alex arrived at the open entrance to the barrow where Bonnie was standing, hackles raised a little, gazing into the shadowy depths. Very cautiously, Alex took a few steps from the light of day into the barrow's darkness and at first thought that her eyes, or her mind, were playing tricks on her as she saw a version of what she had visualised earlier. Lying on her side, knees drawn up to her chest was a woman, elderly, very slight – but clearly of the twenty-first century. Her face had already started to relax into the other-world aspect of the recently-dead and between her thin, clasped hands, rested an envelope.

'That fucking woman,' Josh breathed, looking down with infinite compassion at what remained of Jessie MacKenzie. 'That stupid, thoughtless, fucking Maitland Morgan.' He whipped out his mobile and jabbed into it the figures 999. 'Police, please. Yes, it's Josh MacDonald and tell Hamish that I've found a body in one of the *Sleeping Guardians*. No, there is no possibility of resuscitation. We'll be standing outside the barrow – he can't miss us.'

Josh thrust his hands deep into his jeans pockets and turned his back on the barrow, walking quickly to a large boulder some distance away. Alex followed him.

'Do you know everyone on the island?' she asked gently, trying to coax him out of his silent reverie.

'Yes,' came the terse reply.

'So Hamish is?'

'The sum total of our police force.'

'And Maitland Morgan?'

'The idiot that exchanged clinical practice with me – when I went to the States.'

'Wasn't she properly qualified, Josh?'

'Oh God knows, Alex! In the strictest confidence, I have strong suspicions that there was some sort of affair going on between her and my clinical director. Otherwise I cannot understand how or why such a moron could ever have been trusted with a diverse and context-specific practice such as mine.'

Both sat without speaking, listening to the ever-present whisper of the breeze ruffling the short turf, almost like an invisible hand stroking close-cropped hair. After some minutes a small, dark figure on a mountain-bike started to climb, surprisingly quickly, up the cliff track.

'Hamish.' Josh observed in a monotone. Alex watched the way in which her companion almost visibly shifted himself from dark introspection into a professional and emotionless mode.

'Hamish! Grateful for your speedy response!' Josh extended his hand and shook the slightly breathless, red-headed young policeman warmly by the hand, before walking away with him to re-inspect the open barrow and the fragile human remains that found their last resting place in its dark security.

Alex sat and raked her fingers through Bonnie's thick, curly fur. Her emotions were in turmoil: over the frail and vulnerable old lady who had clearly just lay down and met her end a long way from anyone in her community and without companionship; but overwhelmingly over the man whose depth and complexity filled her mind.

⊹⊱⊰⊰

'Another Scotch please, Rory.'

Jessie's remains had been taken away by helicopter to the mortuary on Benbecula, and PC Hamish Stewart had cycled away as swiftly as he had arrived. A timeless peace once again started to descend on the line of cliff-top barrows as Alex and Josh watched the helicopter until it was a mere speck in the sky.

'I need a drink,' Josh said without preamble.

'Me too. *The Inn?*'

'Hardly much choice!'

And now they sat opposite each other in the sunlit bar of the quayside inn, with Bonnie curled comfortably between Alex's feet.

'So how do you know that this locum drove that poor old lady away from her home, Josh, to die alone in the barrow of all places?' Alex swirled the wine around in her glass, watching the refractions of the sunlight in its red depths.

'Morag.'

'Is this a medical code word for something – an acronym for a set of symptoms?' prompted Alex gently.

Josh drained his whisky and laughed quietly.

'You have such a knack of making me smile, Alex Miller! Morag is my secretary and keeps me sane – or tries to. She told me about a conversation that she had with Jessie MacKenzie after a travesty of a 'consultation' with Doctor Morgan. Apparently, the old lady told Morag that she needed "to find something useful to do" because she "mustn't waste NHS time."'

'But she was probably just lonely!' exclaimed Alex.

'Exactly!' Josh automatically reached out his hand to clasp that of his companion, but checked half-way and returned it to his empty glass. 'You have it in a nutshell. "Human beings can withstand a week without water, two weeks without food, many years of homelessness, but not loneliness. It is the worst of all tortures, the worst of all sufferings."'

'That's so true. In my marriage I was always lonely. But I thought that scientists were supposed to be inarticulate. That's some sound bite, Josh!'

'Not mine – sorry to disillusion you, Alex. It's from one of my favourite authors, Paulo Coelho. Would you like another drink?'

Alex glanced at the clock behind the bar. 'I really should not be sitting here drinking on a lovely sunny afternoon – but, why not?'

'Why not indeed? And whilst I'm re-ordering, think of three of *your* favourite authors. I'd be interested to know who they are.'

'Don't need time to think: Jane Austen, Elizabeth Goudge and Alison Uttley. And yours?'

'Now I *will* need time to think. So be patient.'

Josh was amazed to find that he was smiling as he walked to the small bar and ordered another round of drinks. How could he be smiling when less than two hours ago he had, yet again, mourned the fragility of human life. It was as if Alex brought checks and balances to his intense perceptions. She offered a panacea to pain and an enhancement of pleasure.

'Virgil, Dante and Dostoevsky.'

'Nothing too heavy then! Why those three? And thank you for the wine. I may be found drunk in charge of a dog, Dr MacDonald, and it will be all your fault!'

'Virgil, because the cadences and flow of his language soothe me; Dante, because he is passionate; and Dostoevsky, because he captures the majesty and misery of the human condition.'

Alex sought for a light-hearted comment, but found nothing.

'Alex, Josh, good to see staff and Governors getting on so well.'

'Probably a more complex situation than you realise, Jeanne.' Josh looked up at Jeanne O'Hara who had glided soundlessly into the empty bar. 'Alex and I discovered the body of a frail and elderly member of this community less than an hour ago and, understandably, are still reeling from the situation. This is hardly socialising. It is a sound counter-measure to such a profound shock.'

'Ah, I see. I foolishly thought that it was a continuation of the long and clearly pleasant evening that you had both spent together.'

Josh looked at the amber liquid in his heavy-bottomed tumbler and swirled it round, not giving Jeanne the comfort of a quick response.

'Quite frankly, Jeanne, what I and the teacher-in-charge of the school do in our own time is our own business. And if you will excuse us, we were discussing the timeless impact of Dostoevsky's commentary on the human condition. No doubt you have something to do that is very pressing. I know how constantly busy you are.'

Even Jeanne had the grace to flush and said, 'Yes, I'm just off to school – always things to do there!'

'And there are always things to do in the community, Jeanne, where people live and interact, and children look for models of behaviour that combine study and leisure – the best combination for wellbeing. Goodbye.'

❈

'That was brutal, Josh.'

'That woman gives me the creeps! She literally causes my hackles to rise! Did she see you leaving my house this morning, do you think?'

'Oh probably! She seems to have the knack of materialising silently in the most unexpected places and having the most unfortunate effects: in the back of a classroom when I'm teaching, causing me to lose my thread; behind me when I am having the occasional meal here and chatting to Rory, giving me intense indigestion! Why not on the quayside at dawn?' Alex swirled her drink around thoughtfully. 'I don't know whether I should say this to you, Josh, but she makes me really uncomfortable too. It's as if she is constantly watching and waiting for me to slip up, to make a mistake. And do you know what's most telling of all?'

Josh shook his head.

'She is totally unresponsive to the children. She hardly ever talks to them, never interacts. It seems to me that she only regards each one as a number that feeds into her eternal analysis of data. I've never met anyone in the teaching profession like her.'

'I'm going to have to talk to Jenna about her, Alex. I'm sick to death of social injustice! First of all, that poor woman dying alone – in a barrow of all places that must have seemed to her a place of isolation and security; then this Academy Trust idea Ms O'Hara is pushing so hard. I can't bring Jessie back to life, but I can have a conversation with the Chair of Governors about what you've just told me. Our children live within *this particular context.* I feel passionately about this. Just as that idiot locum failed totally to understand what my patients needed and did so much damage, Ms O'Hara's head seems to be full of academic nonsense that is not important for children who are born, raised and educated in the Western Isles of Scotland. In fact,' Josh declared, draining his whisky, 'I'm going to the Manor House right now. And after that I'm going to ring Clive Bloody Saunders and tell him what I think of his arrangement to put his fancy woman in my medical practice. I'm in the mood!'

There were a dozen things that Alex wanted to say – 'Don't go' 'Can I come with you?' 'Are you sure?'

being a selection. But, exercising immense self-control, all she did was to smile and stroke Bonnie.

'Don't breathe in her direction, Josh! The whisky fumes may make her pass out!'

Chapter 32

'Josh, how lovely to see you!' Jenna MacLeod smiled radiantly and took an involuntary step closer to Josh as she opened the door. She was immaculate in a tweed pencil skirt and matching green jumper, to which was pinned a small enamel version of the MacLeod coat of arms, with its motto *Hold Fast*.

'As always, Jenna, you look every inch the Clan chieftain,' Josh responded, kissing her lightly on both cheeks.

'And to what do I owe the pleasure of this unexpected visit?'

'Jenna, I need to talk to you – seriously – about the school.'

'Well, it must be serious if you come and visit me on one of the only two days per week you actually have time to stop and think about yourself, Josh. Come in and I'll make us some tea, or something stronger if you wish – although,' she inhaled delicately, 'perhaps tea would be better for your liver!'

Whilst Jenna went through the homely routines of boiling the kettle on her Aga and opening a biscuit tin emblazoned with a picture of Edinburgh Castle, Josh told her how Alex and he had discovered the body of

Jessie MacKenzie. As, once again, he vented his anger over the incompetent locum that had been forced on the island, Jenna listened in silence, then turned to him thoughtfully.

'That's terrible, Josh. I wish I had had some inkling of her distress. I would have tried my hardest to do something to help her ... but it's good to hear the return of some of your old passion concerning social justice.' She poured milk into a china jug, then turned to face Josh, resting her back against a pine dresser polished to within an inch of its life. 'I still miss our times together – so much. I know back then you made your position very clear, but sometimes, things change over time?' The inflection in her voice made the statement into a question.

The slow ticking of the kitchen clock marked the seconds, as Josh stared silently into the depths of his mug and Jenna watched him intently.

'Jenna, you know how fond I am of you. I admire you as a fine figurehead of your Clan and an exceptional Chair of Governors of our school – but I don't love you as a man ought to love his woman. All those years ago, after my divorce from Elspeth, when I just didn't know how to begin to be father and mother to my girls, you were amazing. You were such a staunch friend. The times we shared were special, of course they were. You are a lovely and intelligent woman. What man would not have been attracted to you and enjoyed every aspect of you? But when you asked me to marry you, I couldn't say yes, because I realised I didn't love you. I didn't then, Jenna, and I don't now. Some things do change, but others are irrevocable.'

'As always, Josh, thank you for your honesty, brutal though it may be. Do you know what? I think I'll break my six o'clock rule and have a scotch right now. After that exposition, I feel I could do with a spot of Dutch courage!'

'Oh, bugger the tea – and my liver – I'll join you. It's no easier to be honest when you know what hurt it is going to cause, than to be on the receiving end of what you term my 'brutality'.

The shadows lengthened across the soft green lawns of the Manor House as Josh explained to Jenna his misgivings concerning Jeanne O'Hara. She listened carefully, occasionally taking a sip from her heavy-bottomed tumbler.

'So, you are suspicious of her on two counts: firstly, her relationship, or lack of it, with the children; and secondly, the basis on which she is recommending the formation of a Multi-Academy Trust.'

'Yes.'

'She has a cool personality, Josh, and I know that that would not particularly appeal to you …'

'For Heavens' sake, Jenna! I don't regard every woman as a sex object!'

'I'll ignore that. But her credentials are outstanding. We received a glowing reference from James Pinner, the managing trustee of the Edith Warne Educational Foundation, testifying to her drive and focus in establishing the MAT in Kent and becoming its Executive Head.'

'Did you speak to this James Pinner, Jenna, or visit the trust?'

'No. There was no need. And the quality of Jeanne's interview spoke for itself …'

'Alex told me that she was unemployed when she came for interview.'

'Yes. She felt as if her role in Kent was complete and wished to develop her professional practice further by facing new challenges within a different context.'

Josh sat, swirling his drink around thoughtfully. 'All these jargon phrases could come out of a textbook, Jenna. Why did you make two appointments at school? Why not just Alex Miller?'

'Alex is delightful, and a truly gifted teacher. You really ought to observe her, Josh. She enthrals the children. But she is no administrator. She lives and breathes classroom teaching.'

'Surely that should come with the territory, rather than the sort of stale truisms that define Jeanne?'

'But the school won't run itself, Josh! We desperately wanted Alex; but equally we desperately want our school to flourish as a centre of learning in the Western Isles. Just as you are a medical lead, I long for our school – my mother's vision – to be an educational lead. That's the reason.'

'I understand this, Jenna. But I can't shake off my suspicion of that woman. I really can't. I may do some quiet nosing about …'

'Of course. I respect your opinion, as I know you respect mine. Now, can I change the subject? I would like to reinstate the May Ball this year. In my mother's time it was the highlight of the Fragrey year and the island was invaded by MacLeods from all over the world.'

'I remember,' Josh nodded. '*My* mother made herself a new dress for the occasion whenever she could scrape together enough money to buy fabric.'

'Would you come, Josh?'

'Of course, Jenna. But as island doctor and governor, not as your partner. I'm sorry, but you must realise that,

Jenna. If you don't, neither of us will ever move forward.'

'Fine. I'll send out the invitations over the next couple of weeks.'

'I never mean to hurt you, Jenna. Believe me.'

'But hurt there is, Josh MacDonald – intentional or not. And now I must get on with some paperwork.' Cool and regal, Jenna stood up and reached out for Josh's empty glass. Then, leaving her visitor to find his own way out of the Manor House, the chieftain of the Clan MacLeod left the room and no-one, certainly not Josh, could have suspected from her stately posture that she was fighting back tears.

Chapter 33

'Drinking alone, Alex? And at three o'clock in the afternoon? Is this how the teacher-in-charge of the youth of Fragrey spends her Saturday afternoons?'

Agnes joined her at the small pine table in the bar of *The Inn* minutes after Josh had vacated it, and Alex slowly explained how she had discovered Jessie's remains and had run to ask Josh for help, with some vague idea that he may be able to do something for the old lady. As she was talking, she realised that she was speaking slowly and sometimes searching for the right word. After a night of practically no sleep and powerful emotions, the events of the day took on a surreal feel and she was surprised to find that she was blinking away tears. 'I feel as if I've hit a wall, Agnes. I'm totally exhausted.'

'Mm, I'm not in the slightest surprised to hear that, Alex. Enough red wine for you, young lady. I'm taking you home for some good old-fashioned tea and cake, and I may extend my hospitality to your little dog – she looks hungry!'

Agnes's croft faced the road along which Alex had driven from the ferry port – it seemed a lifetime ago now – and its long, rough 'garden' backed on to a pebbly beach and the sea. It was neat, whitewashed and stood out against the green of the island and the intense blue of the Atlantic. Tamarisk, sea holly and Viper's-bugloss were vivid splashes of pink, purple and blue against the white walls.

As the women walked slowly along the quayside and followed the grassy verge, Alex was surprised that she had started to shiver and she wrapped her jacket more tightly around her. Agnes opened the blue-painted front door and gestured to one of two chairs which flanked the stone fireplace, completely filled by a black iron range, which provided heating, hot water and cooking. 'Sit yourself down there, lass. I'll put some more peat on the fire.'

'Everyone here's so kind,' Alex murmured. 'Why are you bothering to take care of me, just because I have drunk too much wine and become maudlin?'

'Because that's not true. You're in shock and you're battling new and intense emotions. And because you are the best teacher that Fragrey has seen in my time. I want to ensure that you stay safe, and that you stay on this island!'

'What do you mean about "new and intense emotions", Agnes?'

'Ah, they don't call me the "Wise Woman of Fragrey" for nothing!'

After several cups of tea and a huge slice of fruitcake, Alex had stopped shivering and felt warm and relaxed, but immensely tired. She observed guiltily that Bonnie had demolished a huge bowl of meat and biscuit and was now lying on her side, her waistline visibly expanded. It must have been a day since she had eaten and Alex was gutted that she had lost count of time as far as the little dog was concerned. She yawned as she and Agnes watched the sun sinking steadily towards the western horizon and lighting a golden-red ribbon of water which seemed to touch the low wall at the end of Agnes' pebbly garden.

Alex got slowly to her feet. 'I love this house, Agnes. It holds a liminal place, touching both the sea and the land; strong walls against the waves and the wind; sheltering a secure home within.'

'Liminal indeed. Times past and future meet here.'

Alex's eyelids were heavy with exhaustion and she felt almost as if Agnes' quiet lilting voice was weaving a subtle spell around her. She stood slowly, straightening her back. 'I must go, Agnes. I need to seek the dubious comforts of Gladys early tonight, I think.'

'Before you go, can I show you something?'

'Of course.'

Agnes led the way out through the back door of the croft, past a range of substantial stone outbuildings.

'This is like a different world, Agnes,' Alex exclaimed, as she followed her companion through an arched door in the wall into a still courtyard lit by the very last rays of the sun. At the centre of the space stood a beehive-shaped stone structure with an entrance barely two feet high.

'It is a different world, Alex,' Agnes smiled. 'Follow me.' They crept on hands and knees under the low lintel and into a warm space illuminated only by a circular hole in the top of the roof. Directly under the opening, on the earth, was a shallow stone basin full of water which reflected the clear blue of the late afternoon sky.

'What is this?' Alex whispered.

'This is where my inner eye perceives the world.' Agnes breathed on the surface of the water and it shifted and shimmered slightly. 'This is from the holy well of Haligrey. It shows Truth that external vision cannot see. Watch!'

The water clouded momentarily, then cleared, and Alex saw the interior of Josh's cottage. She saw his capable hands, serving the dinner which he had cooked for them both, his face, serious, intense, then suddenly breaking into a smile which transformed it. Then she saw her own face and was shaken to the core: mouth smiling, eyes shining, completely enrapt with the man who moved so deftly around the small living kitchen.

'When I talked of your intense emotions, Alex, this is what I meant. Josh MacDonald is a fine man and a great doctor, but there is complexity there, and danger. Be careful.'

Chapter 34

'It's a perfect day for a trip to Haligrey, our 'Holy Island'. It is the Sabbath, after all.'

Alex dragged herself back into consciousness. She had fallen into her bed the previous evening after washing and brushing her teeth and had slept undisturbed until she was awoken by the cheerful voice of Agnes, who was leaning over Gladys' stable door.

'Agnes,' she groaned sleepily. 'What time is it?'

'Eight o'clock and the day is fine and calm. You've had at least ten hours sleep, which is enough for anyone! The holy island looks larger and more vivid than ever – a certain sign that it is calling us there.'

'Calling or not, Agnes, I must have coffee! Would you care to join me?'

The two women sat on the low stone wall behind the camper van, sipping their coffee and munching on bread rolls and some blackcurrant jam which Alex had unearthed from the tiny storage cupboard above the sink.

'Have you heard of the legend of the *Sleeping Guardians?*' Agnes asked, fastidiously brushing bread crumbs from her faded jeans.

'I have not! But I'm sure you are going to tell me!'

Agnes grinned. 'You're right – I am! The legend was brought to my mind by your finding dear Jessie yesterday. The story goes that in one of the barrows that are called the *Sleeping Guardians* there is an entrance to a cave, deep and beautiful, decked with precious gems and silver carvings. Years ago, almost at the dawn of recorded time, a king and a small band of his retainers, fought off unimaginable attacks to keep Fragrey safe. This was so long ago that we do not even have the king's name. Wave after wave of invaders, of monstrous animals, of plague and famine and ferocious weather hit the island but the king and his men protected it – sometimes by battle, sometimes by diplomacy, sometimes by practical actions, sometimes by prayer. This continued for centuries because in those days the life span of humankind was very great. But on this earth all glorious things do end and eventually the king and his followers became old and frail and the safety of the island was weakened. The people of the island, in thankfulness for the reign of peace, built a burial chamber fit for the monarch and his men, and constructed a barrow to shield and protect it. At grey dawn one summer's day, the king and his retinue marched slowly up the track to the cliff top and entered the barrow and its burial chamber. From that moment they existed in legend only. It is said that great power lies in the barrow and that, in times of need – either of an individual, or of our island – the barrow will draw to it anyone who seeks sanctuary.'

'Like poor Jessie?' asked Alex, feeding bits of bread to Bonnie.

'Like poor Jessie.'

'You speak the legend as if you believe it, Agnes.'

'Alex, I have lived long enough in this world to allow my mind to be open to everything. Who is to say that this story is not true? Why shouldn't it be true? Why shouldn't truths deeper than history, and more powerful than death itself, exist to sustain us when we need hope and a perspective beyond what we call the real world?'

'Why not indeed, Agnes. But why do you want to take me over to Haligrey again?'

'For two reasons: the most important is that each time a person visits the island their relationship with it deepens. They see more, and further; they hear the almost inaudible and they are open to a range of emotions that they can perceive there and there only. Secondly, because we didn't get as far as Aelfric's tomb, I think that you ought to see it. It is unforgettable.'

'Well, O wise-woman who can read my mind, the answer is I'd love to go again, on both counts! I'm reasonably awake and no longer feel in danger of eating grass along the way because I'm so hungry, so let's go! Rory has offered to dog-sit when necessary, so I'll just take Bonnie to him, then I'll be with you.'

Less than half an hour later, the women rolled up their jeans and threw their shoes into Agnes' boat, before they dragged it along the shingle behind her croft and into knee-deep water.

'I thought you kept *Frigg* in the harbour, Agnes,' Alex commented, jumping lightly aboard.

'From time to time she has to be repaired or de-barnacled, or sometimes painted, and it's easier, and cheaper, if I do it here.

Unlike the last time Alex and Agnes had crossed to the island, today the sea was completely calm. There was no vestige of a breeze and the dip and splash of the oars as they entered and left the water seemed to echo across the straight between Haligrey and the Fragrey. Neither woman spoke, as each was lost in her own thoughts, their minds soothed by the creak and splash which marked their progress to the island. Agnes sifted, as she often did, through the stories and myths which were as real to her as the world which surrounded her; and Alex played and re-played her conversations with Josh.

After what seemed only a matter of minutes, the boat drifted onto the soft white sand of the *beach of homecoming*. The silence and heat of the day were intense on the small island. Together Agnes and Alex hauled the small boat higher up the beach and walked, still without speaking, to the holy well. Alex smiled as she watched the water surge out of the hillside into the stone trough where, centuries earlier, the monk whose presence on the island she still felt so vividly, had touched the earth. They cupped their hands and drank: the water was ice-cold and tasted faintly of peat.

Alex followed her companion up the path which led to the green hollow and the small stone and turf-roofed building which had been Aelfric's home. But this time, instead of remaining there, Agnes walked on, climbing the far side of the grassy bowl and descending a steep slope on the other side, before disappearing into a thicket of low-growing trees.

As she stepped inside the enclosing warmth of the small wood, Alex was reminded of mediaeval paintings that she had seen in art galleries, and photographs of manuscripts from the same era. The trees were impossibly lush and she noticed with astonishment that they were fruit trees – apple, plum and damson mostly, but with the occasional angular pear. All were laden with blossom, and strewn across the vivid green grass which carpeted the wood were scattered primroses, violets and wood avens. Butterflies fluttered, rising and falling in a mystical soaring dance.

'But how can this be?' Alex whispered. 'There are no trees on the Western Isles ... This is like an enchanted forest imported from a softer and gentler setting.'

'But in this place, all things are possible: new life and healing and beauty beyond imagining. Come, follow me.'

It was impossible to be certain of distance or time in this wood beyond the world. But Alex judged that they must have reached its approximate centre when Agnes stopped and knelt on the damp turf. She reached down her right hand and lightly caressed a stone cross, inset into the earth. 'Here he is,' she whispered.

Alex, too, laid her hand flat upon the turf and it was almost as if she felt a great heart beating – a steady thrum, a pulse of nature that went beyond the moment.

'Is he still alive, Agnes?'

'Alive? What does "alive" mean? Were you alive, Alex, when you lived with your husband? Are the tens of thousands of people "alive" who never notice the changing seasons, or the nesting birds, or hear the dawn chorus? I believe that energy – pure, passionate energy – never dies. I think it is transformed into something sublime, timeless, eternal. I feel that here. I think you do too. Aelfric "died" a thousand years ago. Did he disappear? I don't think so.'

Drinking in the mystery and beauty which surrounded them, they sat in the dappled shade of the wood, enveloped by the intoxicating scent of spring flowers ... for minutes ... for hours.

It was Alex who first noticed the stars pricking the dusk of the sky. 'But we came here this morning, Agnes! How can this be?'

'In some places, time either doesn't exist or moves differently. This is one of them. I can navigate by the stars, Alex, and find my way towards the lights on the quayside at Heillstath. We should go now. You need to say goodbye to this place. Your life will not be the same when you see it again.'

Alex once more laid her palm on the stone cross that lay on the earth and was silent for some minutes.

'Alex?'

She shook herself. 'Sorry, Agnes. I'm coming.'

Chapter 35

Josh stared out of the Georgian sash window across the green space below, sprinkled with trees which were dramatically foreshortened from this perspective. The vista which spread in front of him seemed to encompass the whole of Scottish history and pre-history: Arthur's Seat, the plug of an extinct volcano and a site of human occupation since the Iron Age; Edinburgh Castle, a royal residence since the twelfth century; and the network of railway lines proudly declaring their origin in the Industrial Revolution. Josh was proud of his national identity at any time, but the powerful visual statement made by the capital city of his country made his heart swell with pride.

Turning from this source of pleasure to the elegance of Clive Saunders office, where clearly no expense had been spared, filled him with a cold fury. What a travesty that a man held in such regard within such a fine country could have acted so shabbily. Josh had worked out exactly what he was going to say to his line-manager, whom he knew to be smooth and articulate and, as his mother would have said, 'as slippery as a snake.' He had already been waiting for nearly an hour and his temper, already pushed almost to its limits, was about to erupt. But finally, the oak door swung silently open and the Clinical Director of Medicine for the Highlands and Islands of Scotland stood urbanely before him, extending a well-manicured hand.

'Josh! Always good to see a colleague from the outposts of the empire! How goes it?'

'I haven't come here to make small talk, Clive. I have some data that I would like to discuss with you – in private please.'

The elegant PA got to her feet with practised grace and sashayed over to the door which led to the general office. 'I'll get coffee,' she said, gazing from under her long lashes at the tanned and toned man who had unexpectedly brought a touch of excitement to her turgid daily routine.

A little of Clive's studied bonhomie evaporated as he led Josh back into his inner office. Without preamble, Josh whipped out a slim file from his black briefcase and laid it firmly in front of his clinical director.

'As medical professionals, Clive, we both know how important it is to evaluate the impact of a strategy after it has been implemented. I have drawn up figures from my practice records during the period of my three-month secondment to the States which show the profile of patient care during that period. Out of the four hundred and fifty patients registered to my practice, one hundred and fifty of whom require ongoing observation, one hundred and twenty-five were seen by Dr Maitland Morgan. Of this number, none made follow-up appointments. On my return, two hundred patients made appointments to see me within the first two days. Cases of diabetes had not been monitored or had been told to go to the nearest large hospital; one child had cancer, which was missed by the locum; and one very elderly woman committed suicide.'

Josh lay his hands firmly on the desk in front of him. 'Do you think that this data indicates an appropriate professional standard of care on the part of the locum you placed within my practice, whilst I was on a secondment that you specifically recommended?'

Clive Saunders flicked through the figures, dates and graphs in the file. 'Well, it seems to me that she was probably just easing into the job, Josh. She is young and ...'

'What, Clive? Attractive? Your mistress?' Josh got to his feet. 'These figures are *appalling!* I believe that you put forward a woman who, if not your mistress, was certainly a favourite and in doing this, you put in jeopardy vulnerable, socially inexperienced people, who felt less than safe, and whose health was damaged by the locum's ineptitude.'

'Josh, this is extreme. Do you think you have been overdoing things again?'

'Clive. Stop this bullshit! I work hard – I couldn't do my job if I *did not do so.* I'm professionally on top of my work and clearsighted enough to see what my next step must be.'

'To return to the States to complete your research project? I was surprised and disappointed when Brad told me you'd left ...'

'Really?' The scorn in Josh's voice was palpable. 'I had no choice but to return when I heard that the symptoms of a wee girl whose sister had died from lympho-sarcoma were "diagnosed" as teething troubles! I intend to report you to the General Medical Council for incompetence, and possibly gross misconduct.'

'You'll never win, MacDonald!'

'We'll see about that.' Josh whipped the file from Clive Saunders' desk, replaced it in his briefcase and left without another word, only too aware of the tightening band of pain around his forehead, signalling the onset of another migraine.

Chapter 36

From conversations on the quayside between fisherman gutting their catch, to groups of people chatting outside the island store, two topics reigned supreme: the Leavers' Service at the end of the Summer Term; and the May Ball.

The children had responded enthusiastically to the idea that they should perform a version of the turn-of-the-year boat burial. It possessed all the elements that attract young children irresistibly: drama, action, and a strong touch of the macabre. The children had involved their families in every aspect of the event. Mothers and grandmothers designed costumes and jewellery suitable to the era when boat burials marked the end of earthly life for Viking warriors. Fathers and uncles fashioned swords and shields from wood and painted them in the brightest reds, blues and yellows that they could find. And hardened fishermen talked at length to sons and daughters about the appropriate design for the boat that was going to be made, or possibly adapted, for the occasion.

As a preamble to the May Ball, Jenna MacLeod had taken a school assembly and explained to the children the importance of determination with reference to the

origin of the motto of her own family – *Hold Fast.*
'When my ancestor, Malcolm MacLeod, the third
chieftain of the Clan, was returning home down a
narrow track through Glenelg, he met a wild bull. The
huge black creature blocked the chieftain's path,
lowered its head and pawed the ground but, instead of
running away, Malcolm was determined to pass and
decided that the only thing he could do was to wrestle
with the animal. The bull was many times the man's
weight and size and the odds that the Clan chief would
be killed were overwhelming – but he was cheered on
by his men who stood at a distance. They yelled "*Hold
fast, MacLeod!*". He did and eventually he managed to
leap onto the bull's back and cut its throat with his dirk.
Ever after, the dogged determination of the MacLeods
to stick to their goal has been marked by the words,
Hold fast!

'It was the dearest wish of my mother, Lucilla, that
my family – scattered as it is all over the world – should
be given an annual opportunity to be reunited here in
the centre of our Clan territory. She chose the best time
in the natural year for this in my opinion – May, when
our world is waking up and showing her full glory. The
May Ball has not been held since my mother's sad
death some five years ago, but this year I intend to
reinstate it. I am *determined* to do so, and I am
determined to share this occasion with you all. The
families represented by all of you,' Jenna made a
sweeping gesture across the assembled children 'will
be welcomed, of course. And MacLeods – please put
up your hand if you belong to our proud family – will
be invited to the reception beforehand.

'I have talked to your teacher, Mrs Miller, and
explained that I would love you all to be involved in

this island celebration. I have asked whether you can produce invitations, programmes and posters, based upon the story I have just told you, maybe also drawing upon aspects of our beautiful island itself. Thank you, Mrs Miller. Thank you, children.'

Serene and regal as ever, Jenna rose to her feet, as did the children in respect for her status, and left the school hall.

⊰∦⊱

Summer had started early and, once again, the sky was a pale, washed-out blue, as a heat haze shimmered between earth and heaven. Looking at the rich and stimulating environment in which they lived, Alex made the decision that after lunch she would take the children outside for the afternoon session.

'We have a lot to do!' Alex told her class with a happy smile as she joined them on the playground. 'The May Ball is only a week away and we need to work hard on the project that Ms MacLeod has given us – but all this can be done indoors, in our classroom. Because today is such a perfect day, we should take our learning outdoors and I thought that we could make a start on our end-of-year production.'

'What, building a boat, Miss?'

'We will be building a boat, Rory, or at least modifying an existing boat but, as with all stories, it's best to start at the beginning and trace it through. By the time the Vikings had started to settle in our island, marrying and merging with the people of Fragrey, the *Sleeping Guardians,* the barrows, were already old and had become a site of great reverence. The people of our island would have processed down from this hallowed place to the quayside with the body of the warrior who had died, maybe after a short ceremony to celebrate his life. It would be powerful, it seems to me, if we went to the cliff-top and re-enacted their procession from there. People could gather on the quayside and watch our progress down to the harbour. What does everyone think?'

'Fabulous, Miss! Can I be the dead body?'

'We haven't talked about casting yet, Angus.'

'The end-of-year festival is dramatic because it is dark and people carry flaming torches, Miss. We will be doing our production in July and it doesn't get dark until midnight. What will we be doing about our torches, Miss.'

'Really good thinking, Fiona! I have a couple of ideas – but what do you all think?'

'We could still carry them, but you wouldn't see them very well.'

'That's one possibility, Elizabeth.'

'Or maybe instead of torches we could carry musical instruments and play the soul of the dead person into the afterlife.'

'A really great idea, Gemma! I hadn't thought of that one myself!'

'We could carry flags in flame colours and wave them.'

'Do you know, you have all come up with much better ideas than I had myself! Let's go straight out onto the cliff path. Who has a watch and would like to record how long it takes us?'

'I've got my Batman watch, Miss, that my granny bought me when I learned to tell the time!'

'Excellent, Archie! You can be our timekeeper then.'

Alex knew that the route they would follow would normally take her about twenty minutes, walking at her fairly rapid pace, and imagined it might take approximately half an hour for the children.

'Who knows a good song that we can sing to help our marching along?' she asked.

'*Mairie's Wedding*?'

'That's got a good rhythm, and maybe we ought to sing during the walking part of our performance, but do you think that a wedding song is appropriate to a funeral procession? Are there any more ideas?'

'*The Road to the Isles?*'

'*The Skye Boat Song?*'

'My Daddy loves a piece of music called *Rowing from Islay to Uist,*' Gemma said softly. 'But I'm not sure whether there are any words to it. He says it is a Hebrides rowing tune.'

'Could you hum the tune to us, Gemma?'

'I can.'

The music was lyrical with the poignant undertow of so much associated with the Hebrides, and Alex felt her eyes prick with tears as the young girl's voice rose and fell in a wordless ululation. Soon the tune had captured the imagination of all the children, who started to join in as they swung along to the haunting rhythm.

⸻

To say that Josh had not had an easy day was a gross understatement. He had had another agonising appointment with the Logans, who seemed to be fading away at the same pace as their little daughter. Josh had very serious concerns about the wellbeing of Neil and Jeannie as well as a sort of pent-up fury at how cancer could be depriving the frail little girl of life before she had really started to live it. Nothing he could say touched the parents: they left as pale and desperate as when they had arrived.

In the middle of morning surgery, he had received a phone call from the General Medical Council in response to the case he had brought against Clive Saunders. It was no surprise to learn that they required further evidence. The usual good-humoured banter about coffee with Morag was lacking as he flung open his door and, without preamble, brusquely demanded a drink. 'I understand that you are worried about your patients, doctor, and about the complaint against Dr Saunders, but don't take it out on your faithful secretary!' She had placed his coffee – rather too firmly – on his desk, spilling a few drops on the polished surface. Atypically, she had ignored this and stalked out, flushed, and with her head held high. Josh took a deep draught of the bitter strong drink and gazed into the depths of his cup as if seeking inspiration. How would he ever persuade the GMC to believe him above Clive Saunders? He recalled the sneer in his Clinical Director's parting words 'You'll never win, MacDonald!' Perhaps he wouldn't. Perhaps one could never really win against the tide of illness, injustice and death against which he constantly fought.

Josh stood up and crossed to the window of his consulting room. A grassy bank swept down to the track which led along the quayside and up out of the town to the cliffs which protected it. The room was stuffy and crowded with the painful memories of the morning's consultations, so he flung open the window to take a deep and steadying breath. Listening to the sounds of nature was comforting: the sweet song of the woodland birds and the harsh cry of the gulls and, everywhere, the sound of the sea, soft today, but timeless and never-ceasing. Then gradually he became aware of another sound, a musical sound, but pure melody without words. This swelled until it obliterated all sounds except those of the gulls and then, his heart catching at the sight, he saw the line of children, hair blowing in the warm breeze, faces lifted to the sun, humming a tune he recognised from his childhood. At their head – tanned, slender, laughing, strode the woman who had started to dominate Josh's mind. The laughing band seemed to epitomise life and hope – everything that Josh yearned for – and at that moment he would have given almost anything to run out of his surgery and join them. But the only socially-acceptable gesture towards this longed-for freedom that he could make was to open the window wider and wave. 'Afternoon off, Mrs Miller?'

'Certainly not, Doctor MacDonald! We are undertaking research for the Leavers' Service!'

'The research being, how loud you can sing? Or how happy you can make the children?'

'Both – and much more!' Alex laughed.

Josh found himself smiling in response. She had done it again! Where everything had seemed unremittingly dark, Alex had shone her unwavering light.

Chapter 37

'Aye, Scotland's boasting this year!' Rory Cameron poured Alex a large glass of Merlot and handed it to her with a smile. 'Jamie McKye was saying only yesterday that he usually lambs his ewes in snowstorms, not a heatwave! And how's your steak this evening, Mrs Miller?'

'Compared with the sludge I usually manage to produce on my camping stove, absolute ambrosia!' Alex mumbled, adding 'but if I don't slow down, I'll have to order Rennies for pudding!'

'Alex, why do you not come and have your evening meal – at the very least – here with us more often?' Rory frowned.

Alex glanced swiftly around the empty bar. 'Is Jeanne out tonight?'

'Yes. She's having supper with Jenna MacLeod. They're talking through some of the arrangements for tomorrow's Ball.'

'Well, in that case, I can be honest. I feel so uncomfortable with Jeanne, Rory. She always gives me the impression that I am being weighed in the balance and found wanting – in every way! Teaching, appearance, dress code, behaviour …'

'How about the transformation you have brought to our school? Even Jeanne likened you to the Pied Piper when you walked your children up the cliff track the other day.'

'Let's not forget that the Pied Piper imprisoned the children of Hamelin in a hillside,' Alex pointed out, taking a large mouthful of wine.

Rory grimaced and nodded. 'I do know what you mean about Ms O'Hara. The whole atmosphere of *The Inn* has changed since she moved in here. More than one person has told me that she makes them nervous sitting silently, sipping her water and gazing at her computer screen, or at them. Locals never come in here – into the snug – any longer. Almost without exception, they stay in the bar, and I don't think they fully understand what she is doing in the school either. Everyone knows that you are the teacher-in-charge, and that says everything. But Administrative Head …'

'Ah well, Rory, I never mind someone else taking paperwork off my desk! I respect Jenna and I am sure that she believes that she is doing the best she can for the school.'

'Aye – and for the name of the Clan MacLeod!'

'Will you be going to the May Ball tomorrow, Rory?'

'If there's a dance to go to, I go! Never missed a single May Ball when the old lady was organising them. Sadly, though, my Catriona doesn't share my enthusiasm and she seems to be increasingly feeling her age. You're going, Alex?'

'I love dancing. Try to keep me away!'

'Then, if I may, Mrs Miller, please may I reserve the first dance?'

'With the greatest of pleasure, Mr Cameron.'

Scotland was indeed 'boasting', Alex reflected, as she walked swiftly towards the Manor House the following evening: golden and still, it was redolent of mid-summer rather than the usual chilly May Day eve. Against all expectations, Alex had been able to borrow a plain white mid-calf dress from Agnes, who told her firmly that she 'didn't do dancing'. It fitted her perfectly, skimming her slender figure; and moved as if it had a life of its own to the lively Scottish dance music she had listened to, and tried to move to, in Gladys' cramped confines. Paired with a jade-green scarf, slung across one shoulder instead of a plaid, Alex felt as if, tonight, she would not disgrace her role within the community. She also felt comfortable as a woman, which, whether she acknowledged it or not, was central to her peace of mind when she was likely to come into contact with Josh MacDonald. She hadn't spoken to him since the brief exchange from his surgery window, but his dark intensity haunted her dreams. Some nights she woke, hot and yearning, remembering the frank – and at one point passionate – exchange when they had known each other only as *Star* and *Alex* on the beguiling Twitter platform. Sometimes she lay listening to the dawn chorus and reflected on what she had learnt of the man since she had met him: his deep caring for his patients, his intellect, his passion. And then she twisted and turned on her hard bed, desperately trying to rid her mind of what she longed for. Of his opinion of her, she had no idea. The potentially dangerous evening, and the long night of conversation, that they had spent together at his cottage had left her unsure of whether he still desired her as a woman now that he had met her in real life.

As she approached the lights and manicured gardens of Jenna's home, she reflected, for the thousandth time, on how Josh's physical presence had dominated her thoughts since that first, excruciatingly difficult, Governors' meeting. All her life she had longed for a man who stimulated her mind as much as her body and in Josh, she knew, without a shadow of a doubt, that she had found him. But Agnes' warning that he 'was dangerous'; Jenna's proprietorial possessive pronoun when she had talked of '*my* friend, Josh MacDonald'; his aggressively male presence on Twitter; and the strictly hands-*off* approach that he himself had taken since his return from the States – everything nudged and nagged her to believe that she was deceiving herself if she thought Josh wanted any sort of relationship with her.

By a gorse bush that seemed to be holding a personal celebration of the wonderful, sunny Spring evening by its very colour and vigour, Alex stopped and settled her uneven breath. Tonight – Josh MacDonald or no Josh MacDonald – she was resolved to retain her calm and professional demeanour. Inhaling deeply and re-affirming her intention, she strode on, more slowly and with a steady determination.

Alex had never stepped inside the Manor House before and, passing through the stone arched entrance straight into the great hall which was crowded with flowers, she was astonished at its elegance and sophistication.

A waitress unobtrusively proffered a tray full of champagne flutes, 'Madame?'

Almost without thinking what she was doing, Alex smiled, took the nearest, and sipped. Her brain was in overdrive, trying to assess the situation and determine exactly how she should act during the evening; but she succeeded in appearing calm and untroubled through immense self-control. Alex recognised a scattering of people amongst the Governors and families from her school, but there were others she had never met before, and to those she simply smiled and nodded. If she was aware of how she was presenting herself to others, she was acutely conscious of how she herself was being observed. Jeanne O'Hara, in a classic black cocktail dress which bespoke 'designer' in its every minimalist line, watched her, unsmiling, under lowered lashes. The Reverend Mike Whitfield hovered attentively at Jeanne's elbow with eyes for no-one but her. Rory smiled and waved, gesturing to his watch, whilst Jenna greeted her with outstretched hand, commenting warmly on the array of children's art work which rested, it seemed, on every surface in the Manor House. But it was on Josh that Alex's gaze came to rest: self-contained, immaculate, the bold red and black of his Clan tartan accentuating his dark beauty. Desperate not to appear to stare, Alex chatted to those she knew, but was hyper-aware of Josh's thick, dark hair, his broad shoulders and his voice, as he effortlessly engaged in conversation with all those in the room who wished to talk to him.

Jenna, smiling, approached Josh and took from him his half-empty champagne glass, placing it on a polished console table. Inclining her head, she stretched out her right hand which, with slight hesitation, Josh took, and together they moved onto the parquet floor to open the dancing. The first dance was a waltz and, as the well-matched couple circled, Jenna held Josh's glance intensely with her own.

After completing one turn of the space cleared for dancing, Jenna and Josh were joined by a scattering of other couples, and Rory approached Alex to claim his first, promised dance, inclining his head and proffering her his arm. Rory was a large man, who seemed quite ungainly as he went about his work, but on the dance floor he was light-footed, and skilfully steered Alex around and in between the other couples.

'I've never seen a gathering of people dressed in their Clan tartans before, Rory,' Alex observed. 'You all look magnificent!'

'Aye, and some more magnificent than others,' Rory replied. 'The chieftain is positively radiant tonight! And being in the arms of our good doctor will crown her evening.'

Anything Alex thought of saying seemed puerile or pathetic. She longed to seek reassurance from the dependable man in front of her that Josh was impervious to the cultured beauty of Jenna MacLeod; and that just because Jenna and Josh opened the dancing together didn't indicate any particular intimacy. But she said neither of these things, instead switching the conversation rather awkwardly to the display of the children's work which surrounded them.

The quartet came to the end of *Westering Home,* and Rory bowed gallantly over Alex's right hand. 'You are as graceful a dancer as you are a gifted teacher, Alex. The island is lucky to have you.' He escorted her back towards the refreshment table where the soft light from crystal candelabra danced and shimmered across glass and china.

'Thank you, Rory, that was lovely!' Alex responded, flushing slightly at the compliment.

'Miss, would you dance the Gay Gordons with me, please?' Archie MacLeod, the yellow and black tartan clashing somewhat with his carefully slicked-back ginger hair, stood solidly before her.

'I would be honoured, Archie. Thank you for asking me.'

Alex anticipated the challenging logistics of a dance which requires the woman to dip and twirl under the arm of her partner, but looking down at the earnest, well-scrubbed face of the small boy, she just didn't have the heart to refuse him. Beaming, Archie led Alex onto the parquet floor and solemnly bowed as the musicians struck up *Scotland the Brave.* Alex was a good five foot ten inches tall, and Archie perhaps a foot shorter, but laughingly, she dipped and bowed to fold her height under his arm and they managed to complete the dance without catastrophe. Breathless with the extra effort of accommodating her partner, Alex returned to the refreshment table – this time to find the longest, coolest drink she could lay her hands on. One of the ever-attentive waitresses was immediately at her elbow: 'What can I get for you, Madame?'

'Thank you for your attentiveness, Alice, but I will serve the lady.' Josh stood slightly behind Alex and, although she hadn't heard him approach, she could feel the heat of his body only inches from her own. Much of a height, she turned and managed to look into the depths of his changing grey-blue eyes, holding her gaze steady – but as for speaking, or moving further, this was at that moment beyond her.

'Alcohol or soft?' he prompted gently.

'Something thirst-quenching please … the efforts of the last dance took their toll on me!'

'You were splendid! Sparkling water – medically prescribed!'

Alex had always been preternaturally aware of the shape, colour and form of the human hand. Anything plump or pale or skinny she found repulsive and now, glancing down at Josh's hand, which held out to her a glass of spring water, she appreciated the strength of form, the long, tanned strong fingers and neat, well-manicured nails below the cuff of the crisp white shirt.

'Thank you.'

'I know I am a poor comparison with your previous two partners, Alex, but would you do me the honour of dancing with me next?'

Alex never knew what made her do it, but she curtsied deep in acquiescence, holding her skirts wide and looking up laughingly into Josh's eyes, where she saw an expression that quickened her pulse and her breath.

The quartet – this time joined by a vocalist – started to play one of the most beautiful of classic Scottish songs, *My Love is Like a Red, Red Rose*. Alex flushed as she listened to the words which could have been written specifically to describe her tumultuous feelings for the self-contained, complex man who held her so surely and guided her with grace and skill around the crowded room.

> *My Love is like a red, red rose*
> *That's newly sprung in June.*
> *My Love is like a melody*
> *That's sweetly played in tune.*

People had told Alex on many occasions that she had an open and expressive face that was all too easily read and now, terrified of her feelings being betrayed, she lowered her eyes to rest somewhere on her partner's right shoulder.

'Tu m'enivres.' The quiet intensity of Josh's voice made her lift her eyes to his, where she saw passion and longing that paralleled her own.

'C'est la même chose pour moi …' she whispered, and felt Josh's arm tighten on her waist and pull her infinitesimally closer to him.

'Alex, after this show of wealth and power is over, meet me by the *Sleeping Guardians*.'

And, almost as if making a vow, Alex said, 'I will.'

Chapter 38

For Josh, letting Alex go from within the circle of his arms was one of the hardest things he had ever done. He watched as she moved across to talk to parents of children in her school, almost following her with his body as well as with his eyes, as there was a lightness and energy about her movements that filled him with joy. As for Alex, it was as if Josh's hands rested on her still, so intense had been the experience. For both, the rest of the evening seemed never-ending. A succession of partners presented themselves to each, and each smiled and made conversation politely, but remained overwhelmingly aware of the presence of the other, whether they could see them or not.

Eventually, at around midnight, the last dance was announced and, once again, Jenna MacLeod almost imperiously beckoned to Josh to join her as her partner. Unsmilingly, he did as he was bidden. Rory claimed Alex once again for the final dance and, as they circled amongst the other couples, Alex caught glimpses of a low-key drama which seemed to be unfolding between the Clan chieftain and Josh. Jenna had raised her chin and once again held her partner's gaze with her own. Then Alex glimpsed Josh's almost curt shake of the head and the faint colour that crept into Jenna's face. At the end of the dance, Josh bowed, his face still implacable, turned on his heel and walked to the front door and out into the twilight of the Scottish early summer night. Alex saw that Jenna was keeping her emotions under control with some difficulty – but this she managed to do, smiling and shaking the hands of her guests courteously as they left.

'Fancy some company walking home?' Rory asked Alex.

She had been anticipating this and had already decided to accept. The route from the Manor House to the *Sleeping Guardians* passed *The Inn* and she had decided that it would be too conspicuous for her to follow Josh directly.

'Jenna, thank you for such a lovely – and memorable – evening. It is my first experience of a ceilidh and I have loved it!' Alex's thanks were entirely genuine and she felt real compassion as she saw the strain on the face of her Chair of Governors.

'I'm so pleased you enjoyed it, Alex,' Jenna responded graciously. 'It's good to have you with us as part of the island family.'

As Alex transferred her jade green pashmina from its role as sash and wrapped it around her shoulders, she noticed that Jeanne O'Hara lingered, tidying serviettes on the refreshment table and blowing out the candles in the crystal candelabra. Mike Whitfield shadowed her every move, trying to open a conversation with her but being met only with the occasional patronising comment. First to arrive, last to leave, and conspicuous by not having danced a single time. Why did everything about Jeanne cause a jarring note?

On their way back to *The Inn,* Alex and Rory chatted inconsequentially about the evening and about island matters in general, Alex quickening her walking pace until the elderly landlord was almost trotting to keep up with her.

'Good night, Rory, and thank you for your company this evening.'

'Good night, Alex.'

Her fists balled with impatience, nails digging into her palms, Alex shut the stable door of Gladys behind her. How long should she wait before she could safely leave the purlieu of *The Inn* and climb the cliff path? At least she was not concerned about Jeanne's prying eyes as she should still be safely at the Manor House pursuing whatever devious plan she had in mind. Alex traced Rory's progress through his home through the sequence of lights being switched on, then extinguished: in the kitchen, the hall and finally the bedroom, leaving the building in darkness. In her turn, Alex flicked off Gladys' dim interior light and, not stopping to change, she jumped lightly down the steps of the campervan and flew along the quayside. Josh had had at least twenty minutes start and she was unsure how long he would be prepared to wait for her. Although she had started to get to know the man, there was a wildness and unpredictability about him that gave an edge to their relationship: there was so very much still to discover.

The civilised and sophisticated context of the May Ball paled into insignificance in comparison with the power of Nature, as she was shaking herself awake from the cold sleep of winter and early spring. Out here, the noise of the ocean surged in Alex's ears, the wind tore at her hair. Out here, it was May Day eve

– the ancient Beltane. As she gained height above the town, lying dark behind her, Alex became aware of beacons – the lighting of the Beltane fire – burning at high points on Fragrey and other neighbouring islands, including the holy island of Haligrey. But despite the beauty of the night and the power and promise of the ancient ritual which surrounded her, to Alex it was like an ancient cinematograph, two-dimensional, flickering and unreal. Her single thought was to reach Josh. Randomly, as she ran, she recalled other high points in her life: the anticipation of Christmas when she was a tiny child; the joy when her girls were born; her fulfilment when she qualified as a teacher – but that anticipation, joy and fulfilment were as nothing compared with the single-minded longing that she now felt to see and touch Josh.

She was still running when she was stopped still in her tracks. Josh said nothing but held her at arms' length as if not quite able to believe that what he was looking at was real, then he pulled her to him hard and seemed to envelop her with his arms, his lips, the scent of him.

The short hours of darkness of the Scottish early summer night had started to lighten, and when she was eventually released, Alex saw Josh's face more open and unguarded than she had ever seen it before. She touched his cheek gently. 'Tell me what you are thinking, Josh. I can't read your face.'

For what seemed an interminable length of time, Josh held Alex at arms' length, before starting to speak, almost inaudibly, before pulling her once again towards him, hard. 'Alex, five months ago I stood only a few metres from this spot, intending to kill myself. I felt alone and useless against the power of illness and death. What saved me was a card from Carrie Logan, the wee girl I was telling you about, who died. She had decorated it with a rainbow and a picture of a unicorn and she called me "her bestie". The card made me change my mind. It gave me a glimmer of hope that somewhere there would be something that would make my life worth living again. This may sound fanciful, Alex, but I believe that I've found this in you: you are honest, you always ring true, and you bring a light and a kindness into the darkest situation. I have no idea what the future holds, but I know one thing right now – overwhelmingly. I want you.'

Calm, smiling, Alex with infinite gentleness stroked Josh's cheek and whispered once again, 'C'est la même chose pour moi …'

Effortlessly, Josh lifted Alex and carried her into the nearest of the *Sleeping Guardians* that stood, sheltering and shadowy, behind them. He spread his plaid on the sandy, warm earth and knelt before her, very slowly loosening her clothing. 'Beltane is a day which celebrates fertility, the eternal renewal of life. People think of these barrows as places of death and ending, but to me they are symbols of constancy, of familiarity. I want to drive back darkness with you here tonight, Alex.'

Her white dress slipped to the ground off her slender shoulders and, looking at the man before her, Alex thought that she had never felt such complete awareness – of his masculine beauty, of the cool air which flowed around her breasts and thighs, of the fading stars outside the barrow, and of the warm, and welcoming earth that spread before them.

'I want to be inside you, Alex.'

'And I want you there…'

Chapter 39

Rolling over on to her side and hugging her knees to her, Alex laughed softly: she had never dreamt how cosy a tomb could be! The ground seemed to be hollowed to hold their bodies. It was warm – unbelievably warm – and as she stirred, she was aware of the sun rising and striking its light directly through the open entrance to the barrow. During her sterile marriage to Dave, he had without exception been asleep when she awoke – sometimes snoring, sometimes hot and restless. But this new morning, when she opened her eyes, it was Josh who, propped on his elbow, was gazing down at her, as awake and aware as she was herself. The tension and anguish that she had seen a few hours earlier had evaporated with the night, and the man whose love-making had taken her to points of ecstasy which she thought existed only in literature, or myth, looked utterly relaxed and at peace.

'"*She is all States, all Princes I, Nothing else is …*"' Josh murmured, threading a tendril of Alex's thick blond hair through his fingers and moving it slowly around her nipple.

'"*Compared to this, all honour's mimic, all wealth alchemy*". I used to read John Donne's poetry too, and weep, thinking that such love could never be mine.'

'Just in case you're unsure, Alex …'

The sun had climbed higher above the horizon when Josh sat up once again and ran his hands through his short hair. 'This must be the best view from a tomb ever!' he smiled; and she, looking at him, and gently pulling away the plaid that he had drawn across his belly, affirmed 'It must be …'

'Alex, how shall we take this forward?'

'Carefully,' she answered, laying her head on his shoulder and now wrapping the plaid around them both.

'You know I still have this tedious GMC complaint against Clive Saunders to deal with. And it's taking far too much of my time and thought. That and investigating Jeanne O'Hara's motivation. And, perhaps most difficult of all, trying to persuade Jenna that she and I simply do not have any sort of future together, ever.'

'I feel sorry for Jenna,' Alex whispered softly, tracing the line of her lover's cheekbone.

'Ach, so do I,' Josh said, pulling her to him once again.

'Tell me about Jenna.'

'Ah well. It's not something I am particularly proud of Alex. When my wife left me, I was completely at a loss as to how to manage my two wee girls. As the only medical practitioner on the island, I had – and still have – hardly any time at all for myself, let alone my daughters. Jenna was kind. She took the girls to school and picked them up at the end of the day, taking them back to the Manor House until evening surgery had finished. At first, I used to pick them up and take them home for supper, then Jenna started to invite us to eat with her and gradually this became the norm. As you know,' Josh paused for a second, gritting his teeth, 'my default position with women is to have virtual relationships, but because Jenna was there in person, she seemed to take up the vacant position as my partner quite naturally. She is a lovely woman with a formidable intellect and – I know this sounds crass – but we slipped into an affair, which clearly meant a lot to her, although as far as I was concerned it was merely convenient.'

'Josh! That poor woman.'

'I know. As I said, Alex, this is not something I am proud of – but I want to be completely honest with you. I have so many flaws and shortcomings that I do not particularly like myself!

'Matters came to a head when she invited me around for dinner one evening. It was quite a formal occasion. I asked Morag to babysit the girls for me and I made an effort to look my best. Jenna had too. At the end of the evening, when we were chatting over a couple of whiskies, completely out of the blue, she asked me to marry her. It shocked me that I had to give my answer no thought at all. I just said no. When she asked me why I had refused her I said simply that it was because I was not in love with her. I wasn't then, and I am not now.'

'Put like that, it sounds so brutal, Josh. As if you made use of her.'

'There are aspects of my character that I hate, Alex. I did make use of her. I had fallen into the habit of using sex to escape from the harshness of life – almost as an antidote, or a drug. Whenever I met an attractive woman, I seduced her if she appealed to me, and with each act of seduction, the word 'love' became more remote, more meaningless. Sex was the panacea for death and despair and lives ruined by illness.'

Alex sat, cross-legged and silent. Wrapping his plaid around his body, Josh knelt in front of her. 'Alex, I have been as honest as I can be. With you I can't be anything else. But please say that I haven't disgusted you so much that you no longer wish to have anything to do with me. When I sent you that pornographic photo and you rejected it – and me – I couldn't get it out of my mind. I kept re-playing the joyful, honest exchanges that we had had before that point and I felt bereaved – there is no other way of expressing it. You intrigued me, and I thought because of my pitiful sex-pest games, I had lost you.

'When I saw you here for the first time in school, I realised that the woman I had been attracted to on social media was a mere shadow of the fun-loving, caring and lovely woman who stood before me. I saw how hurt you were to encounter someone who had caused you at best discomfort, and at worst pain, and I could, once again, have jumped off that cliff. I was obsessed by trying to make you understand how deeply I was sorry for what I had done, but I never imagined that this would be possible. It was a huge gamble when I asked you to dinner at the cottage, but I saw such understanding and forgiveness in you that I started to hope that possibly we could have a future together. But we can't go forward from *this* point, Alex, if I hadn't honestly explained about Jenna – and more importantly about that aspect of my character that has made me loathe myself for the past years.'

Alex was pale, but she smiled and held her hands out to Josh. 'It's on a par with sleeping with someone you don't love for more than twenty years. Just going through the same boring and meaningless ritual because of duty. When I met you, I believed that I had found something wild and passionate and dangerous. And I loved it. And now, I think I …' Alex stopped and looked into her lover's face. At first, she could detect no emotion, but gradually as he smiled his expression changed from showing only habitual tension and repression to an infinite tenderness. For many minutes they sat silently and looked at each other as the sun rose and filled the place designed to hide the darkness of death with the untouched light of a new day.

'"*Morning has broken, like the first morning,*"' Alex whispered softly.

'Alex, we need to go. It's the last thing I want to do, but we can't stay in a neolithic barrow indefinitely – however atmospheric!'

'What are you going to do about Jenna? Are you going to tell her about you and me, Josh?'

'I must. But not yet. Don't you think we need to ease our relationship forward gradually? From being governor and teacher, to being an item together in what appears to be a mere twenty-four hours might appear a little foolhardy. Do you see what I mean?'

Alex nodded. 'Yes, I do.' Then added tentatively, 'Should we start to be seen together do you think?'

'Yes. Perhaps prising Bonnie from Rory's company and taking her for a walk together, or attending any ceilidh that's going. Maybe going to the occasional film that's shown in the village hall – that sort of thing.'

'Agreed! Now what's the best way to seal a promise?'

'If we had longer, I would show you the very best way! But let this be a gesture of good faith.' Josh took

Alex's hand and kissed the palm, folding her fingers over the place where his lips had rested. 'Goodbye for the present, Alex.'

'Goodbye, my Star of the Sea.'

In an instant, she was gone and for Josh the world became once again a darker place.

Chapter 40

Alex's foremost thought as she ran down the cliff path was thankfulness that it was Saturday. To have to concentrate on teaching, when all she wanted to do was to play and re-play the memories of the unforgettable night that she had just spent with Josh, would have been not just difficult, but impossible. She almost danced down the track as she remembered what had been said and what she had felt. But for a moment she reflected seriously that when she had told Josh that she had 'loved' the wildness, passion and danger of his character, she had almost gone on to say that she loved him.

Mentally, she reviewed the meagre provisions that she had stored in Gladys and decided that – Jeanne or no Jeanne – she would go to *The Inn* for the Scottish equivalent of a full English breakfast.

'Good morning, Rory,' she sang out as she entered the familiar dark-panelled snug. 'And what a perfect morning it is! Hello Bonnie – how are you, lovely girl?' The little dog wagged her way into the snug at Rory's heels. 'She seems very happy, Rory, and very settled. Are you going to offer her a permanent home?'

'Hello, Alex. This is an unexpected pleasure! Have you actually decided to forego your muesli and coffee for a decent first meal of the day? And yes, we are. Catriona has lost her heart to the wee thing. She says that she is better company than I am!'

Alex laughed. 'I have indeed decided to abandon the subsistence diet I follow in Gladys – I'm starving! What's the biggest, most calorific breakfast on your menu today?'

Rory hesitated for a moment before saying, 'Catriona wasn't feeling too good first thing, Alex. But I know that she loves cooking for you because you enjoy her food so much! I will see how she's doing. Meanwhile, would you like a coffee? At least I can produce that for you!'

'I'd love one, Rory,' Alex replied with a concerned frown. 'Look, if it's too much trouble, please don't worry your wife. I can easily eat in Gladys. I was only teasing about my subsistence diet.'

'Now, don't fret yourself, Alex.' Rory spooned ground coffee into the shiny new machine that had graced the snug for several months, and flicked a switch. 'A couple of months ago, Catriona told me that she felt that she needed help in *The Inn* and so we advertised. The new girl is arriving on Monday – we interviewed her via, erm, *Scoop?*'

'Skype, I think Rory. Is your wife ill? Has she seen Doctor MacDonald?' Alex flushed as she mentioned Josh's name and recalled how someone had told her years earlier that when you are in love with someone you find every opportunity to talk about them.

'She hasn't seen Josh – no. There's nothing specific. But let's see how she is after the new girl arrives and she has more time to herself.'

Catriona Cameron came into the snug several minutes later, smiling and tying on her apron.

'So good to see you, Alex.' Then, swiftly looking around the space before speaking, she added 'It's nice to have my cooking appreciated!'

'Are you all right to do this, Catriona?' Alex asked anxiously. 'The coffee is wonderful – anything else would be a bonus!'

'I'm fine, lass. Just a wee bit tired. Now, has that useless lump of a husband of mine told you what a full *Scottish* breakfast looks like?'

Alex smiled and shook her head.

'Weeell… haggis, fried tatties, sausages, eggs and bacon. How does that sound?'

'Utterly perfect! Thank you, Catriona.'

Thankfully, Alex had almost finished her breakfast when she felt, rather than heard, Jeanne O'Hara enter the snug. Bonnie gave an appropriate sharp bark, which rather wickedly brought a smile to Alex's face.

'And what can I get for you this morning, Ms O'Hara?' asked Rory.

'Oh, just the usual, thank you, Rory,' came the flat response.

'Right, so that's half a grapefruit, one slice of toast, no butter, and black coffee?'

'Correct,' came the reply, as she opened her laptop. 'We don't often see you in here, Alex. Out enjoying the scenery early this morning, were you, and working up an appetite through exercise?'

'As always Jeanne, your instinct, or should I say your ubiquitous observation, is completely correct. What was your observation method this morning – curtain twitching, or binoculars? And the scenery, and the exercise, were spectacular, thank you. Bon appétit!'

The innuendo, almost the sneering tone, in which Jeanne had asked the question infuriated Alex and convinced her that somehow she, and possibly Josh also, had been spotted earlier that morning. She had seen no sign of Jeanne, but the woman had a knack of being exactly where she was *not* wanted. Alex knew that Josh intended to leave the barrow some minutes after she herself had, but if Jeanne had for some reason been systematically spying on her, then perhaps she had watched first her own, then Josh's, return down the cliff path.

Despite having had negligible sleep, Alex felt restless – partly because she still longed to be with Josh, and partly through her anger at Jeanne. She changed the now rather grubby white dress for jeans and a light sweater and headed without further thought towards Agnes' cottage.

The self-styled 'Wise Woman of Fragrey' was not at home, although as was the custom on the island, her door had been left unlocked. It was a perfect morning and Alex decided to wait for her friend's return outside the croft, on the pebbly shore. She moved aside several sharper stones and leant against a warm, smooth boulder. Lying back and gazing straight up at the clear blue sky and soaring seabirds, Alex's eyes half-closed, as she remembered the feel of the earth under her body in the barrow and the heat and hardness of the man who had enveloped her.

She knew that she must have drifted off to sleep because the sun was nearly overhead when the soft splashing of oars awoke her and her eyes flickered open once again.

'A sleeping beauty!' Agnes laughed softly, as she pulled Frigg clear of the small waves that advanced and slipped away again on the strand. 'And, by the look of you, Alex, a very fulfilled one. Coffee?'

'I'd love some, Agnes,' Alex yawned. 'Where've you been?'

'Haligrey.'

'Was it you who lit the Beltane fire there?'

'It was.'

'But no one lives there, Agnes.'

'Don't they, Alex?'

Inside the herb-scented croft, the women sat opposite each other, on either side of the black, cast-iron range.

'Why did you come to see me?' Agnes asked, pouring the coffee.

'A combination of things … one of which was anger …'

'Never a good feeling – you did right to come.'

'Jeanne O'Hara. I think she hates me and, for some reason, wants to harm me in some way.'

'You don't mean physically?'

'No, Agnes. I think she wants to damage me professionally, tarnish my reputation. But I cannot imagine why. I don't like the woman that much' – Alex pressed her index finger and thumb closely together to illustrate the extent of her dislike – 'but I have been determined to work together with her for the good of the school.'

Agnes gazed down into the murky depths of her drink and swirled it around the thick stoneware mug. 'The woman is devious. She has her own plans and I believe that she thinks that you will block them in some way. I know Josh MacDonald was going to make some enquiries about her previous career history. He feels that certain things just do not stack up: the way in which she was not in post when she came for interview being one; the nature of her reference being another. I wonder if he has made any progress. I know how busy he is.'

She watched the play of emotions across Alex's face. 'Has anyone ever told you that your expression is as easy to read as a child's?' she asked gently.

Alex nodded. 'Too many times, Agnes!'

'As soon as I mentioned Josh's name, your eyes shone, then your whole face lit up. There was a combination of longing and tenderness which even an ancient spinster like me can easily decode. Was Josh MacDonald the other reason you came to see me?'

'Probably – but I had no idea how I was going to start to speak to you about him; nor did I have any idea what I wanted to ask you, or tell you. I just want to talk about him.'

The brass carriage clock on the dark oak mantel-shelf ticked away the seconds.

'That is the way of love. Josh is one of the most complex men I have ever known. One side of his character is all light – his care for his patients and his skill as a doctor are exceptional and he has a great capacity for love. Another side of his character is dark and potentially dangerous – to himself and to those who love him. He has experienced more than his fair share of tragedy in his life, and each loss, each betrayal, has damaged him further.

'He adored his mother and was deeply scarred as a human being when she died. I believe that he felt guilt that he had not been able to provide for her more and that he had been away at medical school when she was dying. Above all, I believe that he blamed himself for not somehow being able to cure her.

'Josh's father drank himself to death, and because he was determined to leave a world which no longer held the woman he loved, he was deaf and blind to the pleading and reasoning that Josh applied, to try to bring him back to his senses.

'Josh's wife, Elspeth, lived on the island only briefly at the start of their marriage. Whereas Josh seemed wedded to Fragrey itself, she was wedded only to her ambition. Did you know that she was a junior registrar in Edinburgh during their married life? She took the job that Josh had vacated when he returned to the island to set up his general practice here. She was a beautiful woman – but cold – and, we all felt, calculating. When Elspeth was with Josh, she was witty, charming, utterly radiant, and could wrap him around her little finger. When their girls were born, on the surface they appeared a perfect family, but Elspeth insisted that she take their daughters back to Edinburgh with her for most of the time. She claimed that Josh was "too busy" to care for them properly, whereas she could afford live-in childcare. This she did until she returned with them one Easter to tell Josh that she was pregnant and that the father was a consultant surgeon in the hospital she worked in. I believe that Josh was prepared to accept the unborn child as his own, but Elspeth returned once again to the mainland, this time leaving the girls with their father, and had an abortion. Josh once told me that he could have forgiven unfaithfulness, but never taking a life, even at its very beginning.

'Jenna MacLeod made a bold play for Josh almost as soon as the ferry carrying Elspeth away for the last time had sailed beyond the horizon. They had an affair for a couple of years, but it was always driven by Jenna, not by Josh. All his emotions seemed to have died, to have shrivelled away. The whole island was worried about him, as we watched him working himself to the point of breakdown. But Josh's way is to take on more – and more – until what would overcome most people seems to heal him. I cannot explain this. I can only tell you what I have observed.

'Fate seemed to stop tormenting him for a while: his girls grew up and passed their Advanced Highers; Jenna seemed to accept that Josh didn't want any sort of romantic relationship; and he was asked to take on quality control in General Practice across the Western Islands.'

Agnes paused and looked down for several seconds at her hands which were clasped hard on her lap before continuing.

'But then, completely out of the blue, his elder brother Hector was drowned. Hector was a self-styled 'adventurer' who had never married and hadn't had children. He had been refurbishing his father's fishing boat with a view to sailing it to Iceland – following the route his father would have taken on his fishing trips. He decided that the boat was seaworthy and ready to start making short, trial trips, and one November day he set out to sail around Haligrey. You've seen how a storm can blow up out of nothing here and, when he was part-way across the channel, a vicious November sleet storm started and he was unable to handle the boat alone. It blew wildly off course and sank somewhere out there – maybe between here and the Holy Island, maybe on the far side, facing the orchard thicket. The waters are deep there and neither the boat, not Hector's body have ever been found.'

'That's terrible, Agnes! I knew that Josh had a brother, but that was all!' Alex exclaimed. 'How would you ever begin to cope with a loss like that? So near to home. And never to find the body! What was Hector like?'

Agnes smiled sadly, 'Very like Josh to look at – but it was as if, when life qualities were being handed out to the MacDonald family, Hector had inherited all the light-heartedness and hedonism, and Josh the seriousness and sense of social responsibility. Whereas Josh always seemed to be searching for a meaningful vocation, a serious relationship, Hector was a dilettante. He tasted women and moved on; he never settled to a career, but swam the furthest, ran the fastest, climbed the highest. He was utterly charismatic and we watched with real concern to see how this loss would impact upon Josh. It seemed to many of us as if it might be the thing that pushed him too far into the darker aspects of the MacDonald family character and that he may take extreme measures to leave the pain – or even leave his life – behind.'

Alex stood up, frowning. 'Was there no one to support him?'

Agnes shook her head. 'The defences that he has built around his character are impenetrable – well, we all thought they were,' Agnes smiled. 'But he did take decisive action: he started an exercise regime that would put an elite athlete to shame. Morning and evening, we would watch him run along the quay and up the cliff path. To the right of the track lie the traditional farming lands of the MacDonalds. They go back untold generations and are bounded by the barrows that stand on the cliff top. He told me once that the burial mounds, the *Sleeping Guardians,* had become for him a symbol of constancy, a sort of unchanging certainty in his life.'

Alex fiercely blinked away tears. 'Constancy' and 'Certainty', the words echoed Josh's own and she knew that was why Josh had chosen to love her there, in a burial mound – to most, a shockingly unsuitable place for love-making, but for him a complex symbol of security.

Agnes continued, 'All of us feel that he has been betrayed by the system he serves. Morag Kitchener, his devoted receptionist cum secretary cum slave, always follows protocol and confidentiality to a 't'; but sometimes when we meet in our spinning circle, she is apoplectic about his line managers. She never mentions anything specific, but consistently voices her disgust at how they treat a man of such integrity.'

'So when you say that Josh is 'dangerous' what did you mean, Agnes?'

'Half the women on the island are, or have been, in love with him, Alex. Jenna MacLeod is a powerful woman and I do not know how she would deal with a rival to the feelings she herself holds for Josh, and I don't know what professional harm she would cause him. He works himself too hard, and I'm not certain what inner strength or power sustains him, but I think that it could be his position as healer here on this island. I believe that it is beyond precious to him that people depend upon his skill and knowledge to cure them. His professional status is not empty vainglory, but is what centres him and makes his life worth living. If that professional role were to be destroyed, then I do not know what would happen to his mental and physical wellbeing. We all have an inner sustaining power. For me it is the unseen world of the spirit. For Jenna it is the glory of the great family of which she is chieftain. For Rory it is the community that he seeks to strengthen through his role as landlord and as school governor.'

Alex leant forward, her face quiet and thoughtful, and lightly touched Agnes' clasped hands. 'And for me, what is my "inner sustaining power"? Do you know, I've never really thought about it until this moment, but maybe a *seeker of everyday magic* isn't too shabby a description.'

Agnes laughed quietly. 'Maybe it's not. Forgive my ramblings, Alex, but I thought you needed to know some of the background to Josh MacDonald.

Chapter 41

Jeanne O'Hara smiled calculatingly at the images produced by the colour printer in the school office. Alex, stifling a yawn, and half-turning to wave goodbye to Josh just outside his cottage on the quay, the early morning sun sending a rippling banner across the sheltered water of the harbour. Alex again, dancing down the track from the *Sleeping Guardians*, her white ball dress crumpled and dirty and her hair flying around her head in a wild halo. And finally Josh, self-contained as always, but with a smile of utter fulfilment, striding down the cliff. Because the images had been taken on her mobile, the date and time of each were clear, and the last two images were shown to have been taken on May Day eve, just ten minutes apart.

She touched the screen of her iphone. 'Jenna, could I come over to the Manor House, sometime? I need to discuss something with you.'

'Of course, Jeanne. But if it's not urgent, could we make it next week do you think? My cousins are staying with me until then. That's one of the benefits of the May Ball – maximum exposure to family!'

'What day and time would suit you?'

'Say next Monday – a week tomorrow – at eleven? Thanks Jeanne.'

Alex was exhausted. It was all very well giving the children full responsibility for writing, producing and directing their dramatic re-enactment of the Fragrey boat burial, but the process was much more gruelling than if she herself had been author, director and producer. She had to gently correct anachronisms, modify language and steer the boys away from the enactment of endless, bloody battles. It was six o'clock before she closed the school door and stretched long and languorously to ease the stiffness out of her neck and shoulders, before walking briskly home to make some sort of supper – probably, she reflected ruefully, omelette again. She knew that Josh's surgery ended at six and strained her eyes to see if she could catch a glimpse of him, leaving his place of work just as she was leaving hers, and the mere anticipation that she might see him sent waves of longing through her. Many women – most women – would have texted or phoned Josh, to seek reassurance or elicit compliments, but Alex projected her own honesty and trust into her relationships. She always had done – with David, her husband, with Diana and Chloe, her daughters, and with her close friends. Too often this trust was misplaced or abused, but Alex knew no other way. So, her longing for Josh unabated, she hugged to herself the beautiful secret of what had been between them and what lay between them still.

After the most cursory of checks to see whether some unexpected delicacy lurked in the fridge or cupboard of Gladys' compact kitchen, Alex sighed slightly and unearthed eggs, herbs, cheese and mushrooms and started to prepare the supper she had anticipated. As she chopped and beat and grated, Alex felt more settled and happier than she had for years. She poured herself a glass of red wine and found a Sting album on her phone, which she started to play as she danced around the compact space of her kitchen/ bedroom/living quarters.

Every breath you take, Every move you make
Every vow you break, Every step you take,
I'll be watching you.

She laughed out loud as she thought how the lyrics of the song could describe Jeanne O'Hara's spying on her, and started to sing along with the music, hamming up the performance and using the wooden spatula as a pretend microphone.

'Hello Mother! Been at the vino again?'

'Diana!'

'Is that all you can say?'

⊰║║⊱

In his surgery, Josh re-read the email from the General Medical Council:

We have spoken to Mr Clive Saunders MBE MBChB FRCS who utterly refutes the allegations that he used his position of authority and influence to appoint to your practice on a temporary basis a newly-qualified medical practitioner who failed to meet the basic standards required for safe and effective general practice.

Unless you can adduce significant support for your allegations, this case will be closed.

'Doctor MacDonald – Josh – it's nearly seven o'clock. I have my spinning circle tonight and I can't stay much longer. You really must go home too!'

'Ah, Morag, before you go, just come and look at this! It's not what you know … etcetera …'

Morag read the email over Josh's shoulder and exclaimed with impatience, 'But all the islanders could support what you say, doctor! We would do so without hesitation!'

'And do you think the great and the good at the GMC would listen to the likes of fisherfolk, subsistence farmers, crofters? They wouldn't, Morag.'

The practice secretary stared at the computer screen intently as if it would somehow give them both the answer they were looking for – which in a way it did, when a new notification arrived with a *ping* in Josh's Inbox.

Hi Josh, it's Brad here. Hope all is well in that obscure island of yours with the impossible name? How's that little girl you were so worried about? Do drop me a line, Josh. It would be good to hear from you.

Josh leapt up from his seat, picked Morag up in his arms and spun around, 'Eureka! I'll nail the bastard yet.'

'Do you provide a translation, Doctor MacDonald, or is this some sort of initiative test?' asked Morag, flushed and slightly breathless.

'Brad Jackson is a good man, Morag. He is honest and straight-talking and had suspicions himself about the integrity of Clive Saunders. Perhaps the GMC will listen to a world-famous neuro-surgeon who is the

Senior Clinician at one of New York City's leading hospitals.'

Morag nodded her neat head. 'Now will you go home, doctor?'

'After I have emailed Brad, Morag. Yes, I will.'

⊰⊱||⊰⊱

'What are you *doing* here, Diana?' Alex asked blankly.

'My God, what a welcome! I don't see you for a couple of years and all you can do is to bombard me with questions!'

'Hardly bombard. I just have no idea why you're here, that's all.' Irritated, Alex noted that she was responding in her habitual way to her daughter's hectoring tone. Diana always seemed to be accusing Alex of something, and Alex always felt pushed into a position where she had to justify herself. She remembered the relief she had felt when, in leaving her home in Kent, she believed she had also left behind the undeniably toxic relationships with the three members of her 'family'. Then, like a wave, guilt flooded through her – the old pattern, the same old exhausting pattern.

'If you pour me a glass of wine, I'll explain everything to you.'

Sighing, Alex complied.

'Ha! Judgmental as always I see! I can drink with complete moderation now, Mother dear. Why am I here? I'm the new chef at *The Inn.* The old girl who does the cooking is clearly out of her depth and wanted some new ideas and energy. She and her overweight husband interviewed me on Skype and – here I am!'

'I see.'

'Aren't you pleased that I'm here? Think of all the things we can do together! Just like old times. We can walk and swim and have supper together. I've so missed all the things we used to do, Mum.'

This was something else that tied Alex's brain in knots: the reminders of the genuinely wonderful times that she and her daughters used to enjoy together, but *fifteen or so years ago,* when the girls were in their early teens, not now when they were in their late twenties and seemed to have thrown away all the care and love that Alex had lavished on them through their lives. Alex took a deep breath – it always felt as if she was walking through a minefield when she talked to Diana – and she chose her words with extreme care in case she triggered an explosion.

'What happened to your last job, Diana?'

'Well, if you'd bothered to keep in touch with Dad, you would know! They expected me to work ridiculous hours. No overtime was ever paid and the accommodation I had was more like a hostel than anything else. This place seems different, though. My room is old-fashioned – like my employers – but clean enough and spacious. The hours are manageable and, I think there is a real possibility of taking over the restaurant in the future.'

'You said you saw the same potential in the last place though …'

'You are such a negative person, Mum. No wonder Dad couldn't stand living with you anymore! Is there any more wine?'

'*I* left your father, Diana.'

'Ah, always the control freak. You're always in the driving seat, aren't you? Well, I bet you won't be expecting *this* news: Dad and your friend Sarah are an item! She was really kind to him when you just dumped him like an unwanted parcel. Dad has instructed his solicitors to start divorce proceedings against you.'

Alex sat down. 'Sarah? Are you sure?'

'One hundred percent! Anyway, I've got to go. Early start in the morning. Goodnight.'

Alex watched the orange door of the stalwart old vehicle that had, to this point, been her sanctuary, open and shut, and held her head in her hands. She had forgotten how uncomfortable Diana always made her feel: under attack and a complete failure as a mother and as a human being. The peace of her life here, the simplicity, the hours of Yoga and meditation, Josh – oh God, Josh! How could their relationship ever flourish, when Alex was constantly fighting off feelings of her own shortcomings.

There was still light in the sky and, almost surreptitiously, checking to see whether she was being observed by her own daughter or by Jeanne O'Hara, Diana slipped silently out of Gladys and made her way along the quay to Josh's cottage.

Chapter 42

'Alex!'

'Josh, I'm really sorry to disturb you when you are probably doing research or something, but …'

She never finished the sentence. Josh shut the door firmly behind her, pulled her to him and all her angst, all the frustration and hurt vanished as he kissed her eyes, her cheeks, and finally her mouth. '*Never* apologise for coming to see me, Alex. When I see the school, or walk past *The Inn* I have to exercise such control not to run and do this …' He kissed her once again. 'Or this …' And he took her by the hand and led her up the twisting dark wood staircase to his bedroom which nestled under the heavy slate roof.

Alex only gained the most fleeting impression of ceiling timbers, white walls and blue-striped curtains and bedding, because all her attention was on the man who stood in front of her. As if following a reciprocally beautiful ritual, each took off an item of the other's clothing until they stood naked in front of each other.

'You are the most beautiful man I have ever known,' Alex breathed.

In the neat, hidden space under the sloping roof, hours passed as Alex and Josh discovered and rediscovered each other, until finally they lay quiet and silent in each other's arms. Gradually, Alex started to notice details of the room: photographs of two lovely dark-haired girls who bore a striking resemblance to the man who lay still and half-smiling beside her; a book of Latin poetry on the pine bedside table and a photograph of a fishing boat, with the name *Star of the Sea* painted on its prow.

'What are you thinking?' Josh asked her, tracing the line of her eyebrows with his forefinger.

'About you – that you're my safe harbour.'

'I meant about my palatial dwelling place.'

'It's perfect – like you, understated and in the best of taste.'

'Behave, Alex! Why did you come and see me tonight?'

Alex lay back on the white sheets. 'Lots of unpleasant and difficult reasons. I shall feel like an utter traitor, but here goes.' And gradually she told Josh about her daughters, about the way in which Diana made her feel wretched and an utter failure as a mother, about how she had always loved them unconditionally, but now felt bullied and manipulated by them. And finally, she tried to explain her fears about her life here on Fragrey being changed because of her daughter's unexpected arrival.

Josh reflected for some time, then said, 'That's so difficult for you, Alex. I can understand how you feel, but you don't need me to tell you that, with substance abuse, the intrinsic person disappears. All the pain, the manipulation, the bullying – it's the substance that is causing these things.'

'*Hate the sin, love the sinner?*'

'Something like that,' he smiled. 'If I were a religious man, I might have used those very words. And as for you and I, as for our relationship being spoiled, it would take more than such things to change it.'

'That black and white photograph, Josh. Is that your father's boat?'

'Aye – yes, it is.'

'Is that why your beautiful Twitter name was *Star of the Sea*?'

'No, Alex. My mother's name was Molly – Molly MacDonald. She … I don't often speak of her, Alex.'

'You don't have to now. Come here. You need a cuddle! Remember I have won cuddling competitions!' Alex wrapped her right arm under Josh's head and neck and pulled him to her. She felt his body relaxing against her, no longer hard and male, but compliant and childlike.

'I want to tell you about her, Alex. She is the only other woman I have ever really loved. She was the mainstay of our family. Always there, always doing her best, loving, caring. I continue to honour her with this,' and he showed Alex a neat tattoo of a simple radiant star on the outside of his left thigh. 'I broke my thigh when I was fifteen and it was the worst thing that could have happened to me at that stage in my life. I was playing in the island under-seventeen football team and it was in a particularly brutal game that the accident happened. I thought my world had ended. But my mother cared for my emotional needs, just as the doctors met my medical ones. Hector had just climbed the *Old Man of Hoy* and was being fêted for his physical prowess by the local papers. I felt an utter failure.

I always felt in his shadow. This tiny reminder is scant enough, but when I see it, I think of her.'

Alex's every sense was sharpened. Clearly, Josh's guard was down. He was talking of something that meant so much to him that to interrupt would have been brutal. But the words *the only other woman I have ever really loved* had stopped her in her tracks, just as Josh had caught her in his arms when she was running to meet him on their magical Beltane Eve. She was certain that he meant that he loved her as much as he had loved his mother, and once again, Alex's lack of false modesty didn't prompt her for a second to ratify her belief. She *knew* that this was what Josh meant.

'One night I asked my mother why my father called her his *Star of the Sea* and she explained that people used to call Mary, the mother of Jesus Christ, Stella Maris, Star of the Sea, because they felt that she protected all sailors. My father believed that Mother prayed for him when he was at sea and he called her that name for protection, just as he named his boat, for the same reason. I remember she talked about Latin as "a very old language that folk don't speak any more." It was the very first time I had ever heard tell of the language that has brought me such intellectual pleasure. Of course, she couldn't read Latin – bless her, she had left school at thirteen. But she squirrelled away facts that could be helpful to her boys and shared them with us for the best of reasons.'

Josh moved his face over her breasts, the stubble causing a sensation that was a mix between discomfort and pleasure. 'My brother Hector was a wild man! He had made a vow to honour the name of MacDonald with feats of extreme endurance – of stamina to make the eyes water! But my father's boat, *Star of the Sea*, which Hector intended as an epitaph to our parents, ended as an epitaph to him. He was drowned trialling her seaworthiness. I love this island, Alex,' Josh propped himself up on his elbow, 'but the sea I love and hate with equal passion. It took my brother; it deprived my mother of her husband for months of every year during the years of their marriage; it aged my father before his time. But it surrounds and holds this island like the metal of a ring holds a gem. It is the changing and timeless setting for Fragrey. If I was not here, I would cease to exist as a man. That is why I could live nowhere but this island …'

'I love you, Josh …'

Josh looked down on the gentle, fair face of his lover and pressed his eyelids tight shut. When he opened them, Alex saw the very essence of the man. 'And I love you, Alex. Heart of my heart. Mind of my mind. My woman.'

Chapter 43

Alex left Josh's cottage just before dawn. The night had been so precious that she could not bear to have it spoiled by mundane concerns to do with being spied upon by her colleague or her daughter. It was cool and she folded her arms against the pre-dawn chill as if she were folding to herself the beautiful memories of the night. In the last seven hours, she had learnt more about the man who was rapidly becoming her lodestone – the settled point of her world – than she would ever have imagined possible. And every small fact that she learned she stored away in her memory box of treasures.

Alex had, as usual, left Gladys' door unlocked, since security was never an issue on the island, and now she opened it as quietly as a cat. The grey light of dawn was just seeping into the sky and she could see sufficiently well without having to turn on the lights. She was almost unsurprised at what she saw: her small store cupboard door stood open, showing that the second bottle of wine that she had last bought at the town store had gone; and a tell-tale ugly red stain had marred the beige carpet that Alex had been so proud to have in her mobile home. Diana had indeed arrived on Fragrey.

'Has anyone told you, Morag, that you have the loveliest smile?'

'Good Morning, Doctor MacDonald. Not for about thirty years they haven't, no! Busy surgery this morning. Coffee now, or later?'

'Now please, Morag. I'm just going to quickly check my emails before I see the first patient. I want to see whether Brad Jackson has come back to me yet.'

'Right you are, doctor.'

Brief and to the point as always, Brad had responded without delay. *Anything I can do to help, Josh. I'll put a statement together today and mail it over to you soonest. Best, Brad.*

'Success, Morag!' Josh exclaimed, grinning widely, as she set down his mug on his desk.

'It is good beyond belief to see you so happy, Josh.' Morag lay a maternal hand on the shoulder of the man she respected so much and who was now looking at her with such joy in his face that it was difficult for her to witness. She understood how deeply he felt – everything – and if something, or she suspected, someone, had brought about such transformation, she dreaded what would happen if the agent of that joy was ever removed. 'Tell me to mind my own business if you wish, but have things come right between you and Jenna?'

Josh smiled wryly and shook his head. 'Not Jenna, Morag.' He paused for a long breath. 'But everything is right between Alex Miller and me.'

'Alex Miller – the schoolteacher? Josh, she has only been here a few months. How could you possibly have formed a relationship, which has obviously had such an impact on you, in such a short space of time?'

'You know sometimes how you look at a view – or something you have woven, Morag – and the harmony, the proportions, are just right; and you think to yourself that if you were to work on that landscape or that garment for a thousand years you could never improve it? Well, that's the feeling that I have for Alex: there is such rightness between us. I feel completed, Morag, as I never have before.'

Sighing deeply, Morag bit her lower lip. 'Josh, how about Jenna? She is a powerful woman and is never crossed by anyone. What will she say, what will she do, if this news ever reaches her?'

'Not if, Morag – but when! I must find the right time to tell her. I value her deeply as a friend, but that is all. I have told her this until I have literally run out of words, but I'm by no means sure she has accepted it.'

Between Josh and Morag, there was a quiet understanding and a companionship beyond words. Each remained silent, lost in their own thoughts for some time, before Morag coughed quietly and said, 'Lisa Logan is your first patient, doctor.'

'Thank you, Morag. Please show them in.'

Lisa's treatment had been going well and she seemed to be holding her own against the heedless killer that destroyed lives and families mercilessly. She came into Josh's consulting room holding her father's hand.

'Please may I hold rabbit again? I am a very brave girl, doctor!'

Josh turned away, ostensibly to unearth the white rabbit from his desk drawer, but in reality to mask the emotion that he knew would show in his face.

'Here we are, Lisa! And you are *always* a brave girl!'

Lisa Logan was particularly chatty that morning and, as Josh ran through the next steps with her parents, she explored his room, chattering continually to the toy rabbit. 'When can I go to school, doctor? My big sister Carrie loved going to school. She used to come home and try to teach me what she had learned during the day. I'm a really big girl now – nearly four and a half!'

Josh smiled encouragingly at the frail little girl. 'You *could* start in September, Lisa.'

Jeannie Logan looked desolate, her doubts about the time that her child had left written clear on her face. 'September, Josh?'

'Strictly speaking that's when Lisa should start. But would you like me to see if she can attend, maybe some mornings only, for the rest of the term? There are only five weeks left.'

'I think that would be good …'

'We would monitor her energy levels of course.'

Jeannie gave an exhausted smile, 'It is one of her little ambitions, doctor.'

'Consider it done.'

Chapter 44

Usually, Alex couldn't wait to get back to Gladys after a day's teaching. She still felt a thrill of possessive pride when she caught sight of the garish vintage vehicle nestling up against the grey rock of the hillside behind *The Inn*. It was Gladys who had provided her escape route from the endless tedium of her marriage. It was Gladys who had – slowly to be sure, but with complete steadfastness – covered the seemingly endless miles from Kent to Scotland. Gladys was her refuge, her place of safety. But this evening Alex sighed, as she realised that she felt as if this was no longer the case. She didn't feel safe or secure there anymore. She felt as if her space was about to be invaded by her daughter at any moment; and that her privacy had been breached.

So, on this particular evening, Alex walked slowly and thoughtfully through the fields from school, down the road and along the start of the quay into the courtyard behind *The Inn*. She realised that she would almost have been surprised *not* to see that Diana had taken over her home: the top of the stable door was open and heavy metal music blared out far too loudly. Her daughter's voice was raised above the cacophony of the sound as she talked to someone on her mobile.

'Mum's the same as ever, Dad – buttoned-up. You're well rid of her. Sarah's a much better bet – much more fun. Yeah, the job's going great – absolute piece of cake. OK – love to Sarah. Speak soon.'

'I've decided to cook you dinner, Mother dear!'

'Aren't you working this evening, Diana?'

'No – evening off. The Black Widow is out to supper apparently, and there are no bookings for this evening.'

'The Black Widow?'

'Oh, the woman who lives here – something O'Hara?'

'What's on the menu then, Diana?' Alex asked, trying desperately to sound upbeat and enthusiastic, whereas in reality she would have infinitely preferred yet another omelette and her own company.

'Linguine with spring vegetables and garlic pesto.'

'Sounds amazing!' As always, the tension between what her daughter could potentially achieve and what she actually did achieve was acute. Diana was a gifted cook – she just lacked reliability.

'Wine?'

The inevitable question: 'Not tonight, thank you. Water will do fine.'

'Well, it just so happens that I have a Chardonnay that would be the perfect accompaniment. I'll go and get it.'

'No, really, Diana …'

'Don't be boring, Mother!'

Alex ran her hands through her hair. What on earth was she going to do about this? Instead of day after glorious day being full of discovery and fulfilment, her life had returned at a stroke to tedious predictability.

'Ta-da!' Diana pronounced dramatically as she returned, brandishing a bottle of chilled white wine.

'Let me pour you a glass, Mum,' she wheedled. 'You just sit and relax and I'll create a culinary masterpiece.'

Alex sat, flicking through her phone for messages and sipping the wine – which, actually, was delicious – as Diana launched into the preparation of dinner. Each woman was totally engrossed in her own world and so a soft knock at the door caused Alex to spill some of her drink on her jeans, and her daughter to curse under her breath as she splashed hot oil onto the gas stove.

'What the fuck?'

Alex took the two steps to Gladys' door and looked out.

'Josh!'

'Alex – I need to ask you something …'

Alex urged caution with a slight warning frown. 'You've not met my daughter, Diana. She is cooking us supper this evening. Would you like to join us?'

'Not sure I have enough ingredients, Mum,' Diana started, then turned to look at their unexpected visitor. 'Ah, but – erm, I'm sure we will make it go round.' Flicking her eyes from his tousled black hair to his tanned legs, Diana unceremoniously dumped her cooking utensils and beamed at Josh, saying unnecessarily, 'Hi, I'm Diana. I'm the new chef at *The Inn.* And what do *you* do?'

'Hi Diana, pleased to meet you,' responded Josh, slipping into formal mode and extending a hand. I'm the doctor here.'

'Don't tell me you've heard a lot about me – that would be just too predictable!'

'I have heard the headlines, yes, but not a lot.'

'Diana, I think the vegetables are burning,' Alex warned, moving over to the stove with a wooden spatula.

'Just leave it will you, Mum! Drink Josh?'

'Erm, no thank you – I'm fine. Got to do some research tonight.'

'What is it with you guys around here? Everyone drinks water or nothing at all! Are you going to take up my mother's invitation to stay and eat with us?'

'I can't – but thank you both.'

'Well, I'll leave you to ask my mother whatever it was you wanted to speak to her about.'

'That's good of you.' The distinct note of cynicism was lost on Diana, but Alex flushed as she turned to face Josh. 'How can I help?'

'What would be your response to having little Lisa Logan come into Reception class for a couple of mornings a week for the rest of term, Alex? It's one of her dreams that she should attend school like her sister Carrie did.'

'Perfectly possible in principle, but how's her health at the moment – her energy levels?'

'She's responding well to the treatment …'

'Two minutes, Mum!'

'I'll say yes, Josh. Let's provisionally book in Monday and Thursday mornings.'

'Thank you, Alex.' Josh smiled at her and took both her hands in his and held them hard for a few seconds, letting the gesture communicate the words he couldn't speak. 'I'm really grateful. It will mean the world to her. Catch up with you at school, maybe. Good to meet you, Diana.'

'And you, Josh!' she sang out as she piled pasta in a garlic and pesto sauce topped with steamed vegetables onto two plates which she carried over to the folding table cum bed base.

'He's *fit as!*' she pronounced emphatically. 'What's the connection?'

'He is the doctor Diana – everyone knows him.'

'Well, I'd certainly like to get to know him,' her daughter drawled thoughtfully.

The food was delicious and Alex made a sterling effort to hold a conversation with her daughter, but almost everything she said was belittled or ridiculed. This was the sort of situation that Alex had forgotten: the mindless emotional attrition that was, quite frankly, exhausting. She couldn't wait for the evening to end.

'Was that OK then, Mum?'

'It really was lovely, Diana. Thank you again.'

'Well, don't expect to be spoiled like that every evening, will you. Some people have to work hard for a living, not come swanning home at six o'clock.'

Alex bit her lip. 'I quite understand.'

'I wish you weren't so *correct*, Mother! A bit of spontaneous swearing or bitchiness would make you so much more interesting. I bet Josh appreciates a spontaneous woman …'

'Good night, Diana. Hope work goes well tomorrow.'

Alex sank her head into her hands. This was impossible! In the company of her daughter, she became someone else – someone who was definitely 'buttoned up' – someone with whom she, Alex, could never become friends! A repressed woman who would never do Yoga on a clifftop in the moonlight, or make love with someone in a Neolithic barrow, or row over to the Holy Island with a woman who professed to have second sight. If Gladys' engine would still work, she decided there and then that she would move on somewhere else, anywhere else on the island, as long as it was a fair distance from *The Inn* and the daughter who made her feel like a shadow. If Diana had her day off today, then Alex would have relative freedom during the rest of the week to explore the island for suitable lay-bys, even small car parks where she could potentially park Gladys. She would move on as soon as she could.

Chapter 45

'I've scored two goals in a single week, Morag – perhaps my luck has changed!'

'Coffee before or after the revelations, doctor?'

'After! Do you remember I told you about my suspicions concerning Jeanne O'Hara?'

'The most unpopular incomer on the island? Yes, I do.'

'Well, I've been in communication with the Chairs of Governors of several Multi-Academy Trusts in Kent …'

'Sorry, doctor, I don't follow. I am a simple Practice secretary.'

'Far from simple, Morag – this is educational jargon. A Multi-Academy Trust is a number of schools which work together under the management of an executive headteacher. Ms O'Hara was executive headteacher of the White Raven Academy, near Faversham. The operational structure of an academy trust is complex, but basically individuals or corporate entities sponsor and have a say in the proper operation of the trust and the running of the schools.'

'Like the Governing Body to which you belong?'

'Yes, in a way. Jeanne O'Hara's principal reference was from James Pinner, the managing trustee from one of the academy sponsors. It's taken me forever but I have found out that the White Raven Academy Trust had to be dissolved because it became no longer "financially viable". That would explain why Ms O'Hara was technically unemployed when she came for interview. I'm in the process of establishing the credentials, or otherwise, of Mr Pinner who is, apparently, director of a charitable educational foundation of which the CEO is – guess who?'

'Well, you lost me in a couple of places there, Josh, but I imagine it could well be Jeanne O'Hara?'

'Spot on, Morag.'

'So, this would suggest that there is too close a relationship between the Administrative Head of our school and her referee.'

'Yes.'

'I feel I need coffee too, Josh, to get my head around all these complexities. What are you going to do about all this?'

'Well, I need to get final verification from Companies House, and I must speak to the Charity Commissioners, but my first step is to tell Jenna, as she was the prime mover in the appointment of Ms O'Hara. I think that Jenna was carried away by a barrage of educational jargon and a very slick and persuasive act.'

'Right! Definitely coffee time, Doctor MacDonald!'

⊰∦⊱

Gradually, and much to Alex's relief, the Leavers' Production was finally making progress. She felt that they had experienced a real breakthrough that morning when Gemma Blisset had written a genuinely moving elegy about the passing of an era and the challenge of entering another. As always at mealtimes, Alex was starving and was tackling a large ham and cheese sandwich when her mobile pinged. Ever since their Twitter days, neither Alex nor Josh had used their mobiles to communicate with each other, preferring the completely random personal meetings which they were now able to enjoy. But, opening her phone, to her surprise, a text from Josh flashed onto the screen:

Fancy going to a ceilidh on Thursday night? Super sophisticated venue of the village hall? J xxx
Love to! xxx

'How can you eat that quantity of food and retain your figure, Alex?' Jeanne had glided into the staffroom and was looking at the half-finished sandwich with amused tolerance.

'Because I am hungry, Jeanne. The children and I have been out most of the morning. I've not checked the number of calories related to the thousands of steps I have taken, but I am certain that they total far less than the calorific value of this sandwich! Don't you eat anything?'

'Just an apple.'

'And water?'

'That's right.'

'Well, I'll take my caffeine fix and cholesterol-laden lunch to my classroom and leave you in peace, Jeanne.'

⊰∦⊱

'That dish of a doctor came into the bar at lunchtime today!' Diana announced gleefully.

'Really?' Alex fought to keep her voice even.

'With a woman who looked a bit like a horse – well-dressed though …'

'Like a horse? Was she wearing green, Diana?'

'Yes – long face, hair up.'

'Jenna MacLeod.'

'Are they an item? And could I have a quick glass of wine before my evening shift starts, Mummy dear?'

'Mummy dear doesn't have any wine left,' Alex retorted with a certain amount of asperity. She would have loved a glass, but any wine that she bought seemed to be removed almost immediately by her daughter either directly, or surreptitiously. It's coffee, tea or water.'

'I'll get one in the bar then. Are they an item?'

'I don't think so.'

'They seemed in very close conference together, arranging some sort of meeting – I thought probably a date.' Diana looked at her mother from under lowered lashes, checking for some sort of reaction which might indicate that the relationship between Alex and Josh went beyond that of patient and doctor. For as long as she could remember, Diana, and to a lesser extent her sister, Chloe, had perversely sought to shake their mother's calm equilibrium. Diana had already decided that if Alex and Josh *were* together, then she would, without much difficulty, be able to seduce him, in order to dent what she saw as her mother's smug and self-satisfied attitude. But all Alex said was, 'I expect it was school business.'

Disappointed by the apparent calm of Alex's reaction, Diana flounced out, to find wine and engage somewhat hectically with the evening's food preparation.

Chapter 46

The village hall was probably the most unprepossessing building Alex had ever seen. It looked as if several mobile classrooms had been joined together at some time in the past to form a featureless rectangle, with a dais at one end on which the band was gathered. A bearded giant on a piano accordion chatted to the hall caretaker, pointing to the sound system and clearly asking for it to be moved to a more prominent position. The other members of the band – a slight woman on fiddle and a youngish man on flute – chatted and laughed together at one side of the stage. But, as with everything on this island of contrasts, people had tried to make the best of what they had. Vases of wild flowers had been placed randomly on the small tables clustered around the dance floor and black and white photos of Fragrey through the ages marched in regimented, horizontal lines along the whitewashed walls.

'I think I'm developing paranoia!' Alex had explained to Josh when she suggested that they meet at the ceilidh, rather than beforehand. 'I have started to listen for footsteps following me, or the glint of binoculars tracking my movements, shadows behind bushes and the sound of a drone in the sky!'

'You're not serious?'

'No, I'm not. But I do feel that Jeanne and Diana are pretty interested in my movements and, until people know for a fact that you and I are seeing each other, I won't feel comfortable visiting your house, for example. As for you boarding Gladys – beware, because she may well have been taken captive by my daughter!'

'I met up with Jenna at *The Inn* the other day, Alex, and asked whether I could go over to the Manor House to discuss a couple of things with her. She got quite animated, because I think she anticipated that I was going to try to rekindle our relationship rather than, as compassionately as I possibly can, I finally have to put an end to her hopes. I need to talk to her about Jeanne O'Hara too.'

'Ah, can you share with me?'

'I feel I need to talk to Jenna first, Alex. However uncomfortable Jeanne is as a colleague, boringly I think we need to follow the protocols of school governance.'

'Of course. You are very formidable in this mood and I daren't disagree! See you at seven thirty then?'

'A thousand Jeanne O'Haras wouldn't keep me away, my love,' Josh had replied softly,

Alex couldn't help smiling to herself as she contrasted the last social event that she had attended with the present one. At the May Ball, champagne flutes had appeared as if by magic at her elbow and the entire ambience of the Manor House was the ultimate in sophistication. Here in the village hall, there were short, orderly queues, where islanders with plastic cups waited for red or warm white wine to be poured from wine boxes. She joined the queue for red wine, chatting to Elizabeth Currie's mother, a statuesque farmer from the centre of the island.

'My Lizzie loves school now Mrs Miller! She takes after me, you know, happier with the animals than with numbers or writing. She used to feel she wasn't up to much at school, but she runs along now every morning. She can't wait to go! I think she feels much more at home with what she is learning with you than with Miss Meredith. Things like the theme of the Leavers' Production, it's part and parcel of island life, isn't it? Whereas all that algebra and stuff, well, what's the use of that may I ask?'

'Evening, Mrs Currie.' So rapt had Alex been, listening to the most precious source of information about a pupil – a parent – that she had not noticed Josh arrive at her side. 'I quite agree with you! The Governors are delighted that our attendance rate has shot through the roof! In fact, the children often come to school when, from a medical viewpoint, they ought really to stay at home.'

'Yes, doctor, you need to look after Mrs Miller! She is like gold dust to this island.'

'I – we – will most certainly look after her. I promise you that.' And gently, almost invisibly, Josh pressed his thigh against Alex's.

Mrs Currie's florid face beamed and she turned to chat to a neighbour in front of her in the queue, whilst Alex mouthed, 'Behave!'

Josh and Alex joined a table with Rory Cameron, who grinned widely. 'My favourite partner again! And twice in one month!'

'Ah, you have to share her tonight, Rory,' Josh laughed.

The landlord's eyes flicked from one to the other of the couple sitting opposite him and, if anything, his smile broadened. 'I see! Well, that's just fine with me.'

Maybe the glamour and sophistication of the May Ball was absent, but the energy and sheer sense of fun at the village hall ceilidh had Alex laughing out loud. She danced every dance, mostly with Josh, but also with Rory, and a couple of times with parents. The contrast between her other partners and Josh was vivid: she and he were exactly matched in rhythm, length of step and timing, and the elderly islanders smiled and nodded to see such joy shining from the face of their new teacher and such quiet fulfilment in the face of the doctor they all loved.

The interval was set for nine-thirty and the band, who had put everything into their music, gratefully drained their drinks. Alex and Josh were once again in the queue for red wine, chatting quietly, when there was a slight commotion at the door and they turned at the raised voice of the caretaker. 'I'm sorry, lassie, but quite honestly I think you have had quite enough to drink already this evening.'

'Oh, get lost! Who are *you* to tell me what to do?'

'Go home and sleep it off until morning.'

'No. I'm coming in! At least something is happening in this dead and alive hole at last.'

'Oh God. It's Diana!' Alex groaned, shutting her eyes to block out the sight of a flushed and swaying figure trying to push past the caretaker.

'Come with me. You need fresh air and water.'

When Alex opened her eyes again it was to see Josh, his hand under her daughter's elbow, firmly steering her out of the Village Hall. She caught fragments of Diana's slurred response. 'Fine, I'll take a proper medical opinion from *you* any time … not shit from that old goat!'

Alex's hands were shaking so much that she could hardly hold her plastic cup still as it was refilled and she went sadly back to join Rory at their table. Diana was getting much worse. She had arrived less than a week earlier, but already she was behaving like this. Rory looked thunderous. 'What does she think she is doing!' he hissed between his teeth. 'She was supposed to be in charge of *The Inn* tonight but she's clearly been drinking for some time! That young lady and I will have to have a frank exchange of views tomorrow! I'm sorry Alex.'

'I think I'll call it a night, Rory, if you don't mind. I'm er, a bit tired. Thanks for the dances and your company.'

'And thank you, Alex. I'm sorry I took you from the doctor's arms for even a small part of the evening! It's so good to see such a look on Josh's face once again. Everyone loves him here on Fragrey, you know. There have been times in the past when we have all thought that he was just working himself to death. He looks now as if he has all the reasons in the world to live his life to the full.'

Choking back a tangle of emotions which included her love for Josh and an aching longing for him; frustration and anger at Diana's behaviour; and respect and friendship for the man sitting opposite her, whose concern and compassion showed so clearly on his face, all Alex could manage to say was 'Goodnight, Rory.'

Chapter 47

'Mm, that's *nice,*' Diana mumbled as Josh put his arm around her waist to stop her falling over.

'It's not meant to be *nice*,' Josh said grimly. 'It's just necessary. Do you realise that the water is only a metre or so away?'

'No bloody idea…'

'Even if you could swim, you would certainly drown if you fell into the sea in your present state. Why on earth did you get so drunk? Do you have any idea of the impact this sort of thing has on your mother? I need to text her to let her know you are relatively all right.'

'My mother … my mother … why the hell bring my *mother* into this? Mrs Boring Buttoned-up Prude.'

Josh said nothing, but had a flashback of the beautiful woman who had matched his passion with her own, loving him again and again until all he could think of, taste and feel, was Alex. Awkwardly, he managed to pull out his phone from his jeans pocket and one-handed started to text Alex.

'You fancy her, don't you? You fancy *my mother?*' Diana started to laugh raucously. 'You could do so much better for yourself than her. How about me?' She made a wild gesture and managed to knock Josh's mobile out of his hand. It slid across the cobbles of the quayside, followed the curving line of a mooring rope, and fell into the harbour.

Josh bit his lip thinking of all he wished he could say, about the waste of the young life that he saw before him, the distorted, bloated features and slurred voice, not to mention the sheer inconvenience of losing his bloody phone! But he realised that virtually nothing would penetrate the alcoholic haze of the woman who was staggering at his side, so all he actually said was, 'You need to sober up, Diana. Come home with me until you feel more yourself.'

'I knew it! It's me you fancy!'

'I do not, as you put it, "fancy" you. But as a doctor I have a duty of care towards any human being whose health is in danger.'

Josh hauled Diana along the quayside and propped her up against the front of his house with one shoulder whilst he opened the door.

'Mm – cosy. Where's the bathroom? I feel …' and Diana promptly illustrated how she felt very graphically by vomiting on Josh's rug.

Josh always took as much time as was necessary with his patients, whether that was minutes, hours, or in some cases, like the Logan girls, months. He was meticulous, caring and kind, listening to personal worries, reassuring, and working around the clock for their wellbeing and social care. But with self-imposed excess, like drunkenness, he was disgusted, both as a man and as a doctor. For a human being to become animalised and to deliberately put themselves in a position of danger was almost impossible for him to bear. But now, watching the young woman vomiting helplessly in front of him, he thought of how Alex had carried, given birth and cared for Diana, and cared for her still. And, through his love for Alex, this prompted him to say, 'Sit there. I won't be a minute.'

He came back with a bowl of warm water, a flannel and a towel and proceeded to wash and bathe Diana's face and hands. By now she was slipping into unconsciousness – hardly sleep – and he decided to let her, as the impulse to vomit should subside if her tortured digestive system could have some respite. Carrying her with some difficulty to the small sofa at the back of his living room, he laid her on her side, covered her with a soft mohair throw, and turned his attention to cleaning up the mess on the floor.

A quarter of an hour later Josh stood and looked at the now pale face of the young woman who was in a deep, alcoholic stupor. Occasionally she made a slight moaning sound, shivered and retched. Josh's instinct was to contact Alex and reassure her that he would keep a close watch on her daughter, mainly to make sure that if she did vomit again, she did not choke and suffocate. But he didn't have a house phone and without his mobile this was impossible. For a split second he wondered whether he could run to *The Inn*, speak to Alex briefly and run back to his cottage, but if something happened to Diana whilst he was out, he would never forgive himself. After several minutes' careful thought, Josh decided that he had no option but to remain on watch at Diana's side until he was satisfied that she was out of danger. Pouring himself a stiff whisky and wrapping his plaid around his shoulders, he pulled up a chair and sat down, preparing himself for a long and uncomfortable night.

Alex tossed and turned on her hard bed. After Rory's steady, measured footsteps returning to his home, there had been no sound, either in the small courtyard behind *The Inn*, or in and around the building itself. She was surprised that Josh hadn't contacted her. That was really unlike him, she reflected, as he was the most considerate and emotionally empathetic man she had ever known. The dawn chorus came and with it the reassurance that Alex always felt when some of the smallest animals in the natural world brought her such intense joy. Smiling and curling her knees into her belly, she hugged to herself the thought that, whatever had happened, there would be some logical explanation for the lack of contact from the man who had become the centre of her world. Finally, with that comforting thought, she drifted into sleep.

⊰∥⊱

'Do you want coffee?' Josh asked, stretching stiffly as the bedraggled figure finally roused itself from the sofa.

'No. I feel terrible. I will just go home and catch a few more hours sleep. See you around.' Diana swayed to her feet, steadied herself on the back of the chair on which Josh had spent the night and walked cautiously – as if seeing which parts of her body still worked – towards the door. The lack of thanks, the gracelessness of Diana's behaviour prompted Josh to speak. 'If you carry on like this, Diana, you will die. And before you die you will lead a half-life where the first thing you think of in the morning is when you can have your next drink. Your mother has told me you have real talent, but that you lose job after job through your behaviour, through this addiction. You *can* get help! But you need to want to change, Diana. Rory Cameron is a decent man and he was looking forward to your support in his business. This is your chance to succeed and to overcome the addiction that constantly pulls you down. Ask for help – please – I can help you!'

'How dare you lecture me like that! And how dare my mother talk to you about me and say things like that! I have lost jobs – yes – but only because the tossers who employ me don't see how talented I am. Sometimes they are jealous, sometimes they just don't know what they are talking about. *The Inn* are lucky to have me. They won't get rid of me. Who else will they get? I'm going. And perhaps in the future you can mind your own bloody business and let me get on with my own life. And if you do fancy my mother, you would make a perfect pair: self-satisfied do-gooders with an exaggerated sense of their own importance.'

The slam of the door made the windows of the little cottage shake; and the combination of anger and wretchedness which overwhelmed Diana meant that she walked along, head down, lost and wandering in her own confused private world. She didn't see a shadow stir in the alley that led to *Pleasant Row* and point the camera of a mobile phone in her direction, capturing the moment when she flung out of Josh's cottage; the angry tears that stood unshed in her eyes; and her hunched, defeated walk along the quayside back to *The Inn.*

Chapter 48

'Tea or sherry, Jeanne?'

'Just water for me thank you, Jenna.'

Jeanne O'Hara sat at the table set in the window of the morning room in the Manor House, opened her briefcase and pulled out a manilla A4 envelope which she placed on the highly-polished mahogany surface. Jenna returned, smiling, with a small tray, and sat down opposite her visitor.

'I'm so sorry I couldn't see you last week, Jeanne, but I know you understand how important family is.'

Jeanne nodded politely.

'So what did you want to discuss with me? Is it about becoming an academy, or some other school matter?'

'It is another matter, Jenna – or rather several other matters – related to the school in general, but crucial, terms. Please open this.' Jeanne slid the envelope over in the direction of her Chair of Governors. 'I have printed off these screenshots from my mobile,' Jeanne continued. 'You will see the exact times and dates when they were taken. I will give you several minutes to digest the relevance of this and then maybe we can talk about them.'

Frowning, Jenna slit open the envelope and drew out the ten or dozen photographs which it contained. To the images of Alex descending the cliff on May Day morning, dishevelled and joyful and of Josh just minutes later, his face showing the quiet contentment of a man utterly fulfilled, Jeanne had added the photos which she had taken of Diana leaving Josh's cottage on the morning after the ceilidh – her anger, her tears, her unkempt appearance.

Jenna's face drained of all colour as she studied the images intently. The one of Josh she looked at particularly closely, stroking her finger lightly over its surface as if to enlarge the image. Then, regal as always when under emotional pressure, she lay them face down on the table, interlaced her fingers on her lap, and looked hard at Jeanne.

'Perhaps you would care to explain the significance of these to me.' It was an order rather than a request.

'Certainly. For some time now I have suspected that Alex Miller has been having an affair with Doctor MacDonald. The way they interact together is a main indicator. We must remember that Alex is *Mrs* Miller – still a married lady – and her role as teacher-in-charge of the children brings with it the most intense responsibility to model morality and decent behaviour as well as educating the children academically. The photographs on May morning show two people who have, in my opinion, been engaged in an assignation, and I believe that the state of Alex Miller's dress speaks for itself. I have not led a purely monastic life and I recognise the look of triumph of Doctor MacDonald's face: it is indicative of sexual conquest and satiety.'

The colour came rushing back into Jenna's face as she reflected that never, during the course of their affair had Josh remotely looked as he did in the photograph.

'I don't know whether you are aware that this young person,' Jeanne flipped the photos of Diana face up again 'is Alex Miller's daughter.'

'I had no idea.'

'Mike Whitfield tells me that she made an absolute spectacle of herself last Friday, when she rolled up at the village hall ceilidh, extremely drunk – indicative of her parenting I think. Josh left Alex, with whom he had spent the evening, and escorted her daughter, Diana, out of the hall. No one knew why or where they had gone and neither was seen for the rest of the evening. This photo shows that Diana Miller left Doctor MacDonald's house at four a.m. And *this* photo, in close up, shows how upset she was. I believe that the doctor seduced the young woman and then ejected her from his house at dawn.'

Jenna stood up sharply and turned her back on her visitor, looking out of the window to regain her poise.

'So you are saying what, precisely?'

'That two key figures in our school and in the life of this island are behaving with a degree of impropriety – indeed, immorality – that is unacceptable. Alex Miller is a married woman having an adulterous affair with one of her Governors; and Josh MacDonald is a seducer who appears to have slept with both mother and daughter. I certainly think that he ought to be removed from the governing body of the school, and possibly reported to the General Medical Council. As for Alex Miller, I think she should be dismissed for gross misconduct.'

Jeanne O'Hara was a strategist and never did anything without being fairly sure of the outcome. She had expected outrage from the Clan chieftain who upheld vigorously the morals of both school and island, but what she hadn't expected was a curt dismissal.

'I see that you have sifted your evidence carefully, Jeanne, and have presented a powerful case. Please leave me to consider what you have shown to me and to decide upon an appropriate course of action. Goodbye.'

Jenna held open the door for her Administrative Headteacher and escorted her without a word across the polished wooden floor of the hall to the massive arched and studded front door of her ancestral home. Without a word she shut the door firmly and walked, almost blindly, to the nearest deep leather armchair, into which she subsided, covering her face in her hands, weeping as she had not wept since Josh had ended their affair over twelve years earlier.

⇥||⇤

Unsuspecting of the drama that had just been enacted within the walls of the Manor House, Josh smiled quietly to himself as he walked swiftly over to see Jenna. He recalled how he had pushed a note of explanation under Gladys' stable door on his way back from surgery the morning after the ceilidh. The only scrap of paper he could readily lay his hands on was an appointment card, on which he had written:

Sorry not to ring, Alex, but Diana managed to project my mobile into the harbour! D very sick so sat up with her to make sure she didn't choke. Seems fine, but fragile, this morning. See you soon, my love xxx

Alex had written *ASAP please!!!* next to the *Time of Next Appointment.* She had such a gift of making Josh

269

feel that the sun was always shining and that all would be well; it was that emotion that flooded through him now. He took the three stone steps up to the front door of the Manor House at a bound and rang the bell.

'Hello, Josh.' Jenna spoke in a monotone and he had never seen her so rigidly defensive.

'Jenna, I need to speak to you.'

'And I to you, Josh. But I will listen first to what you have to say.' Almost like an automaton, Jenna walked across the hall and, once again, into the breakfast room where barely three hours earlier she had faced Jeanne O'Hara.

'Sit down. What do you wish to say to me?'

Josh had not known how Jenna was going to greet him. It was usually with the utmost warmth and an affectionate touch, but now, today, she sat pale and composed looking directly at him with dark-shadowed eyes.

'Two things: firstly, I am in love with Alex Miller. I wanted to reassure you, Jenna, that there was nothing second-rate or shabby about the relationship which you and I had together. But I explained to you then, and I re-iterate it now: I did not, and I do not love you. You will always be the dearest of friends to me, and I know how much Alex respects you. I would like to think that in time the three of us would grow closer together in friendship.'

'And the second?'

'Is to do with Jeanne O'Hara. I suspect that she is in the midst of perpetrating fraud as far as our school is concerned. I have written notes about my findings, and links, phone numbers and names are on this piece of paper. The Academy trust that she headed in Kent became financially not viable and that is why she was unemployed when she came here for interview. She is CEO of a charitable educational foundation of which her sole referee is managing trustee. I believe that she intends to establish the Western Islands Multi-Academy Trust and defraud sponsors of investment monies.'

'Is that it? Is that all you wanted to tell me?'

'Yes. Jenna are you all right?'

'Am I all right, Josh?' Jenna flung back her chair and banged her fists on the table. 'Am I all right? No, I am not all right. Look at these!' She picked up the envelope containing the photographs which Jeanne had left with her and fanned them out in front of Josh.

'Where did these come from?' he asked frowning.

'Jeanne O'Hara brought them this morning.'

'Her purpose being?'

'Oh, minor things! To accuse Alex of an adulterous affair with you. Alex is still a married woman, or did you not know that? Has she not told you? To accuse you of infringing school governor protocol. And to accuse you of seducing Alex's daughter and throwing her out of your cottage at dawn. She suggested that the GMC should be informed of your immoral conduct; and she strongly recommended that Alex should be dismissed instantly for gross misconduct.'

'And you believe her, Jenna?'

'Here is proof in black and white, for God's sake! What do you think I believe?' Jenna was shouting now, and tears were flowing unchecked down her face.

'In that case, I have no option but to resign as governor of the school and you need to make your own decision about referring my conduct to the GMC. But please listen carefully to what I am about to say, Jenna. Alex and I are in a relationship together. She told me the first time she met me about her husband, who is now in the process of divorcing her. I love her and I believe that she returns my love. Do what you like to me, but do not, I beg you, deprive the children of the best teacher that they are ever likely to have in this school. Who will take her place? Jeanne O'Hara? She never interacts with the children and parents simply do not know what her role actually *is!* As far as Diana Miller is concerned, she was drunk and I cared for her as any competent medical professional would have done. I sat at her side all night so that she did not choke on her own vomit. Believe me or not, as you will, Jenna. You should know by now that I do not lie. However brutal the truth is, I tell it. Check out the details of what I have told you about your Administrative Head. They are true. Then make an *informed* decision about the educational future of the children of this island. Please, Jenna,' and Josh forcibly took both Jenna's hands in his own, 'please do not let your personal feelings impact upon your professional decisions. The Jenna I know and respect would not do that. I need to leave you to reflect calmly upon what I have just said. Goodbye.'

Struggling to keep his eyes focussed on negotiating the stone steps of the entrance to the Manor House and the irregular paving of the path leading down across the gardens, Josh tried in vain to fight off a blinding headache that was, as usual, accompanied by a lightning storm across his vision.

Chapter 49

'What a mess, Josh!' Alex lay on her back, looking intently at the timbered ceiling of Josh's bedroom. 'Such a tangle: some things are true, some things are untrue, and some hold partial truth …'

'I know one thing that's irrefutable, Alex: I love you.'

'Come here.' Alex wrapped her slender brown arms around Josh's shoulders and waist and drew him to her. She reflected, not for the first time, that this must have been a position of comfort for Josh when he was very young because he became relaxed and compliant. Once again, she became conscious of the child beneath the carapace of energy and drive that the world equated with Josh MacDonald.

'What do you think Jenna will do?'

'Until today I would have said she would act always as the model of reason, but she was beside herself this afternoon, Alex. She was beyond reason.'

'So she may sack me and report you to the GMC?'

'She may do one or both those things.'

Alex exhaled sharply. 'And if she does, what then for us? Should we just drive away in Gladys? Camp in Timbuctoo? Roost on Mount Sinai?'

'Gladys would never get that far … but you don't sound as devastated as I thought you would be, Alex.'

'Taking refuge in silly banter is a strategy that I have adopted over the years for self-preservation purposes! Believe me, Josh, I am utterly devastated at the prospect that unfair, twisted behaviour is threatening us as individuals, and also throws a taint over our relationship.' Alex gently released Josh and sat cross-legged on the bed. 'Why is it that the world in general, and certain people in particular, seek to spoil and destroy anything pure and beautiful?' Seeing Josh reach for a packet of paracetamol on his bedside table, she was instantly concerned. 'Do you have another migraine?'

'Just the vestiges of a lousy one that started after my meeting with Jenna. It's nearly passed now. But to answer your hypothetical question, yes, sadly I agree that the desire to spoil and hurt is certainly one of the less attractive aspects of human nature. It occupies my mind far more than it ought. But now my vision has finally stopped jumping about all over the place, I need to shower and change before surgery and the range of problems that human nature holds in store for me this evening!' Josh rolled Alex onto her back and stroked her hair back from her face. He lightly kissed her eyes, her nose and finally her mouth, then jumped out of bed. 'If I don't go now, I never will.'

'Can I have another appointment soon, please?' Alex grinned.

'In my professional opinion, you need to see your doctor daily!'

'Dad's filed for divorce and he's citing adultery as the cause,' Diana pronounced gleefully later that evening.

'His own?'

'No, yours. Everybody seems to know all of a sudden that you and the sexy doctor are an item.'

'But your father doesn't live on Fragrey …'

Diana ignored Alex's comment. 'I overheard Rory and Catriona discussing it; and the Black Widow was on her phone to someone called Jamie. I think he announced his name as James Pinner. I just happened to overhear her conversation …'

'What, in the bar?'

'Well, no, in her room, actually.'

'You were listening at her door, Diana!'

'Are you sure of him, Mother?'

'Sorry, what do you mean? Sure of Doctor MacDonald, of Josh?'

'Yes. Do you trust him – absolutely? Do you never wonder why he says he fancies you, rather than anyone else? Are you sure that he is pure as the driven snow and doesn't have any nasty habits which he hides from most people for most of the time?'

'I do trust him, yes. And as for "nasty habits", what do you mean?'

'Oh, ways in which he gets a sexual kick – maybe social media, maybe other stuff. You do know I spent the night at his place, don't you? You know he put his arm around me – and so much more that I could tell you ...'

'I believe he put his arm around you, because you would have fallen over otherwise – possibly into the harbour! And as for anything else, how would you know? You were almost insensible.'

'Mm. That's what you think, Mum. Be careful.'

Alex watched her daughter leave, but her toxic words lingered insidiously: *"ways in which he gets a sexual kick – maybe social media, maybe other stuff"*. Wasn't that how she and Josh had first met, via social media? And wasn't the language he had used, and she had followed, been explicitly sexual? And the photograph that had made her block him … Had he stopped using Twitter? She had never thought to ask.

⊰❘❘❘⊱

'Hi, could I register with your practice, please?' Diana asked Morag a couple of days later. 'I have a problem I need to see a doctor about.'

'Of course. Could you please fill in these forms with your medical history, contact details and so on. You can do it right now if you wish. Here is a pen. There is a table.'

'Right, that's all done. When is the first available appointment?'

'One moment.' Morag scanned the computer. 'There is a cancellation this afternoon, as a matter of fact. Two o'clock?'

'Perfect.'

An hour later Josh walked into the surgery, showered and changed, and anticipating the sort of cases he would be dealing with that afternoon and evening.

'Two things, Doctor MacDonald: one you will, I am sure, be very pleased about; the second perhaps will not be so welcome.'

'Fire away, Morag.'

'A letter from the GMC confirmed that the evidence received from Dr Jackson has led them to take the case against Clive Saunders very seriously indeed.

Dr Sanders has been suspended until the investigating tribunal meets next month.'

'Fantastic!'

'And Diana Miller has an appointment with you at two this afternoon.'

Josh groaned. 'Did she say why she needed to see me, Morag?'

'I'm sorry, doctor, she did not.'

'Well, don't be far away at two, will you?'

Morag smiled. 'As always, I shall be here at your side.'

The Surgery waiting room was packed with the variety that made this practice irresistible to Josh. Hector Fraser wanted a prescription for Viagra; an old farmer had cut his hand badly and needed stitches; Maggie Jenner, who was nearing her confinement date, had been feeling unwell recently with acute headaches, and so on – a vivid cross section of life that Josh's lightning intellect and empathy sought to understand, support and mend.

Diana sat quiet and unusually demure, dressed for once in a skirt and blouse, feet planted flat on the floor and knees together.

'Diana Miller, please come this way.'

'Hello, Doctor MacDonald.'

'And what can I help you with today, Diana?'

'I have a lump in my left breast, doctor.'

Josh had been dreading something like this. 'I see. Please go behind the screen whilst I ask my secretary to act as chaperone.' Josh got to his feet and walked to the other side of his consulting room to indicate where the screen and couch were, but before he had taken two steps, Diana screamed loudly and repeatedly. Leaping to her feet, she tore her blouse open and ripped her bra, to reveal most of her breasts, which she then raked with her fingernails.

'Are you all right, Doctor MacDonald?' Morag appeared at the door, but appeared to freeze on the threshold. 'What is happening here?' she asked, in a dazed voice.

'This young lady appears to have succumbed to a fit of hysterics, Josh replied without emotion. Can you sort her out please, Morag? I'll be outside.'

The patients in the waiting room looked startled, as Josh walked out of his consulting room.

'What's happened?' asked Maggie Jenner, laying her hands protectively on her swollen belly.

'To be honest, I don't know,' Josh responded. 'A new patient seems to have had some sort of emotional melt-down that requires female intervention and Morag is sorting out the patient.' He sat down at the computer at Reception, scrolling through messages sightlessly. The bitch – the disgusting bitch. Alex's daughter or not, that young lady was trouble. He knew exactly what she was up to: to discredit him professionally, to ruin his relationship with Alex, and all because of what? Jealousy, spite, maybe boredom? Or just the destroying poison of her addiction. He knew that he was in shock and so concentrated on the meaningless screen in front of him, praying that he would not miss any symptoms or indications in his remaining patients. He anticipated the tightening band of pain around his forehead and the start of the too-familiar vision distortion as he tried to focus on the computer screen.

Ten minutes later, Morag exited Josh's consulting room with Diana's arm linked extremely firmly through her own. She turned to Josh and spoke softly, barely audibly, 'I am going to take this young person to her mother. I need to speak to you later, Josh.'

He nodded imperceptibly, then turned to his next patient. 'Not long now, Maggie. Let's go and see how things are getting on.'

Chapter 50

Morag certainly didn't want to arrive at the school with Diana in her current state, so she rang Alex.

'Hello, Morag! Is everything all right? Is Josh OK? It's not like you to ring me – certainly not at school.' Before answering her phone, Alex had satisfied herself that the children had settled to their writing task, which was to create a dramatic dialogue between two of the Vikings accompanying the body of their leader down to the quayside where the boat was moored, ready for its final despatch into the vastness of the ocean.

'Alex, there's been an incident at the surgery, and Josh is all right, physically at least. But your daughter was involved and I really think you ought to come so we can talk face to face.'

'On my way!' Alex turned to her class and said, 'Please can you stop writing and listen for a moment. I have to go home unexpectedly, and I have to go now, I'm afraid. I'll ask Ms O'Hara to come and work with you until the end of the afternoon.' There were a series of quiet groans as the children heard this announcement but, obedient to a fault, they were ready to settle without further complaint to the task that their beloved teacher had given them. 'See you all tomorrow! And I expect the most *spectacular* work!'

'So why do you have to leave your children in the middle of the afternoon, Alex?' Jeanne raised a carefully-shaped eyebrow.

'It's something to do with Diana, my daughter,' Alex replied hesitantly.

'Ah, the one who made a spectacle of herself at the village hall ceilidh!'

Alex took a deep breath and sunk her nails into her palms hard. 'I need to go now, Jeanne. The only option is that you will have to go and work with the children until the end of the afternoon.'

'But, I er, have emails to catch up on.'

'Are you a qualified teacher, Jeanne?'

'What do you mean?'

'Well, you seem to find every sort of excuse *not* to be with the children in this school. Just for once, you have the opportunity to prove I'm wrong. So, go and *teach them* Jeanne. I will see you tomorrow.'

Alex covered the distance between the school and Morag's neat house in record time and rang the bell, twice, impatiently.

'Alex, thank you so much for coming. Diana is through here.'

'My god, Diana! What happened to you?'

Diana sat, wrapped in a blanket, with blood still seeping through her blouse. Her eye make-up had run and she appeared to be shivering.

'That fabulous doctor friend of yours tried to rape me, Mother!' Diana pronounced shrilly. 'Look!' She pulled open Morag's blanket to show her ripped clothing and the deep scratches across her chest.

Alex was utterly silent as she assessed the situation. She was one hundred percent certain that Josh would never have done such a thing, and she knew, because she loved and relished all the minutiae about the man she loved so much, that Josh's nails were short and smooth, and that it was impossible for him to have inflicted the injuries that she was looking at.

'You're a liar, Diana,' Alex said in level tones. 'Morag, can you telephone – I think his name is Hamish – the police constable for the island, and ask him whether he could come here, please.'

'You believe that sexual predator before your own daughter!' shouted Diana.

To which Alex calmly replied, 'If you mean Josh MacDonald, then yes, I do believe him above and beyond your sad, twisted schemes, Diana.'

Morag, white as a sheet, simply said, 'Thank God!' and sat down suddenly.

⊰⊱

'Weell, this is a turn up for the books, Mrs Miller.' Hamish Stewart scratched his head thoughtfully. We'll need DNA samples from Doctor MacDonald and from Miss Miller to establish who actually did this damage to her, erm, chest. Could you drop back to the surgery please, Mrs Kitchener, and explain to the doctor what is happening. If he could come along here directly after surgery, we can take the DNA and the matter will be concluded.

'With pleasure, Hamish.' Morag, put on her jacket and left. She had felt completely out of her depth that afternoon, having to face the sort of things that she had sometimes seen, and deplored, on the television. Sadly, she reflected that most incomers brought such a different world with them, a world of violence and hatred and complex intentions, a world that the island did not wish to embrace. And then, unbidden, she smiled, remembering Alex's cold and disbelieving face as she looked at her daughter. There were two people at least that would never believe that Josh MacDonald could ever have caused the attack alleged by the strange and disturbed young woman who, unbelievably, was Alex Miller's own daughter.

'Doctor MacDonald, Josh!' Morag called as she entered the surgery, deserted now of patients. Everything was utterly silent, utterly still.

'Josh?' Morag's voice became insistent, concerned.

'Josh! Oh my God!'

Josh was at his desk, head laid quietly on his folded arms. At first sight there was no sign of life, no movement, no breath, and for a fleeting moment Morag wondered whether he had taken something to leave forever the world that kept dealing him pain and difficulty. She crossed the consulting room, and turned his hand to take his pulse, and then she saw the rise and fall of Josh's chest – shallow but there – and felt the beat of his heart, strong enough, under her shaking fingers. Whatever had happened had not been brought about by Josh himself. Without hesitation, Morag dialled 999. 'Air Ambulance please. This is a medical emergency. The doctor has been taken ill suddenly.'

Chapter 51

The mechanical sounds, the hums and occasional bleeps from the monitors, gradually started to permeate Josh's consciousness. Which patient was he with? In which hospital? He blinked his eyes open and saw, unbelievably, that it was he who was the patient, he to whom the array of wires and tubes were attached. And, resembling nothing more than the sort of pale marble statue that he had seen in cemeteries in Glasgow and Edinburgh, Alex sat at his side, eyes wide and full of love, her hand on his.

'Alex.' Josh hardly recognised his voice: it was dry and harsh.

'Josh, Josh my love! It's me, Alex!'

'I am not so far gone that I don't recognise my own!' Josh tried to adopt a light tone, but felt as if his head was about to explode with the effort. 'If it doesn't sound like a cliché – where am I?'

'In Edinburgh. In the Murrayfield neuro-surgical hospital.'

'Alex, why?'

'The consultant will have to explain to you, Josh, in medical terms. I need to get a nurse now, because you are actually conscious again – thank God!'

'What date is it?'

'June 10th, Josh.'

'What? I have lost three weeks of my life, Alex!'

'Shh! My love. Be calm and quiet! I will be back before you realise it.'

Josh tried to sit up in bed when the tall, thin consultant neurologist came into his room, but the network of wires and tubes to which he was connected prevented him from moving more than six inches.

'Fraser Jenner, Doctor MacDonald.' The consultant reached out his hand and shook Josh's gently but firmly.

'Why on earth am I here, Mr Jenner?'

'I will not patronise, or demean, you with a less than honest answer, MacDonald. You have a brain tumour that is impacting upon your senses: sight, speech, and latterly, consciousness itself.'

Josh remained silent for minutes, until he somehow managed to kickstart his professional enquiry, 'And the prognosis?'

'About 95% inoperable. If the most skilful surgeon could be found with this specific specialism, then there may be a chance. But the quality of life that you would lead after such an invasive operation would, itself, be open to another hazarding guess, on a sliding scale of between ninety-nine and zero percent depending upon the success of the operation and the skill of the surgeon.

'I see. Have you told Alex, my partner?'

Fraser Jenner smiled. 'I have. What a remarkable woman! She is insistent that whether you have one day, or a thousand years, and I quote, she will make every day count twice!

'I love her, Fraser.'

'I'm not surprised, Josh. I'll ask her to come in again, shall I?'

'Please. And is it absolutely necessary that I am attached to quite so many tubes? I just want to sit up!'

The consultant smiled. 'I'll get you disconnected!'

⊰)|(⊱

'There is no overwhelming medical reason why you should stay here in hospital, Doctor MacDonald. To speak bluntly, we can give you pain relief to take away with you, to go wherever you think it right to be. If there was some treatment that we could administer here, a procedure that I could undertake, then I would not hesitate to do it. But there is not.'

Josh, now freed from the panoply of tubes and connections, sat up in bed, listening intently to the consultant.

Alex straightened her shoulders. 'Fine. That's quite clear then. We will leave this afternoon, Mr Jenner, and thank you for being so frank with us.'

Fraser Jenner pursed his lips, 'Believe me, Mrs Miller, if there was anything at all I could do, any vestige of hope, I would do it.'

'There is always hope, Mr Jenner. Whilst there's life, there's hope.'

⊰)|(⊱

'That was one of my mother's favourite sayings, Alex. "Whilst there's life, there's hope."'

'Well, it must be right then! But for now, just sit back, my love. We'll soon be back on home territory again.'

'What happened, Alex? The last thing I remember on that day is saying goodbye to my last patient, going back into my consulting room and taking yet another handful of tablets for the migraine that had started after Diana left the surgery. Well, what I thought was a migraine ...'

'What time is it, Josh?'

'Four o'clock.'

'And how long is the flight back to Benbecula?'

'Fifty-two minutes.'

'It will be just about long enough,' sighed Alex.

'After Morag phoned for the air ambulance, she rang me to explain that you had collapsed. I couldn't leave Diana, not because I felt for her in any way, but because she is a consummate actress and I didn't want her to pull the wool over Hamish's eyes. Morag is really quite remarkable, you know,'

'Oh, I do know.'

'She told me that she was going to swab the inside of your mouth and, as soon as the air ambulance arrived, she would return to do the same to Diana. Within twenty-four hours the DNA tests could be completed and then everyone would have a clear picture of the truth. You were taken away to Edinburgh.' Alex stopped her narrative, squeezing her eyes tight shut. 'It was the hardest thing I have ever done, to watch that helicopter circling and taking you away. I took Diana back to *The Inn* and explained to Rory in the briefest possible terms what had happened. He is such a dear man! He just squeezed my arm and said that he would sit outside Diana's door to prevent her leaving and "let her accuse *him* of attempted rape, if she liked!" Morag had to phone the patients who had already booked into your morning surgery and she explained that you had suddenly been taken ill – that's all. She didn't go into detail.

'The next morning – surprise, surprise – the tests proved that Diana had scratched herself and staged the "attempted rape". There was no trace of your DNA on her. I had been summoned to the Manor House and was just leaving Gladys when I saw Rory as I had never seen him before. He frog-marched Diana to the bus and stood, with folded arms, watching it chug away. He shook his head sadly and returned to the kitchen door, looking, bless him, like an old man. The damage that girl has done!' Alex shut her eyes tightly for a few seconds, before continuing.

'When I arrived at the Manor House, all the Governors were assembled there, sitting around Jenna's very grand dining table.'

'I know it well,' grimaced Josh.

'Jenna accused me of setting an immoral example to the children in my charge. She said I had infringed the rules of governance by having an affair with a member of my governing body. And she even intimated that you had seduced me – and my daughter.'

'What!'

'Shh! Please let me finish. Please don't get upset, Josh. I really do need you to stay calm. I thought the best thing I could do was to remain silent, so I said nothing as Jenna ranted on – sorry, there is no other word for it. Rory and Agnes looked wretched; Mike embarrassed; and Jeanne kept her eyes downcast sipping her inevitable water. Quite frankly I could have tipped it over her head! In the end Jenna stood up and said that the decision of the Governing Body was that I should be dismissed for gross misconduct. The only time Jeanne lifted her head was when Jenna pronounced confidently that "the children would remain in the excellent hands of Ms O'Hara". Finally, she said that she expected me to leave the island at the first available opportunity. She had not mentioned you at all directly, Josh, apart from making the accusations about seduction, and it struck me that she didn't yet know that you had been taken ill. When it was obvious that she had, finally, finished speaking, I stood up and said something along the lines of "I wanted to thank the Governors for the opportunity to teach the most delightful children I had ever encountered." I said that "it had been a privilege and would be a memory that I would carry with me forever." Finally, I told her that you had been flown by air ambulance to Edinburgh because you had collapsed in your surgery. I truly think that she has strong feelings for you still Josh, because she blanched, sat down, and abruptly ended the meeting.'

Josh sat, gazing out of the window of the small plane. He saw the tapestry of blues, greens and browns that was the land and sea-scape of the Western Isles, the home that he loved. Then he took Alex's hand, and kissed it without speaking.

'I'm sorry, my love. I'm so sorry.'

'Josh! I loved teaching the children of Fragrey, but I love you more! If the sole triumphant fact of my coming to the island is that you and I have found each other …'

'But for how long, Alex?'

'For as long as we have, Josh! …then I am happy.'

'What's happened to my practice, Alex? It can't be just shut – like a shop!'

'I know, but I believe that it is in the best of hands.'

'Stop playing at riddles!'

'Just trust me, Josh, please. I promise there is no Maitland Moron there!'

'Morag is running it?'

'Well, of course she is, just like when you were there.'

'Alex, what will become of us?'

'Give me time, my love. I'm working on it! Now belt-up – literally. We are descending!'

Chapter 52

Morag met them at Benbecula airport, driving her ancient Mini.

'Oh Josh!' She carefully folded him in her arms, then held him at a little distance, her eyes scrutinising his every aspect. 'I never expected to see you again looking – looking like this!'

'Alive, as opposed to dead, you mean, Morag?'

'Well, something like that, doctor!' Morag replied briskly, relieved to return to the habitual tone of humorous banter that Josh adopted with her. 'When will you be able to come back to surgery? Do you know yet?'

'We're not sure, Morag,' Alex interjected. 'But we're working on it!'

By the time the ferry had reached Fragrey, Josh looked completely exhausted. He had stopped trying to spike the conversation with his usual repartee and sat, pale and silent, in Morag's ancient vehicle as it drove off the boat. He had taken the first dose of the pain relief prescribed by the hospital in the washroom at Benbecula airport and had been surprised by its swift effectiveness. But now he was becoming gradually aware again of the band of pain around his forehead, and quietly slipped another tablet under his tongue.

'I think we should go straight back to the cottage, Morag,' Alex said quietly, noticing this as she noticed everything about Josh.

'Not to the surgery?'

'No, we'll go first thing in the morning.'

Alex couldn't wait to shut the door of the neat, stone house behind her and Josh, and when she had, she wrapped her arms around the man who was the centre of her world and held him close. Surprisingly, she heard him laugh quietly, 'Don't expect the state of my health to be an excuse for me not to love you, Alex Miller. Until I literally have no breath in my body, I will do this,' kissing her; 'and this' lifting her into his arms and carrying her upstairs.

'As if I would expect anything else?' Alex murmured softly, unbuttoning his shirt and slipping it off his shoulders.

⊰⊱

'Right!' Josh announced the next morning. 'The first job of the day is for me to take a deep breath and visit my surgery, and to descend like an avenging angel on anyone who simpers and pretends to be something that he or she is not!'

'I thought that would be the first call of the day,' Alex chuckled. 'Some things don't change. But Josh, do be prepared for people who see you to press you about when you are likely to return. It's bound to happen.'

'Are you coming with me, or staying here, Alex?'

292

'From now on, if you hadn't noticed, whenever possible I am sticking to you like your shadow, but even closer!'

Hand in hand they left the cottage and walked along the quayside towards Josh's surgery. It was early, only seven-thirty, since Josh intended to arrive at the surgery before his locum, so as to establish a certain proprietorial right to the practice.

Alex was relieved that the quayside was quiet: the fishing boats had sailed hours earlier and people who worked in and around the town had not yet left their homes, so there were no flurries of questions as to the likelihood of Josh returning full-time to his practice. She knew that he was ruthlessly honest and would respond to any queries – about his position in the community or indeed her own – with the truth, and she was not yet sure how they would, or should, handle this.

Morag was at the surgery when they arrived, polishing the reception desk and arranging fresh flowers.

'Do you live here, Morag?' Alex asked.

'It feels like it most of the time,' Morag smiled, adding, 'the doctor is in her consulting room already.'

Alex felt Josh bristle next to her. His hope to gain a psychological advantage had evaporated with the early arrival of his locum, and she dug him in the ribs as she heard him mutter 'female!' under his breath.

'May I remind you that I, too, am female!'

'Not much chance that I forget that, Alex,' Josh chuckled, putting his arm across her shoulders. 'Right, here goes.'

Several quick paces took him to the consulting room door, on which he rapped sharply twice, then opened, with the brisk greeting, 'Good morning!'

'Hello, Dad, how wonderful to see you!'

'Molly!'

Alex stood back as Josh and Molly MacDonald hugged each other tightly, smiling as she saw the thick black hair of father and daughter mingle.

'Why didn't you tell me you were coming here?' Josh asked incredulously, holding his daughter at arms' length.

'Well, you have been a tad incommunicado! Morag phoned my head of department and explained that you had been taken ill suddenly, and asked whether there were any newly-qualified doctors who could come and act as locum for the time being. Professor Leitch spoke to me later that day and I agreed that I would love to come and support your practice until you are ready to return. And here I am!'

'Do you mind if I sit in whilst you see the first few patients, Molly?'

'Dad, of course not – but please remember I am doing my best. I may not give the exact advice that you would yourself, but I always strive to listen carefully, examine the patient thoroughly, and give the correct diagnosis and treatment. When do you think you will be back?'

Josh paused. 'I'm not sure, Molly. We'll have to see. Can you bring me up to date with the Logans? How is wee Lisa?'

'Holding her own remarkably well. But she has flatly refused to continue attending morning school. Her teacher's expectations were, according to her mother, quite simply beyond her. To sit still for an hour at the age of four is impossible! I am young enough to remember that myself.'

Alex exclaimed with impatience, 'I will leave you two until lunch time. If I hear any further updates about Ms O'Hara, my blood pressure would soar dangerously high and I would need medical intervention! I need to leave you to treat the patients you have, rather than becoming another one myself. I'm so very pleased to meet you, Molly.' She shut the door quietly behind her and went out into the reception area to join Morag.

Watching Alex go, Josh wondered just how long he could conceal from her the extent of the medication that he was taking; then, pragmatic as ever, turned with a smile to his daughter and to the cases that she faced that morning.

'She's lovely, Morag – so like Josh!'

'Aye, and she's a good, caring and thoughtful doctor too, Alex. As different from the previous person as day from night.'

'Was she called after Josh's mother?'

'She was. I remember Elspeth, Josh's ex-wife, objecting because she said the name was "old fashioned". But, for once, Josh was adamant. How is he, Alex? Really – how is he? Will he be coming back to the practice soon, do you think? We all miss him so much.'

Looking at the love and concern in Morag's face, Alex's strength faltered at last and she sat down, holding her head in her hands. 'Oh Morag. Has no-one told you? Josh has a brain tumour…'

'But they can operate, surely?'

Alex looked unflinchingly at the older woman. 'They say they cannot, Morag.'

'So all those migraines …'

Alex nodded.

'Is there no-one skilled enough to try at least?'

'Morag, they say not.'

'Oh, lass, I'm so sorry! There's so much unfairness in this world. You lose your job and Josh loses … loses everything!'

'Not quite everything, Morag. He will have me always. Always.'

Chapter 53

Alex spent the rest of the morning in the lee of the *Sleeping Guardians* going through a rigorous Yoga practice, focussing her mind on the beauty of nature and the permanence of this beauty, as opposed to the transience of life. In front of her, on the near horizon, and always at the centre of her soft gaze, was Haligrey, the holy island which, on this day of bright sun and scudding clouds, glowed like an emerald. As she flexed and stretched her body in order to subdue her mind and bring it back under control, Alex remembered the fragrance and peace of the island which had been hallowed by the prayer and right-living of a monk a thousand years earlier. She recalled the energy of the place, the feel of the earth under her palms, vibrating with a life of its own. She thought of the clarity and taste of the water from the holy well which had sprung from the earth at Aelfric's touch. And finally, clear and beautiful in her mind's eye, she saw the wood beyond the world, where the monk rested. As her thoughts and her Yoga practice became one, she knew, without a doubt, the next steps that she and Josh must take.

'How was she, Josh?' Alex linked her arm tightly through her lover's as they walked back to the cottage together.

'She was brilliant, Alex! Brilliant! She listened carefully, asked the right questions, listened once again, and recommended or prescribed. I am so proud of her and completely confident that she can take the practice forward – not just maintain it.' Alex was silent and Josh glanced at her quickly. 'Oh, my love, you are thinking of Diana …'

'I am. I can't help it.'

'I'm not going to give you some trite bullshit. In your place, I would feel pretty grim too. But the fate of a human being is determined by his or her decisions. Sometimes they are good, sometimes they are not. The key is to learn by them. Sadly,' Josh stopped and took Alex's hands in his own, 'some people don't learn by their mistakes. A female deer, or bird, nurtures her young until they fledge. They feed them and support them until they can live on their own. They don't then keep on feeding them and supporting them. They launch them out into the savageness of the natural world to experience and to learn for themselves. This is what you did, Alex! This is what every mother does.'

Josh opened the cottage door and closed it again softly behind them. 'Come here!' Enclosing Alex with his arms he waited until the storm of tears that he had expected subsided again. He lost himself in the fragrance of her soft hair and thought for the millionth time how she had transformed his life.

'I love you, Alex.' She blinked her wet eyelashes free of moisture and smiled once again into his face.

'And I love you, my Star of the Sea. And – I have a plan!'

'A plan for what – how we spend the next hour or so?'

'No! Have you thought what you are going to say when your patients see you again and ask when you are expecting to return to your practice?'

'I'll tell them the truth.'

'And when, day after day, this harsh truth is affirmed, how will you feel, Josh?'

After thinking carefully for a time, Josh grimaced and answered 'Pretty desolate, Alex.'

'That's what I thought. It can't be good for you to stay here on Fragrey and be reminded again and again of your own mortality – it's not helpful!'

'I'm hardly likely to forget it: I think if you were to take a sample of my blood it would be ninety-five percent pain relief! But as for not staying here on the island, I just couldn't face life on the mainland – and I think life for both of us if we were to drive about the Highlands in Gladys might be somewhat cramped!'

Alex laughed. 'Gladys can stay with Rory for the foreseeable future! But I've been thinking about all of the above and I think we should stay a while on Haligrey.'

'Haligrey? It's uninhabited!'

'It's magic, Josh. Don't you remember that I answered the call to be a *Seeker of Everyday Magic*? Come to Haligrey with me, Josh. It's wonderful beyond your dreams.'

'If I do, I'll have to overcome some pretty strong feelings. You've heard about Hector, my elder brother?' Alex nodded. 'Well, to think I might be sailing over his remains, and the remains of my father's boat … it freaks me out more than a bit. And the legends that are centred on the Holy Island, the stories about miracles and monks. Alex, I just can't believe in something that my scientific mind cannot test for. Something that I cannot see, and measure. It goes against my training. I cannot prescribe miracles!'

'Josh, how do you test your love for me? How do you measure it in scientific terms? Could you prescribe something to cure yourself of it? For me to coax Gladys around a thousand miles to attend a job interview and just happen to meet someone who had tried to virtually seduce me on Twitter – how rational are these things? How scientific is the basis of our love for each other; or how likely the coincidence of our meeting in reality, not just online? Josh, open your mind. You cannot know everything. Everything is not based on science or even reason.'

Josh stood silent, holding her clear gaze.

'And the past is everywhere, Josh! Think about the *Sleeping Guardians*. On Haligrey, the past is still alive and real. The island seems to have a life of its own – even its own heartbeat! Please come with me, Josh. There is a little stone and turf-roofed house where the monk Aelfric used to live. I'm sure we could make it habitable – maybe not in the Winter, but certainly during the Summer and possibly early Autumn …'

'And after that, you think there may no longer be any need to create a shelter for me on Haligrey, Alex, because I will no longer be alive? Am I right?'

'You are right in the first part of what you said, but not the second. When I was practising Yoga on the cliff top this morning, the island seemed to be calling to me. I remembered it as an ideal of the most intense life imaginable: colours are more vibrant there, the air is sweeter, and life more vital. I believe that if we go there, you may, somehow, get better. I'm no scientist,

Josh, and I'm certainly no doctor, but there is so much more in life that science *can't* define, or work out a formula for. So much is intense and real – but unseen.'

Josh looked down at Alex's face, slightly flushed with emotion and full of passion as she tried hard to persuade him to do something that went against his medical pragmatism.

'So what intense, real and unseen discoveries will we be able to make in this paradise island, my dearest?'

'Love. Faith. Belief. Hope. All those things.'

'Would it make you happy if we went to Haligrey for a time, Alex?'

'Yes, it would.'

'And could we somehow arrange for food and other things to be brought over?'

'I'm sure that Agnes would do that for us. She rows over to the island quite often.'

'Molly could move in here, couldn't she? She's staying with Morag at the moment.'

'Perfect!'

'You scheming, sexy woman.'

'Does that mean you agree, Josh?'

'It does. And if you can teach me how to have Faith, Belief and Hope as well as the Love I feel for you, then you are indeed a seeker *and finder* of magic.'

Looking at the glowing, expectant face of the woman who loved him and whom he loved, Josh wondered how possible it would be for him to take with him to the island sufficient tablets to ease his increasing pain, and how easy it would be to shield Alex from watching his steady deterioration.

Chapter 54

'Hi Alex. Do you have a few minutes?'

'Molly, how nice to see you! Have you come to have a guided tour of the cottage? It won't take long! Fancy a coffee? I could do with one.'

'Love one – thanks. Is Dad in?'

'No. He insisted that he should start running again. I told him if he wasn't back in an hour I would run after him!'

'He loves you very much, doesn't he?'

'Yes, as I love him.'

'That's all good. As his daughter, it's great to see him so happy – that frown he always used to have has gone. Ironically, he looks better – fitter – than he has for years!' Molly stirred her coffee thoughtfully, before continuing, 'But as well as being his daughter, I am a doctor. Dad's told me about your idea to go to the Holy Island. Is this completely wise, Alex? What if he is taken ill again? What if he needs urgent and expert medical care? You won't be able to use your mobile over there and there will be no other methods of communication.'

'I've thought of that, Molly – and of course you are concerned. I am too! But I can't just watch your father fading away as he is forced to reiterate the bleak details concerning his health to people who care so much about him and who will, without doubt, keep enquiring. I have arranged with a school governor, Agnes Muirhead, that I will light a beacon if there is an emergency. She is utterly dependable and I can rely upon her to keep watch for this signal. If the air ambulance had to be summoned again, the delay would be minimal.

'Agnes sounds an unusual woman!'

'Unusual is the word! Look, Molly, pragmatically, either Josh will recover …'

'But he *won't* Alex! As his next of kin, I rang the hospital in Edinburgh where he was taken when he lost consciousness and they explained exactly what his problem is. Believe me, the neuro-surgical team would be trying a whole range of interventions if they thought that anything could be done.'

'But if he deteriorates, then I want his remaining time to be as memorable and stress-free as possible. You know what he's like, Molly! He is known and valued by everyone and it would be beyond frustrating for him to constantly repeat that he is unable to work because he has an inoperable brain tumour. If we spend the last few weeks of his life on an enchanted island pretending, if you like, that all will be well, at least he would be able to remain positive until the very last moment of consciousness that he has.'

The women looked at each other without speaking, sipping their coffee. In the end Molly MacDonald nodded and said, 'I understand your reasoning. Thank you for explaining – and thank you for loving my father and making him happier than I have ever seen him before. I must go.' She stood up and walked over to

Alex, giving her a light kiss on the cheek, then left, leaving Alex to reflect upon the strangeness of looking into the blue-grey of Josh's eyes in the face of his daughter.

The run had been a struggle for Josh. It was nearly a month since he had taken any sort of significant exercise and that fact alone made it difficult for him to maintain any sort of decent pace. But pain was almost a constant presence with him now and he had to stop at the first of the *Sleeping Guardians* to take his tablets and pause until they had started to take effect. This place held such memories for him. All those years ago, when he had fought off depression by establishing an exercise routine that would put many professional athletes to shame, those mounds had been a reassurance, a symbol of constancy. On childhood walks, his mother had told him how, generations ago, his father's family had farmed the land which dipped away to the right of the path into a shallow valley, and this strengthened the connection that he felt to this place. Less than a year earlier, when he had been the closest to taking his own life that he ever had been, it had been here that he stood, brought back from the brink of suicide by a unicorn and a rainbow. Looking back, he shook his head in bitterness. How could he even have thought of doing such a thing, when he believed that he was fit and healthy and had his entire life in front of him. What a betrayal of his own integrity. Now he would give so much to be able to face ten, twenty, even thirty years, growing old with Alex. As he felt the pain gradually ease, he remembered the night of the May Ball and how he and Alex had celebrated the discovery of each other in the shelter of one of the *Guardians.* And finally, he remembered Jessie McLeod – driven to hide away until she died because of the crass thoughtlessness of an arrogant young woman. Life held so much beauty, so much tragedy; and across all life's events, time passed relentlessly, whilst people died, loved and became ill. At that moment, looking at the clear blue sky which arched above him and the turbulent waters at the foot of the cliff; the resilient little flowers scattered through the turf and the wind which tore at his hair, Josh realised for the first time that life is composed of dark and light elements which run together, challenging and yet highlighting each other. And he realised that the only true way forward is acceptance.

Chapter 55

Alex and Agnes looked at the small stone building with quiet satisfaction: it was as ready as it ever would be for occupation. Conscious always of the too-rapid passing of time, Alex had urged Agnes to make trip after trip, which she did uncomplainingly, to bring an inflatable mattress and bedding; the Calor Gas stove from Gladys, together with necessary kitchen utensils; and soap, shampoo and toothpaste.

'You're right to come here, Alex,' Agnes smiled. 'There is healing in the very air of this place.'

'I need to feel that I am *doing* something,' Alex responded. 'Just sitting in the cottage back on Fragrey, waiting for … waiting for something to happen – I just can't do it. But here we can talk, walk, love each other, watch the stars and the sunrise – just fill Josh's mind with all the beauty of the earth, even if he is in a world of pain physically.'

'Is he, Alex?'

'Yes, I believe so. He underplays things constantly, but I know how often he takes the pain relief that the hospital gave him – and it *is* becoming more frequent.'

'As I have said, you are right to take this action. Wait, Alex. Wait.'

'Time is something I don't have, Agnes.'

The warm late spring had blossomed into one of the hottest summers on record for the Western Isles. The white sand of the beaches burned under foot and the machair was a fragrant tapestry, ablaze with drifts of pure colour. Josh stood bare-legged on *the beach of homecoming* and smiled into the tanned and freckled face that he had come to regard as the centre of his universe. It was Alex who soothed him in the middle of a disturbed night, when he had to get up to take more painkillers, all the while pretending that she didn't realise that this was what he was doing. It was Alex who joked about his 'personal best', which was infinitely worse than it had been but was 'lightyears away' from her own. Alex who stumbled over the unfamiliar words of Latin verse, as she read *The Georgics* to him; and agreed that even though she didn't understand a word, the cadences and rolling syntax soothed and calmed.

'What do you think?' she asked him, smiling.

'It's perfect, my own love.'

And they walked together into the cool, dark interior of the ancient dwelling.

'Food for the body, food for the mind, and food for my inmost being.' Josh looked at the proximity of meal preparation area, the small shelf of his favourite books and the comfortable and colourful bed.

'Which shall we try first?' laughed Alex

'Need you ask?'

'No, Josh. I needn't ask.'

Day followed day with the same gentle routine, and in the contraction of their world both found fulfilment. Instead of an impossible schedule, demanding frequent trips by ferry or plane from island to island, or running until the point of exhaustion, Josh found beauty in the smallest things: the minute fanning of a butterfly's wings; the symphony of birdsong at the start and end of each peaceful day; the myriad stars that scintillated in the ink-black sky. Alex found beauty in Josh: in watching his every gesture and smile, and treasuring every word and expression of love, storing all these things up as memories to sustain her future.

Alex knew Josh was failing: he spoke less and slept more, and she thought of how, in Australia, the indigenous people embrace the ages-old concept of *Dreamland,* the state from which we awake when we are born, and to which we return when we die, to dream through eternity. She loved this term, used to describe the end-of-life destination as, to her, it denoted the gradual retreat from the pressures and stresses of worldly existence, and night after night Alex watched over Josh as he seemed to be slipping further towards this peaceful end.

After two weeks of endless sunshine, the weather broke with a tremendous lightning storm. Josh and Alex, wrapped together under the same plaid that had united them in the Sleeping Guardian when their world had seemed cloudless and full of promise, watched the sizzling zig-zag lightning flicker and dart across the sky. Relentlessly the lightning bolts stabbed the sea around the holy island and the land around their frail shelter, as both watched the unbridled savagery of nature in awe. The sound of discharging electricity was interrupted by a loud crack.

'Has something been struck on Haligrey, Josh, do you think?'

'Certainly sounded like it! Probably one of the orchard trees – they must stand higher than this hut of ours. We'll explore in the morning, Alex. I need to sleep now.'

The lightning continued, illuminating with its intensity the passive man curled quietly in Alex's arms, and the tears which slid silently down her cheeks.

Chapter 56

The next morning Alex and Josh awoke to a fresh blue and gold morning. The world had been washed by the rain and the wet grass shimmered as they ran together to *the beach of homecoming* for their morning swim. Josh seemed rested and more energetic than Alex had seen him for days and he dived into the waves before turning to splash her unmercifully.

'Let's go to the orchard this morning, Josh,' Alex suggested, munching her breakfast hungrily.

'This is mermaid hair,' Josh pronounced, pulling Alex's long, wet hair back from her face and twisting it into a knot at the back of her neck. 'And mermaids can ask for whatever they wish and it will be granted.'

'In that case – apart from going to the orchard this morning – my wish is that you will be healed, completely, and that we can live the rest of our lives together in love and peace.' Alex enclosed Josh's hands with her own and leant back into her lover's arms.

'What would I give for that wish to be granted,' Josh sighed.

'What would you give?' Alex asked, twisting around and shaking her hair free. 'Seriously, Josh, what would you give?'

Josh sat, looking back at Fragrey across the strait.

'I would relinquish my doubts about the good at the heart of human life; my cynicism about human motivation; my lack of faith. All these things would be the most difficult for me to give up, because they have grown as I have grown. If I were healed, I would willingly renounce my negative beliefs!'

'You're teasing – but I'll hold you to it! Come on, then – I'll race you there!'

Panting, they arrived in the orchard – beyond the everyday world in its beauty and strangeness. The tiny fruits were bathed in moisture and shone like gems in the bright sun and at the centre of the trees they saw the object of the lightning strike: a shapely apple tree split neatly down the centre. It had been planted at the head of where Alex believed Aelfric lay: half to the left and half to the right – its perfect beginning fruits scattered across the green grass and flowers.

'What a shame, Josh!' Alex exclaimed. 'It was so full of life and promise and has just been struck down …'

Josh smiled ironically at her and murmured, 'Sounds familiar?'

Alex just looked at the man she loved with every atom of her being and said, 'Yes, it does.'

Without further words, they walked slowly hand in hand to the felled tree and looked at the leaves, curling already in the morning sunshine, still trying to protect the fruits that they sheltered, and the sap being leached out of the trunk as the tree lay dying. The whole scene shook Alex, as she saw in it a symbol of the vigorous, fruitful life of the man she loved being decimated by a silent, unseen killer. 'I can't bear this,' she sobbed, running to the root of the tree, close to where she had felt the steady heartbeat of the island on her earlier visit with Agnes. She lay her hands once again upon the earth, as if trying to heal the destruction, or soothe the tree in some way, and as she looked, she saw that where the roots had been torn out of the fertile soil of the orchard, a rift in the ground had been opened. After only a moment's hesitation, Alex reached her hand down into the soft, dry and friable earth. The hole was deep, much deeper than she had expected and, feeling bolder as the slanting rays of the sun illuminated the dark space, she pushed her arm further and further into the earth until the tips of her fingers felt the rough contours of a hard rectangular object. 'Josh, there is something down here!'

Josh's longer reach eventually brought out the object: a wooden box, the carved images on its lid partially filled and obscured with soil. Blowing and brushing the soil away carefully, he set it down between himself and Alex. It measured about forty-five centimetres by thirty and gradually they made out a range of exquisite carvings on the lid and the sides. On the lid, a rainbow arched from left to right, spanning a choppy sea and, breaking the waves, were the powerful, curved tails of marine mammals.

Excitement ran through Alex like the lightning that she had witnessed the previous evening – 'Mermaids?'

'Probably!' laughed Josh. 'A rainbow and mermaids! We should open this, Alex.'

'Yes, we should. But I just don't know what it will contain Josh. It's near to the place where Aelfric is supposed to be buried – maybe its contents are a bit, well, grisly?'

'I thought you were the one to have faith, Alex.'

Carefully, slowly, Josh eased off the lid of the box and held it over its bottom section for several seconds. 'Here we are then,' he announced, as they both looked down into the ancient interior.

'That's the last thing I expected to find,' Alex murmured.

Neatly fitting into the rectangular space lay a book: front and back covers were made of wood, carved like the lid of the box in which it had lain for centuries, but this time the images were of the flowers of the island.

'It doesn't make sense that it is so well preserved,' Josh mused.

'Obviously magic – or holy. Or maybe both.'

'As I said, you're the one with faith!'

Laying her hands upon the book and its cover, Alex felt the same sort of energy that she had experienced when she lay her hand upon the heart of the island. Here there was potency, reassurance, hope, and smiling at Josh, she replied, 'Yes, I am the one with faith.'

Chapter 57

It seemed wrong, somehow, to remove the book from its resting place, and so Josh and Alex sat on the grass under the heavy canopy of the orchard trees to open what they had found. It seemed such a weighty thing to do – to look at the contents that had remained hidden since, presumably, Aelfric had closed the book and sealed it in its box over a thousand years earlier, and both were conscious that they held their breath as Josh gently opened the cover.

Hic liber qui Aelfric scripsit
de potentia mundi naturalis

'*Here is the book which Aelfric wrote concerning the healing power of the natural world* – a pretty good start, Alex!'

'Could you translate it – or parts of it – for me, Josh? It looks pretty challenging! All those words with little lines over them, and words which look like abbreviations …'

'I haven't read much Mediaeval Latin, Alex, but I will do my best. I know that contractions and abbreviations are common – bit like texting today,

I suppose. Give me a few minutes to get my head around the first page and I'll have a go.'

Alex watched Josh's eyes flicker over the page of dense script, running again over certain phrases; she saw the lines of concentration on his forehead and around his eyes and thought for the millionth time what a tragedy it was that such a formidable intellect should be destroyed by a disease working away in the very core of his mind. She had made herself a promise that she would try to banish negative thoughts such as this as soon as they occurred and concentrate on the moment – being with Josh, and his being with her – but it was so hard and became harder the more she came to know the man and love him.

'Right, here's an approximate translation – not what I expected from a monk, I must say:

Day 450

Today I have had to fight to keep my mind on the work which I believe that God has called me to do here on this island of blessing. I have felt lonely and have been missing the company of people I used to know – my fellow monks, of course, but above all my family and – to tell the truth, women that I knew and loved before making my vows. I am, after all, still a man, with a man's desires and longings. Daily I strive to subdue the flesh through exercise, running the small circuit of the island until my muscles bid me stop or swimming against the waves which pound this small sanctuary. But today has been hard.'

'I can sympathise with this,' Josh grimaced.

'Please carry on – it's fascinating. Why has he headed this entry up "Day 450" do you think?'

315

'Perhaps because he has counted the days that he has been on the island? If this is so, he has been on Haligrey for about a year and a half at this stage.'

'He has created his own calendar, you mean, referenced only to the time he has spent on Haligrey?'

'In a way, yes, he has.'

'And in doing this, he has made his chronicle timeless, hasn't he?'

'If you keep interrupting, Alex, with your deep and philosophical thoughts, I will never finish this!'

Day 730

I have been here for two years – during which time I have watched the glorious sun rising and setting and the stars adorn the night sky. In the winter, I have been wet and frozen and, in the summer, burnt with the sun's rays – and sometimes I have managed to pray as I believe God intends for me to do. I saw a woman from the big island rowing her boat today, catching fish, I think. She has long fair hair and it shone in the sunshine.

Day 737

Today I watched as the woman landed her little boat on the beach of homecoming and walked past the spring that God revealed to me when I landed. She walked up to the dwelling house I have built and gave me fish that she had caught. We talked for some time. She is as fair as the day. Her name is Flora, a flower indeed.

'You're right, Josh. This is not what I expected Aelfric to write, or think.'

'At least he's made me feel less guilty about my Twitter activities!'

Flicking back to the poisonous comments that her daughter had made about Josh getting his 'sexual kicks' from social media, Alex couldn't help asking, 'Are you still on Twitter, Josh?'

'When my love for you fills my life, Alex? No, how could that be? Soon after you blocked me, I couldn't stand going on social media any more. It seemed such a self-absorbed and indulgent waste of time. Do you want me to continue with the translation?'

'Yes please. I won't interrupt again.'

Day 815

The year is turning. Now there is more darkness than light in the sky and I am left alone to think, rather than to do. Life is harsh.

Day 840

Flora visited me again today. She brought homespun blankets and a sort of vegetable pottage stew. She warmed it on the fire outside my dwelling place. It revived me – as did her company.

Day 847

She came again. This time with fresh milk from her ewes and bread that she has baked. She also brought a basket of fruit from her garden. A storm blew up suddenly and the skies went black. She could not return to the big island and I gave her shelter.

'Josh! Does this mean what I think it means?'

'Yes, I think so – let's read on.'

Day 950

Today Flora told me that she is with child. I could not be sad as there was such joy in creating this new life. She told me that because she will be disgraced if she gives birth to a child out of wedlock, she has accepted the offer of a farmer to marry her. She will try to pretend that the child is his.

Day 980

I pray daily for Flora and our child. And, of course, I pray for the other concerns which God has placed on my heart, but these two come first and last, morning and night. I know not whether she has married her farmer and I have no news of her. Each day is a trial to me, especially as I have started to have such pain in my head that I sometimes cannot think and certainly cannot pray.

Day 1100

Flora rowed over to see me again. She looks more lovely than ever – the joy and blossoming of motherhood have completed her beauty. She is married and is happy enough with her man, who has been asking for her hand in marriage for some time. His name is Kenneth MacDonald and he farms the land to the east of the great barrows which stand on the cliff. The child is a boy and she has called him Angus. Flora has told me that her visits to the island must cease. At least that will leave me free to do God's work again – or at least to try to do so, when the pain allows me. It seems that I am not destined for the joys of this world.

Josh's voice had gradually become quieter as he translated, until Alex felt that he was almost speaking to himself. He then stopped reading out loud and sat, looking at the text in front of him with a thoughtful frown on his face.

'Are you all right, Josh?' Alex asked softly.

'Not completely – my head is spinning, and not through what is eating away at it! Has it struck you that we may well have been reading some of my distant family history, Alex?'

'Well, the name is obvious…'

'My mother used to tell me that generations ago our family farmed the land to the east of the *Sleeping Guardians.* I think that is what the writer is referring to here. So, he and his son, Angus, who would take his step-father's name of MacDonald, could well have been my ancestors. And what's more, Aelfric seems to have been afflicted with severe headaches – not the best genetic trait to pass on as inheritance!'

'It's probably just coincidence, Josh.'

'Someone once told me that there is no such thing!'

'What puzzles me is that the book is supposed to be about *the healing power of the natural world,* but so far it has been a sort of diary.'

'There's more, Alex. Let's read on.'

Day 1800

My reading from the Holy Bible this morning was the letter of James, in which he says 'Every good thing given and every perfect gift is from above, coming down from the Father of lights, with whom there is no variation or shifting shadow.'

My head was very painful this morning and reading this made me think that God uses the natural world to heal and to soothe his peoples. I began to wonder whether there may be a cure for all ills somewhere in the world. Maybe in the depths of the forest there is a plant, or root, that will cure, say, congestion of the lungs; a certain sort of leaf may relieve fever; and just possibly there may be a flower that will take away intense pain. I will start to search the natural world to see whether there, in her bounty, we can find relief for human suffering. Although this island is small, it is fertile with God's fecundity, and promises much.

Day 1807

Perhaps my plan is not such a good one! I ate of a strange leafy plant in the place where I planted the seeds from the fruit that Flora brought to me. It made me sick and my head is still spinning. Surely nature contains plants which poison as well as those which heal.

Day 1814

Today I was very tired. My head was aching insupportably and, to my shame, I slept in the middle of the day, lying under the leafy branches of those young apple and plum trees. I awoke only as the day became cooler and found, weaving its way through my fingers a small, golden, star-shaped flower. I was convinced that God had led me to this in my searching and slowly ate every petal, leaf and each part of the stem of this small plant. It would not be true to say that I immediately felt better, but I felt some vigour return to my limbs and walked home with a smile on my face and prayer on my lips.

Day 1821

It is now seven days since I ate the flower – which, because I do not recognise the plant, I shall call moly, the magical herb I have read of in ancient texts. Every day I have eaten again, and every day I feel a more certain return to my previous strength. May God be praised! His world is indeed the giver of all good things!

The two sat in silence for some time, until Alex said, 'What are you thinking, Josh?'

'I am asking myself whether this is utter rubbish, and as a scientist my natural reaction is to think that it is.'

'Can we just finish it off, Josh, please?'

Skipping many pages, Josh read:

Day 7300

I have now been on the island for twenty years. Since my discovery of the moly, I have searched for remedies for other ills and have found many – more than I ever imagined. I have spent the long summer days drawing the plants and chronicling their virtues. On the pages that follow I have chronicled the secrets of nature that I have been led to unlock. Willow gives mild pain relief and stops copious bleeding; the foxglove can still the too-fast-beating heart. But for the sort of pain and pressure from within the skull which was taking my life and energy, moly is the herb which God has used to heal me.

I know that my time to depart this world is near, so I shall close this book now and bury it where my body shall rest through all eternity. I have seen Flora again, older but still comely, who is now the mother of four. My Angus thrives and will take over the farm from Kenneth MacDonald. Flora will see that my body rests in peace and decency.

Thanks be to God for the life and work to which He led me those years ago.

'Do you still think it is rubbish, Josh?'

'Aspirin is found in willow bark and drug companies still use digitalis from foxgloves for an irregular heartbeat…'

'And moly?'

'Alex, Homer – himself probably a fictional character –writes that moly is the magic herb given to Odysseus to protect him against the siren's wiles! How can you expect me to take that seriously!'

'But Aelfric explains that "moly" is a term that he chose for the herb he did not recognise. Although there is a legend attached to the name, you can't doubt the evidence from this man that he was healed through *something* – whatever its name!'

'Alex, I don't *know* …'

'Would you ever have expected to meet someone you chatted up on Twitter, Josh? And fall in love with her?'

'No.'

'Then why is it more difficult to believe that there is a beautiful plant which could heal you?'

'Your head is in the land of fantasy, rather than reality, Alex. I'm dying! You can dream up all sorts of "cures", but I know what is happening in my head: the tumour is growing until I won't be able to see, or speak, or move. Exactly when this will happen, I do not know. But it *will* happen.'

'And you won't even try to find this moly?'

'No, Alex. It's nonsense.'

'Then there is no point staying here, Josh. Where there is no hope, there is no life. I shall light a bonfire and ask Agnes to pick us up. I can't live without hope.'

Chapter 58

It was as if she had glimpsed Eden and then been banished into the wilderness once again.

Almost as soon as the smoke and flames of the beacon had started to rise into the sky, Alex saw Agnes dragging Frigg down the pebble beach behind her croft and in just under half an hour, she had landed on *the beach of homecoming.* Alex and Josh sat in silence, waiting by the spring and the concern on Agnes's face melted as she saw them.

'Thank goodness it was not a medical emergency,' she cried, running up to them, smiling. 'But you must need something – what can I do for you?'

'We've decided to return to Fragrey, Agnes. I'll explain properly later.' Alex replied, and the three sat in silence as the boat glided over the choppy blue and white stretch of water between Eden – Haligrey – and the island which they all called home.

And now, hours later, Alex was back in Gladys, trying without enthusiasm to cook something edible on the Calor Gas stove which they had brought back with them. She felt utterly defeated. Just when a glimmer of hope seemed to have been offered, Josh had refused to accept it; and ever since then he had been unusually quiet and withdrawn. They had hardly exchanged a dozen words since his resolute refusal to believe that a miraculous cure for his brain cancer was possible; and, after thanking Agnes, he had walked alone and silent back to his cottage on the quayside.

'Can I come in, Alex?' Agnes stood at the stable door of the campervan. 'I have wine!'

'Oh, bless you, Agnes – of course! Although I'm not guaranteeing the liveliness of the company I'll provide, or the quality of the food! This was supposed to be an omelette, but has turned out more like scrambled egg! Would you like some?'

'Why not! Perfect accompaniment to the Merlot!'

Alex, relaxed by wine and warmth, explained how she and Josh had found the manuscript, what it contained, and how firmly Josh had refused to believe that healing for him would ever be possible, whether via a medicinal herb, or a direct miracle. Agnes exclaimed as Alex told her about the manuscript containing details of the healing power of the natural world.

'I knew it! I knew that he had found the key to right-living! And your discovery of his writing is the reason he insisted that it should be left there on the island. I will return and ask him if I may now remove it.'

'Him being…?'

'Aelfric.'

'So all those trips to Haligry were to visit Aelfric, Agnes? He's dead!'

'As I have said to you before, my dear, what does "alive" actually mean? I have spoken to Aelfric with my heart and mind and he has replied with his. But this is a separate matter. We need to talk of Josh and his refusal to take up Aelfric's help. You see Josh primarily as your lover, Alex, but he is also a brilliant doctor whose medical practice is based on scientific evidence. An ancient text, which suggests that possibly a herb or small flower can heal him, doesn't provide any robust evidence at all – just try to think about it objectively. Josh wants to live – of course he does – but to try a remedy which to him must seem almost that of a charlatan would be very difficult for him, if not impossible.'

'And where does that leave him, Agnes? Where does it leave us?'

'In a dark and difficult place of sadness, unless you start communicating again. It only needs one person to say sorry in a situation like this, and actually, Alex, in this case I think it needs to be you.'

❧❦

'I'm sorry, Josh. I understand that you find the account Aelfric wrote difficult to accept. I'm sorry I wasn't more sympathetic.'

'Oh, come here, you beautiful, infuriating woman. How long is it since I've seen you? Less than twenty-four hours, and every minute has seemed like a lifetime.'

Holding Josh as tightly as he was holding her, Alex thought bleakly about her own future: what was twenty-four hours, one single day, compared with the months and years which lay ahead of her without the man she loved.

'But no more Haligrey, Alex. I need to remain here in the real world and make the most of the time left to me to interact with the people whom I have cared for over the years. Molly has had to tell most of my patients what is happening, so I will be spared that, at least. Come back here, Alex. It will be cosy, but there is room for the three of us in the cottage.'

Alex had deep reservations, but tried to laugh, 'Anything rather than return to the palatial life style I formerly led in Gladys!'

'Have you heard about Jeanne O'Hara?'

'No. I've only spoken to Agnes and we just talked about you. And before you become even more conceited, it was along the lines of what a stubborn man you are!'

Josh chuckled. 'Well, she's left the island, and with Mike Whitfield faithfully in tow!'

'What?'

'Morag rang last night – that woman knows my whereabouts by telepathy, I think – and of course, she knew the entire story, gleaned probably from the women in her spinning circle. Very soon after we left, Jeanne persuaded Grace Meredith to come out of retirement and teach the children again. Without a teaching commitment, Jeanne was free once again to follow her plans to make the school an academy and, as she had outlined at the Governors' meeting, she asked Jenna and Mike to join her as trustees. The paperwork was all in place, and as soon as this final practical step had been taken and the trust had been formed, government funding was released. Morag told me that she believes that Jenna also invested a substantial amount of capital from the original endowment left by her mother. Within forty-eight hours, Jeanne and Mike had gone, together with the entire contents of the school bank account, neatly released by the absconders, being two of the necessary signatories to the account.'

‘Jenna must feel terrible, Josh, being deceived like that!’

‘Only you could feel compassion for someone who deprived you of your career here.’

‘Well, I know how I’d feel.’

‘I do think I need to see Jenna, Alex. Would you mind if I walked over there right now?’

‘Of course not. I would say give her my best wishes, but she’d probably spontaneously combust if you mentioned my name.’

‘I’ve been so taken in, Josh.’ Jenna stood in her gracious drawing room looking out over the slope of lawn which dipped away from the Manor House towards the school.

‘Anyone could have been, Jenna. Ms O’Hara was a very persuasive person. Have you told the police?’

‘Yes, of course. I explained the whole matter to Hamish. He looked a bit out of his depth because I think he is used to dealing with petty theft and drunken behaviour, rather than fraud amounting to hundreds of thousands of pounds.’

‘What did he do, Jenna?’

‘Contacted the fraud squad in Edinburgh, and sadly that is as far as we have managed to get. Our ‘Administrative Headteacher’ *and* our minister seem to have disappeared like mist in the morning.’

‘What are you going to do, Jenna? Did you invest any of the monies which your mother left for the school?’

Jenna shook her head helplessly, as if she was utterly exhausted. ‘I did. And now we have hardly any funds to buy resources, and I'm having to pay poor Grace Meredith out of my own pocket.'

'Oh Jenna, I'm so sorry!'

'And you, Josh, how are you?'

'Still here – against all the odds!'

'Are you still with Alex Miller?' Jenna moved impulsively away from the window and stood directly opposite Josh, her eyes at a height with his, clasping her hands together in an uncharacteristic gesture. 'Oh Josh, if you would just find it in your heart to be with me, I would sell everything I had to find the best specialists to make you well.'

'Jenna, no one can do that! Medically, I am beyond help. And I have told you that Alex and I love each other and real love doesn't change. It lasts forever.'

Jenna's green eyes darkened, 'You don't have to tell me that, Josh. I live with that truth every day of my life.'

'You know I've always been honest, brutally honest, with you, Jenna. Can I ask you a question?'

She nodded.

'Was there any vestige of spite, of vindictiveness, in the action you took to dismiss Alex? Were you punishing her for the fact that I fell in love with her?'

'That's two questions, Josh.'

Jenna paced the floor in front of the tall windows in her drawing room for some considerable time, and when she turned to Josh, her arms were folded against her chest in an age-old gesture of defensiveness. 'I owe you honesty. And my answer is "yes" in both cases. I have felt guilty – of course I have – but jealousy is a powerful feeling.'

'And a destructive one. How can you live with yourself for the rest of your life knowing that you have ruined the life and career of the best teacher this island has ever had?'

Jenna turned away, her arms still folded.

'I will leave you with your thoughts and with your conscience, Jenna. You are a fine woman. A fine chieftain. A Chair of Governors that all respect. Don't betray yourself.'

When she turned around, the room was empty and she was left with her thoughts, her regrets and her restless feelings for the man who never failed to shake her to her core.

Chapter 59

'Cocoa, or whisky?' Alex sleepily asked Josh.

'Need you ask? Bet there is no whisky in Valhalla, or wherever I'm going.'

'Bet there's no cocoa either! I'll take it that that's two whiskies, then?'

A firm tap on the front door of the cottage stopped Alex's progress to the dark-oak drinks cupboard to the left of the fireplace.

'Bit late for visitors,' commented Alex, glancing at the clock on the wall.

Josh opened the door on the wild night. 'Jenna! Is everything all right?'

'Yes, perfectly all right thank you, Josh. Please may I come in?'

'What can I get you, Ms MacLeod?' asked Alex, desperately trying to get hold of her emotions.

'Whisky would be wonderful. Thank you, Alex.' Standing as still as a statue whilst Alex poured the whisky into three tumblers, Jenna took a deep breath. 'Alex, I have come to ask you to forgive me for my hasty action in dismissing you; to apologise unreservedly for my behaviour; and to beg you to accept the post again.'

Atypically, Alex didn't respond immediately with a ready smile and an instant affirmation, but sat pale and thoughtful for some time. Jenna drank deeply and looked down at her hands folded in her lap. Eventually, Alex said simply, 'Of course, Jenna. We all make mistakes, and I know how easy it is to do that. I would be delighted to take up the post again. But before we go any further, could you please let me know what the parents have been told?'

'That you were forced to leave through personal reasons. There was such an outcry, especially as Ms O'Hara was such an unpopular teacher. When can you start?'

'Tomorrow?'

'Grace Meredith will be so relieved. Having made up her mind to retire, she is finding her unexpected return to teaching exhausting.'

'Grace will be relieved? So will I!'

⊰||⊱

'Miss, where have you been? I've missed you forever!'

'The important thing, Gemma, is that we are back together again now. And I am not going to leave you again.'

'Miss, we have done nothing about the Leavers' Production!'

'Well, Archie, we will start to do nothing else from now on! Have you had any more thoughts about how it should go? You all know this is your own event and everything that is written, everything that you do, comes from your own ideas. Where are we up to, and what do we need to do next?

'We rehearsed the procession down from the cliff, Miss, and Gemma wrote that lovely poem. When Ms O'Hara was teaching us, all we had to do was to sit still and listen; to learn stuff about grammar – like submarine clauses and indefinable verbs – and to work quietly because she had important things to do on her laptop.'

'Archie, I think you may mean subordinate clauses and infinitives – but not to worry about these at the moment. Yes, Fiona.'

'Well, Miss, we now need to make the boat and decide what we are going to do with it – set it on fire, or just *pretend* to set it on fire. Is there going to be a body on the boat? Where will it go? All those things.'

'Lots to decide, Fiona. I don't think that we have time now to make a boat from scratch. We can, perhaps use an old boat which needs repair and make it look like a Viking ship. I think you said that your dad offered to help us do that, David?'

'He did, Miss. He said he has an old boat that he could mend and paint for us!'

'That's perfect, then! As far as setting it alight is concerned, do you think that this might harm some of the wonderful sea creatures that we have in our island waters?'

A series of solemn nods followed.

'Right, let's think about this, then. We've talked before about using flame-coloured cloth to represent fire. If you decide that this is an acceptable idea, then we could use a mixture of yellow, gold and red cloth, perhaps made up into flags, and to make the spectacle more realistic we could have a "body" on the boat.' A forest of hands shot up. 'But before anyone says anything, I am afraid that I can't risk one of you in there. If you do decide that we will have a body, it will have to be me!

Chapter 60

The next two weeks built to the usual frenzied climax of the Summer term for the children leaving the island school for the secondary school on Benbecula. As an exercise in strategic planning, team work, creativity and empathy, the Viking boat burial project had exceeded Alex's expectations. She watched with delight as the children she had had in her care for such a relatively short period of time blossomed and matured, taking responsibility for the end of year event. Bitterly she reflected on the uselessness of learning arid terms like 'subordinate clause' and 'infinitives', when understanding of personal responsibility, history, ritual and the meaning of life and death itself, needed to be explored.

David Lowe lived with his parents and four brothers in one of the tiny terraced cottages along the quayside, several doors down from Josh. The day after Alex returned to her school, an ancient boat materialised outside the front of the Lowes' cottage. It was a large rowing boat, rather than a sea-going fishing vessel – and was similar in size to Agnes' *Frigg*. Under the overall direction of their father, David and his siblings swarmed over it, with hammers, nails, and paint brushes and Alex watched as it was transformed in four days into a red and yellow-painted Viking boat, equipped with a fearsome dragon head at the prow.

Alex needed something all-consuming and full of energy to distract her as, night after night, she lay sleepless in Josh's arms, trying to commit to memory the feel and the scent of him. She felt as if he were physically drifting further away from her as each day seemed to drain a little more of his immense vitality.

As far as Josh was concerned, the world had become grey and Alex the only point of light in it. His pain came before everything he saw or did and he started to think that it would be a blessing indeed when it was ended.

The night before the Leavers' Ceremony, Josh and Alex lay wrapped in each other's arms.

'I don't know how much longer I will be able to make love to you, Alex,' Josh whispered, tracing the lines of her face tenderly with his forefinger.

'It doesn't matter. Just lying next to you is everything I need – just looking at you, touching you, being with you …'

'Is everything ready for tomorrow?' Josh eventually asked.

Alex shivered slightly. 'Yes, as far as we can prepare for such an event! Call me fey if you wish, but I have a feeling as if tomorrow will be the end of an era.'

'Well, it will be, Alex. That's the whole point.'

'I don't mean it quite like that. It's so difficult to put into words. You know sometimes you are about to go into a building and it looks threatening in some way?'

'I know what you mean. I sometimes used to feel that when I entered patients' houses. There was an indefinable feeling of sadness, almost of darkness, which seemed to emanate from the place.'

'Exactly. When I think about tomorrow, I feel cold – cold to my core – and I'm not sure why.'

'Come here, you beautiful temptress. You often wrap me in your arms. It's my turn now. Come and be wrapped in mine and I will make you warm.'

⊰◈║◈⊱

The seventeenth of July – the afternoon of which the children had chosen for their Leavers' Ceremony – dawned bright and calm. Parents, grandparents, School Governors and members of the island community had all been invited, the children having written out and decorated literally hundreds of neat cards, explaining the significance of the event.

To mark the moving on of the children in their final year at Fragrey Endowed Primary School, The pupils proudly present their own version of The New Year Boat Ceremony.

The children had taken their costumes into the school hall and were excitedly pulling them on. The Spinning Circle had become the Sewing Circle for the time being and had cut out jagged shapes in gold and yellow and red, to represent the flames that would 'consume' the Viking leader as the boat drifted out to sea.

Unaccountably nervous at even pretending death when it was so much on her mind, Alex had tied her hair back from her face and wore a simple white shift and flat sandals. Because the children couldn't carry her, their Viking Leader, she had decided to appear as otherworldly as she could and would process with the children, silent and with eyes cast down, to enter the boat and sail away into the next world. It had been agreed that she would raise the newly made Viking sail when she had drifted far enough from the harbour to have created the appropriate dramatic impact and she would then be towed back to the quay.

All the invited guests, effectively the entire island population, had assembled somewhere along the route. This ceremony was a rite of passage for their children, their grandchildren, cousins, nephews and nieces. Josh stood outside his cottage, struggling to watch the line of children snaking up the cliff path along which, only months earlier, he had run like the wind. Molly at his side slipped her arm through his and pulled him close to her, 'Are you OK, Dad?' she asked.

'Wonderful!' came the reply. 'Fantastic to see this, Molly! But I can't quite make out Alex – can you see her?'

'Yes Dad, she is in the midst of the children, pretending to be dead.' As soon as she had spoken, Molly MacDonald could have bitten her tongue out, as her father looked at her, without speaking, but with a world of pain in his eyes.

'They're coming down the track now, Dad,' Molly commented. 'And moving towards the boat. Six children are laying Alex down – oops, she's slipped a bit at an awkward angle – and are now climbing out. The golden and red flames – just material really, cut to look like fire – are starting to blow in the breeze and the boat is seaborn now. Alex is really amazing. She is utterly still. I can't even see her breast moving.'

'What? How far out are they?'

'Almost to the point where Alex should lift the sail to signify the boat needs to be guided back to harbour.'

'There's something wrong, Molly. I know there is. Where are those bloody tablets?'

Josh flung himself away from his daughter and made his way as quickly as he could back to the cottage. Feeling his way to grab the latest, and strongest, pain relief that he had been sent by the hospital in Edinburgh, he took twice the dose and stood for several minutes waiting for them to take effect.

'Has she made any move yet, Molly?' He asked his daughter when he re-joined her on the quayside.

'No, Dad, she hasn't. And people are getting concerned.'

'So am bloody I! Where's Agnes? Please find her for me, Molly, as quickly as you can.'

Agnes was standing at the far end of the horseshoe of people surrounding the harbour.

'Agnes, Dad's worried.'

'I am too, Molly. Tell him I will launch *Frigg* and that he needs to come with me – you too if you can. Go and guide him here. Please!'

⊰||⊱

Half an hour later Agnes was pulling strongly towards the garishly painted 'Viking' boat. Josh and Molly MacDonald sat together, Josh straining what remained of his vision to try to see the path that the boat carrying Alex had taken.

'I think it's been caught in a current,' Agnes said quietly. 'The speed at which it travelled was far beyond drifting.'

When they caught up with the boat carrying Alex, it had finally grounded on *the beach of homecoming*. Josh got out as quickly as he could and strode towards the smudged shape that he believed to be the red and yellow vessel.

'Alex, Alex, are you all right?'

There came no answer, nor movement, and as all three – Josh, Agnes and Molly – drew close to her they saw why. Alex's hair was soaked in blood, which was seeping from her temple and running down her neck to soak her white shift, turning it to red.

'Alex!' Josh's cry was almost inhuman. It was one with the desolation of the rocks, the merciless pounding of the sea, and the lament of the gulls which earlier generations had believed to be lost souls. Tears streaming down his face, Josh moved forward to lift Alex out of the boat, remembering as he did so the countless times he had carried her in his arms to love her. But now even the power to lift and hold to himself the woman he loved was denied him. The sight of her dead-pale, expressionless face seared itself into his brain, as he remembered her on the previous night – alive and warm. He couldn't bear this – first the tumour's slow leeching of everything that made him tick, his energy and incisiveness, his quick thought and latterly his sight. And now this, to lose the single precious thing that had made his life worth living and for which, he was convinced, his body had struggled-on far beyond the expectations of the doctors treating him.

'Dad, let me examine Alex – please.'

Josh sank to the sand and Agnes lay a hand on his shoulder whilst Molly MacDonald climbed into the boat and gently explored the origin of Alex's injury.

She looked carefully along the length of Alex's body, felt her pulse and leaned her face close to Alex's.

'She's alive, Dad. I think she slipped as she entered the boat and her temple was pierced by a nail that hadn't been driven deeply enough into the planking. It's long, and it drove in with a fair amount of force – hence the blood loss. Ideally, she needs a blood transfusion, and she will certainly need a CT scan. Obviously, our problem is time – or lack of it.'

Josh remained silent and immobile, kneeling on the sand, and neither Molly nor Agnes was sure whether he was in pain, or in shock, or both.

But actually, what was happening to Josh was neither of these things.

He had heard many times that when a person is drowning, the whole of their life is replayed in their mind. And now he was experiencing the same phenomenon, but in reverse. From the golden days he had spent with Alex in the ancient turf house, almost within sight of where he was kneeling now; to the breathtaking weeks when he knew that he was falling in love with her; the unforgettable night in the barrow; the realisation when in the States of how he had been betrayed by his line-manager; his barren times on Twitter, when sexual release had seemed the only real thing in his sad, dark world; his years on Fragrey, loving and caring for the people of the island; his time with Elspeth and her betrayal; his dedication at medical school; his wonderful mother and her death; losing Hector; losing his father.

Like a series of vivid tableaux, these memories moved across his brain, each one becoming clearer. Then, the pageant started again – but from his childhood. And this time it was as if, atom by atom, his brain was being rebuilt. Where only darkness had existed in relation to each episode in his life, now he also saw light. His father had done his best. He had loved his wonderful Molly and been destroyed by her death – but he had loved his family. Hector – bluff, boasting, but a constant and supportive brother. Elspeth had left him the precious gifts of his daughters, one of whom he knew was by his side now. He wouldn't have missed his time on Fragrey. Even though he could not always cure the stream of humanity that surged through his surgery and his life, he had loved them – always to the end. And they had loved him. They still did. He pitied the constrained individual he had been during his Twitter years – but even there, the light had shone and he had found Alex. His line-manager was now dismissed and the Western Isles were a better place rid of his corrosive presence. Alex, Alex – always full of light, always shining, always believing the best, always trusting. Always, always. Her faith in him had been the making of him as a human being. She had shown him that where darkness inevitably existed in this fallen world, its corollary was light.

Suddenly, Josh opened his eyes, and realised that he could see again with clarity: the beloved features of the woman who was the centre of his world; his daughter, pale and concentrating; Agnes, expressionless; and all set within the jewel-bright island. He knew that he was healed, and spoke to Alex as if certain that she could hear him.

'Come back to me, my love. I believe in this everyday magic, the magic and holiness of this island. It has healed me. It has healed you. You told me to believe in miracles, to have faith. You believed in me and transformed me. If that is not faith, if that is not a miracle, I don't know what is.'

Still kneeling, they now realised probably in prayer, he fell silent again and the women looked at each other, with the unspoken thought that after this last burst of energy perhaps, finally, Josh had lost the power of speech in the final throes of his illness.

Time stood still. Against every aspect of her training, Molly MacDonald waited and watched, agonised. Was her father actually dying? Was the lovely, honest woman who had lit up her father's life also slipping away from the world? She knew that she should take charge as a competent medical professional, but felt in her heart that she was watching something beyond her comprehension and so stood silent by Agnes.

The daylight faded and stars pricked the density of the Hebridean sky, when eventually Alex's eyelids started to flutter, and eventually open.

'What's happening?' she murmured, almost inaudibly.

'I'll tell you later,' smiled Agnes.

'Josh?'

Josh got to his feet and walked over to Alex and knelt by her side, holding both her hands in his. Still he did not speak, but looked with such intensity into her eyes that Molly and Agnes knew that the veil of pain and destruction which had been descending upon him over the last months had been torn away.

The four people, drawn together in such extreme and dramatic circumstances, watched each other closely as the hours slipped by. Each was devoutly wishing, or praying to their own particular gods, and the still enchantment wrapped them around in a timeless blanket of peace. They could have been statues, or figures painted on a mediaeval manuscript: no one spoke and only their eyes moved as they watched the gentle miracle being enacted.

The bright morning star had appeared in the sky when Josh finally moved again. His eyes clear, smiling once more, Josh MacDonald stood and lifted Alex out of the boat and held her close.

'My finder of everyday magic,' he said softly, kissing her.

Chapter 61

'You have a visitor, Doctor MacDonald – and I've brought tea.' The diminutive, auburn-haired nurse smiled at the man reading the latest copy of the British Medical Journal in the chair set by the bed in the side room of the hospital, his right leg beating time restlessly to some internal rhythm.

'Well, he or she had better hurry up if they want to see me before my flight back to Benbecula!' Josh replied briskly, jumping up.

'We just need to wait for the discharge papers, doctor. Mr Jenner said he would bring them down personally before your taxi is due at three.'

'And this visitor of mine is … Brad! And, at the risk of sounding rude, what the hell are you doing here?'

'Can I have one of the eternal cups of tea that you British drink? And I'll tell you.'

Josh was genuinely delighted to see Brad's tall, broad frame filling the doorway. The man's kindness to him during his travesty of a secondment to New York City had been the high spot of a period in his life when Josh had felt betrayed, lost and disillusioned. It had been the turning point for him of a rekindling of faith in humankind. Josh poured two mugs of tea and handed one over to Brad, then sat down, resting his elbows on his knees and cradling his mug.

'I'm ready!'

'Impatient as always,' Brad chuckled.

Josh shut his eyes momentarily, recalling how just a few brief days ago, 'impatient' was not a word that anyone would have used about the laborious tedium that life had become to him.

'Does the name "Morag Kitchener" mean anything to you?' Brad asked.

In mock despair, Josh held his head in his hands. 'She's been up to her tricks again!'

'Morag phoned me a week ago. It was the middle of the night in the States, but she wasn't to know that. Superficially, she appeared to be very composed, but I could tell from her voice that she was in deep distress. She explained how ill you were – that you had an aggressive brain tumour that was impacting upon your senses and said that she knew that I was a neuro-surgeon. She asked whether I could come over to Scotland and try to operate on the tumour. She actually said that she could pay for my services if this wasn't possible under NHS Scotland.'

'She said that!' A lump rose in Josh's throat that made further speech impossible. He thought of Morag's small, neat cottage and the derisory income that she and her husband earned. But she was willing to spend all she had on risking an impossible operation to save his life. He had always known her to be faithful, but this was above and beyond generous.

'Well,' continued Brad, 'I felt that we had formed the start of a promising friendship when you were in the States, and I wanted to see for myself what the situation with you actually was, so I booked my flights and arrived on the island whose name should be changed …'

'Fragrey.'

'Yep … on the evening of the day you and that beautiful woman of yours were air-lifted to Edinburgh. The entire island population had, apparently, been outside most of the day, watching for the return of the boat used in the kids' pageant, or the one belonging to that tall, striking woman, Agnes, who calls herself the wisewoman of your island. Morag told me that it was only on the morning of the following day that your daughter, Doctor Molly, had telephoned for the air ambulance – when you had all returned from the 'holy island'. Everyone was puzzled as to why so much time had passed before she did this.'

'You wouldn't believe me if I told you, Brad!' Josh laughed.

'Alex has explained and, quite frankly, Josh, I thought I had walked into some sort of fantasy world!'

'I'm not surprised to hear that, Brad, and as one scientist to another, I felt the same, until …'

'Until I saw the CT scan of your brain, Josh, which shows no sign whatsoever of a tumour – malignant or otherwise. If I hadn't seen the original scans Jenner took, I would have thought the entire thing a fabrication. But I did see them, and quite honestly if I had been asked to operate on that tumour, I would have refused. I could have done nothing.'

'And Alex?'

'The scan showed the point of entry of the nail at the temple and it had stopped only millimetres from her brain. Blood loss was considerable but she refused a transfusion and seems back to what I would consider a healthy normal right now.'

'"A healthy normal" – sounds good!' Alex stood in the doorway of Josh's room, smiling, serene and almost more beautiful than Josh had ever seen her.

'My own love,' he murmured gently, crossing the small room in two strides to take her in his arms.

'Mm, seems like I'm no longer needed here!' Brad Jackson smiled.

'Maybe not here, Brad, right at this moment. But please come back with us to Fragrey. Did you ever meet Morag?'

'No, Alex. My PA booked me into *The Inn* – they really ought to rename that place too, with some advice from a PR company! I left the next morning for Edinburgh.'

'Come back to the island with us, Brad. There are so many people we would like you to meet.'

'OK. I'm due an extended vacation. I will do exactly that.'

Chapter 62

Jenna, Chieftain of the Clan MacLeod
Requests the pleasure of your company to a
Celebration of the recovery to full health of
Doctor Josh MacDonald and
Alex Miller
The Manor House, 7.00pm,
Friday 4th September.

As soon as they stepped through the door of the cottage on the quayside, Josh and Alex saw the elegant invitation card, bordered in the green of the MacLeod tartan and surmounted by the well-known motto of the Clan: *Hold Fast*.

'This is so kind, Josh! We must go – of course.'

Josh said nothing. He just stood back and looked at Alex as if she were the fairest thing that had ever been created.

'Do I have coffee on my nose? Or a bee in my hair?'

'Don't be daft. I was thinking of how my life was fading away, Alex. Sometimes I would look at you, and it would be as if you were on a distant island. Touching you, loving you, became at the end the only real things in my half-life. It was hell on earth, Alex.'

'I know, my love. I know. But it is past now. And you can show me all the sexual excesses that your Twitter followers suggested – who were they again? Pash n'Presh, Sylken Sybarite, Violet Monkey …'

'But none would have dreamed what we are going to discover together, my darling.'

Alex held him, for just seconds, at arms' length, before saying, 'I know.'

⊰≫‖≪⊱

'I could develop a palate for your draft beer,' Brad mused.

'Well, let's hope you stay long enough to do exactly that, my friend.' Josh smiled into his whisky tumbler. 'And then we can introduce you to the subtleties of single malt!'

'Josh, Alex – how very good to see you both!' Jenna almost ran across the snug of *The Inn* for once, her poise and reserve forgotten. She embraced each – lightly, but with feeling, before apologising to Brad. 'I'm so sorry! I'm Jenna MacLeod, Clan chieftain, Chair of Governors …'

'And one of the most beautiful women I've ever met. Enchanté!'

Blushing deeply, Jenna asked, 'And you are?'

Josh answered for his friend, 'Professor Brad Jackson, senior clinician at one of New York's leading hospitals and one of the world's leading neuro-surgeons.'

'And, despite the glowing introduction, nothing special, as you can see,' laughed Brad, self-deprecatingly. 'Will you join us?'

'I would be delighted to.'

With genuine pleasure, Jenna stretched out her hands to Alex and Josh. 'No words can express my joy at your recovery. You will come to the evening in your honour?'

'Of course,' Alex smiled. 'We wouldn't miss it for anything! It's such a generous idea, Jenna.'

'It's the very least I can do. I feel … ah well, no matter. Now is not the time, nor the place, to dilate upon my personal feelings. Er, Professor Jackson, you are, of course, invited to the evening celebration. Will you be able to attend?'

'As they say in my outspoken country – try to keep me away!'

⚜

The next morning, Alex, Molly and Josh sat at the tiny table in the flagged courtyard of the cottage, crowded with pots of herbs and red geraniums, which Josh glorified with the name of his 'back garden.'

'You're quiet, Molly,' said Josh.

'I've been thinking, Dad.'

'Always a dangerous habit!'

'I need to return to the mainland, or at least to move on. You have no further need of me, Dad. You possibly look fitter than I have ever seen you, and I need to get a proper job.'

Josh and Alex glanced at each other. 'Funny you should raise that subject, Molly, but Alex and I were discussing the future last night. Would you consider staying here and becoming my partner? I would be genuinely honoured if you would. You have all the qualities that I would shortlist in a colleague and I need to take up my peripatetic responsibilities again, wandering across the Western Islands …'

'Bit like a Scottish Odysseus …'

'Behave, Alex. Would you join me, Molly? Would a partnership be a 'proper' enough job?'

Molly MacDonald leapt up, jolting the table so that coffee and croissant crumbs mingled into a soggy layer. 'Would I, Dad? I would love to!'

Laughing as he gave her a bear hug, Josh said, 'Right, better get Morag onto the signage people: "Doctor Josh and Doctor Molly MacDonald" – it sounds good.'

Looking frighteningly like her father, Molly's gaze narrowed thoughtfully. 'I can't stay here, though. I love the cottage, but it's just too snug!'

'Well, funny you should say that, but Alex and I have discussed that too.'

'Is there anything that you and Alex *don't discuss,* Dad?'

Looking at Alex with a gaze more eloquent than any words, Josh said simply, 'No.'

'And what was the outcome of your discussions?'

'That we will look for a new home and let you make this your own.'

'Really? Why? That is just too generous!'

'Several reasons.'

'Are they secret, or will you share them with me?'

'Don't be daft, of course they're not secret. First of all, Alex's divorce has come through and we may get married …'

'Oh, that is such good news!'

'I said "may". Love is the important thing between two people, not marital status. Secondly, we would like to make a new home together – looking forward – rather than live in a home that holds shadows of the past for both of us, some joyful, some not so. And last of all, I want to thank you. For coming here when I needed help so badly and for excelling in your role as doctor, when you were under emotional pressure as my daughter. So, the cottage would be our thank you present.'

'Where will you live?'

'Well, that's the slight snag: at the moment we have no idea! We have considered Gladys, but she is a trifle small! But now that we have discussed it, we will start looking – provided you like the idea?'

'Of course I do, Dad. I love the idea. Thank you both. Thank you both very, very much!'

Chapter 63

'Morag, we have worked together now for – how long?'

'Fifteen years, doctor.'

'And most of that time I have joked and engaged in banter with you because the things that we have seen together have been some of the most serious imaginable, and it's been our way of dealing with the tragedies and the stresses of life in this medical practice.'

'Yes, Doctor MacDonald, you have, and it has made me look forward to every day I spend trying to make the practice run more smoothly and trying to support you the best I can.'

Josh firmly took both Morag's hands in his and looked levelly into her faded grey eyes. 'Well, Morag, I am completely serious now, when I say to you that I thank you from the bottom of my heart for your love and service and selflessness. I will never forget your kindness and sacrificial generosity in contacting Brad Jackson. Never!'

'But, doctor, I could do nothing else!'

Morag's homely features showed her emotions clearly: she was more than a little uncomfortable at Josh's outspoken gratitude and was keen to get away to start her meticulous reception and secretarial support for the practice. Josh quickly picked up on her embarrassment, shifting his ground. 'Morag, I wanted you to know that Doctor Molly will be joining the practice, and …'

'Oh, Josh! I am so pleased to hear that! So many patients like her, particularly the young female clients. You will be able to share the burden of your work with her. You won't get as tired any more. You and your Alex will be able to enjoy leisure time together. This is such good news!'

'Yes, all of the above, Morag. I think it is a perfect solution!'

'When does Doctor Molly start?'

'Right now, Morag!' Molly stood at the entrance, holding her shiny new bag and smiling broadly.

'Coffee, doctors?' Morag grinned.

'Black as hell and sweet as …'

'Welcome home, Doctor Molly. Welcome home, Josh.'

'Oh, one final thing, Morag.'

'Yes, doctor?'

'You have been promoted to practice manager. You will need to recruit a receptionist.'

'Thank you, Doctor MacDonald. I shall be pleased to do so.'

⊰║║⊱

Now that the Summer Term had ended, Alex was at a loose end. Ever since she had come to Fragrey to take up her duties as teacher-in-charge, she had had multiple issues on her mind: primarily Josh, her love for him and then his deteriorating health; the devastating visit of her daughter, Diana; the many-layered challenge posed by Jeanne O'Hara; and the mystical pull of the holy island of Haligrey. Now, apart from wondering where on earth she and Josh were going to live, there was nothing particularly pressing in her life.

She had decided that she would have a complete rest for two weeks, giving herself time to recuperate from her accident and taking plenty of fresh air and exercise. She would then spend the next two to three weeks planning the curriculum for the school, in which she really was now sole teacher-in-charge. Then the final ten to fourteen days, she would be in school working at setting up the classrooms for the new school year. Having given herself permission to rest completely for a time, she lost herself in walking – mainly with Bonnie, who had settled so well into her home with Rory and Catriona that she had put on several kilograms of weight – but sometimes by herself, exploring parts of the island that she had not had time to visit previously. She invariably left Gladys behind *The Inn,* as the vehicle was too conspicuous for Alex ever to be able to do anything incognito, and borrowed an ancient bike that Catriona Cameron had no use for any longer.

One August day, Alex was practicing Yoga in the place that had become as special to her as it was to Josh, in the lee of the *Sleeping Guardians.* She felt that with each session the harmony of her body and mind was being gradually restored, and she rejoiced in each graceful, mindful movement.

'May I join you?' Agnes had materialised silently next to her and Alex merely smiled and nodded.

The two women moved together, feeling as if their bodies were drinking in the beauty of the day and the ozone-laden sea air. When they had completed the final sequence of the sun salute, they lay still on the short turf, open to the soothing sounds and scents of the natural world which drifted to their senses. After a few minutes, Agnes sat up and crossed her legs.

'I'm leaving my croft, Alex. Why don't you and Josh live there?'

'Leaving, Agnes? Where are you going?'

'Haligrey.'

Alex sat silently for several minutes looking at the ageless beauty of her friend. She knew that Agnes' grey eyes saw things that she herself couldn't see; and that Agnes' mind perceived truths that most people could not perceive. But all she said was, 'Why Haligrey? How will you manage when the weather turns to Winter?'

Agnes focussed on the horizon. 'Do you remember that I told you about Hector MacDonald?'

'Of course.'

'I was in love with him – and I believe that he was in love with me. When he was lost in *Star of the Sea*, I didn't know how I was going to begin to face the rest of my life. And so I started to visit Haligrey. Rowing out over the last stretch of water that Hector had covered in his earthly life, I felt that I was in some sort of communion with him, even that I might see him again. Sometimes I went at dawn, sometimes at night. Seldom in the full heat of midday. And with each visit I felt increasingly that his presence was somehow inhabiting the island. His and Aelfric's. Many people would think me insane believing this. But you know the island. You feel its life and energy, Alex. You understand what the power there can achieve.

'I decided that I would visit at Samhain, when the veil between the world that we see and the world of the spirit is torn away and the two become one. I hoped and believed that I would be able to see and talk to Hector again on this precious day when unnecessary barriers are removed. And I did.'

'You did, Agnes? You sound so matter of fact!'

'It *is* a matter of fact, Alex. I lit a fire to celebrate the coming together of the worlds of the living and the dead, and I sat facing Fragrey, wrapped in a shawl against the cold. As the flames danced higher and sparks flew into the night sky, I saw a scattering of other fires across the islands, all dancing and celebrating the timelessness of our existence, and then, when I refocused on the sparking logs in front of me, I saw that the darkness had clotted, become thick and was shaping itself into the form of a man. Hector walked through the fire and stood before me, as beautiful and real as he had been the last time I saw him.'

Alex said nothing. She watched the changing expressions, of loss, of doubt and finally of joy which passed over the face of the woman sitting by her side.

'After that first time, have you seen him again, Agnes.'

'I see him every time I cross to the island, Alex. And that is why I need to go there. The little dwelling of Aelfric is sufficient for me.'

'And Aelfric? You say you see him sometimes too.'

'I do. He is the gentlest and most wise of men. Often he just listens, sometimes he shares stories from his own life on earth. He told me about the book that he had written and buried, and which you discovered. I suggested that I should unearth it and try to learn from his writings, but he was adamant that it should be left undisturbed, presumably for you and Josh to find.'

'And so you are going to live with ghosts, Agnes?'

'On the contrary, my lovely friend, I am going to live with two of the most interesting men I have ever encountered.'

Chapter 64

'Just how am I going to start to impress the Lady Chieftain, Josh?' Brad Jackson swirled his single malt around the tumbler.

'Just be yourself, Brad, and for goodness sake, don't call her that within her hearing. She is fairly and squarely *Chieftain* of the Clan MacLeod. You don't need to set out to impress Jenna: you are a man of standing and integrity and you are kind and true to your word.'

'How about physically, Josh? You can't pretend that my two hundred and twenty pounds of relaxed muscle come anywhere near your toned physique. Oh, and Parvati Patel did hint that you were as good in bed as in the operating theatre!'

'I'm surprised at that, Brad! I felt that I'd been down the Siberian salt mines for several decades after she'd finished with me!'

'I'm serious, Josh. Jenna MacLeod excites me. I've never married as you know and, at fifty- five, it's about time. She is graceful, lovely and intelligent. Why do women over fifty gain a further dimension of attractiveness?'

'In Eastern cultures, post-menopausal women enter what is called the 'Temptress' phase. No longer concerned about pregnancy, emotionally and sexually experienced, and having found their true selves.'

'So you think I have a chance?'

'To be honest, Brad, I haven't a clue. Jenna is very reserved, almost always a closed book. See what happens on Friday.'

'Thank you for the advice, doctor. Another point: what the hell do I wear?'

'Now that *is* a complex subject, Brad! It's acceptable for you to wear a universal tartan if your family doesn't have one of its own – such as *Highland Granite, Flower of Scotland* or *Heritage of Scotland* and I bet I can guess which one you will go for!'

'*Flower of Scotland*, because...'

'You think Jenna is as beautiful as a flower? I thought all Americans are supposed to be hard-headed pragmatists, Brad.'

'Dangerous generalisation; it's as bad as saying that all Scottish people are red-headed patriots!'

'Touché! But if you do decide to wear the kilt, you will not find *Flower of Scotland* outside Edinburgh, to be found in one of the shops that cater for all things tartan!'

'I have time. I'll take a flight over there tomorrow. Jenna confided in me about the fraud suffered by your little school here and I can help. Only the other day my Mom said to me, '"Bradley Jackson, it is high time that you found yourself a wife and started to have some pleasure in your life as well as work. I would like to see that before I move on." As I have said to you before, my friend, Mom is always right. Those bank accounts, the money set aside for health care and for my old age, what use are they, Joshua? When I see you and your beautiful, brave Alex together, all I see is love in the moment, and belief that tomorrow will take care of itself. I intend to do my best to marry Jenna and I will come back to this strange island of magic, to make those investments work for the children who are alive now and suffering because their school doesn't have the resources for their learning.'

Chapter 65

As Alex stepped over the stone threshold of the Manor House the following Friday, she was reminded overwhelmingly of the last time she had done so: for the May Ball. How much had happened, and how much had changed since then! In May she was hyper-aware of Josh, but had not fallen in love with him; and above all she was desperately unsure of how he felt about her. The terrible disease that had almost taken Josh's life had not yet been diagnosed and the endless weeks of torment, watching him fade before her eyes, had yet to come. Diana, and the chaos which followed in her wake, had not at that time arrived on the island. In May she had been a married woman, but to her joy, she was so no longer. Looking at the worn stone steps, the flagstones of the entrance hall and the weather-pitted arch over the door, Alex reflected on the changes that the Manor House had seen in its history, then her mind moved on to the vast and seismic changes that the island had seen since its creation. As she entered the spacious reception hall, centred by the reassuring warmth and strength of her man's arm linked through her own, Alex thought of the relentless flow of Time. Smiling at the crowded room and the rows of ancestral portraits on the walls, she reflected how the events that make up human life are played and re-played in slightly different formats: people are born, live, and die and the only thing that matters, that impacts upon the world, is the difference that each person makes, for good or for ill.

Looking to her right, at the clean lines of Josh's profile and the love dancing in his eyes, Alex thought of what he had given to Fragrey: a life of devoted service, working for the good of the community; and what he had given to her: joy beyond her imagining.

Josh, looking to his left, felt every atom of his being rejoice at the gentle and beautiful woman on his arm, her smile conveying to him a million unspoken words of love, faithfulness and fulfilment.

Whatever Jenna MacLeod did, she did with all her heart and, having decided to fête the man she loved and the woman she had hurt, every minute aspect of the evening had been planned down to the last detail. An archway of cream roses had been set up just inside the entrance door to the Manor House and, as Alex and Josh walked through it, a ripple of applause filled the reception hall, the staircase and the elegant room beyond. Once again, the event had become a whole-island celebration as patients, parents, crofters and fisherman crowded the space.

Jenna walked briskly up to the couple and embraced them both, with a hug longer and warmer than anyone had ever seen her give before. From the left, some of the youngest island children ran up to Alex with baskets of wild flowers and posies and placed them in their hands, blushing and giggling. Then, from the right, Morag walked steadily forward, carrying a shallow blue box. She stood in front of Josh, smiling with a wealth of feeling in her expression, whilst Jenna started to speak. 'As Clan chieftain and chatelaine of Fragrey it is my very pleasant duty, from time to time, to take the decision to grant the freedom of the island to one of its people. Tonight, I am utterly delighted to grant this privilege to Doctor Josh MacDonald, for his outstanding and selfless service to the community of Fragrey for nearly thirty years. Morag?'

Morag opened the blue box and took out a large, silver medallion on a heavy chain, engraved with a bass relief of the cliff-line of the island, the *Sleeping Guardians* prominent on the skyline. Unable to speak through sheer emotion, she reached up to place the chain over Josh's head.

'Josh, welcome as Freeman of Fragrey!' Jenna beamed to thunderous applause.

The quartet took up their instruments and started to play the first dance of the evening. It was the same group of musicians that had played in May, and Alex smiled into Josh's eyes as she recognised the music that had so moved her then, and moved her again now. Then she had felt that Robbie Burns' words mirrored her growing feelings for the beauty and rightness of the man who had now claimed her for his own and held her tightly in his arms:

> *'My love is like a red, red rose*
> *that's newly sprung in June,*
> *My love is like a melody*
> *that's sweetly played in tune.'*

But tonight, it was the second verse that spoke deeply to her. She softly sang the first two lines as Josh held her hard and they started to circle and turn to the music.

> *'Till all the seas run dry, my dear,*
> *And the rocks melt with the sun'*

Then Josh pulled her closer, and his voice mingled with hers as together they completed the words of the beautiful poem:

> *'And I will love thee still my dear,*
> *Whilst the sands of life shall run.'*

Epilogue

Extracts from *The Fragrey Gazette November 2018 – July 2019*

10*th* November 2018

The former Administrative Headteacher of Fragrey Independent Endowed School, Ms Jeanne O'Hara has been apprehended for fraud by the Metropolitan police. Bail has been granted to her and the former vicar of Heillstath Kirk, Michael Whitfield, until the hearing in the Magistrates' Court, expected to be in the New Year. It is thought that some, but not all, of the funds with which the pair absconded in June, have been recovered by the police.

1*st* May 2019

The marriage was celebrated between Alexandra Catherine Lawrence, formerly Miller, to Joshua Joseph MacDonald, in the Kirk, Heillstath.

The Wedding was conducted by the newly-appointed minister of the island. Dr Molly MacDonald was best woman, and Agnes Muirhead, matron of honour.

21st June 2019

The wedding of Lady Jenna Lucilla MacLeod, Clan chieftain, to Professor Bradley Morris Jackson took place under special licence at the Manor House, Heillstath. Doctor MacDonald held an unusual dual role, that of giving the bride away and acting as best man for the groom.

Professor Jackson will take up residence at the Manor House.

About the Author

Alex grew up in the North of England and because her father, who was a well-known jazz musician, inspired her to try anything that life threw in her path, she enjoyed an eclectic childhood, before heading off to University to study English. This philosophy has stayed with her always and is reflected in her novels, which are about ordinary people who face extraordinary situations and frequently pose the question 'What if?'

She now lives in the Yorkshire Dales with her loyal labradors and husband, who has the patience of a saint when it comes to her unconventional lifestyle. Before settling into life and full-time writing in her beloved Yorkshire, she enjoyed various careers in London, and high-profile positions in education in the west country.

Alex has two highly individual grown-up daughters, whose influence is threaded through much of her work. The inspiration for this book, *A Seeker of Everyday Magic*, was a memorable summer that she spent on an archaeological dig on the Outer Hebrides. The peace and purity of the land and the warmth of the people have stayed with her always.

Alex is passionate about exploring the beauty of the natural world and has been fortunate to be able to see many parts of it, inspiring her to regularly practise Tai Chi and Yoga with her like-minded friends.

If you have enjoyed *A Seeker of Everyday Magic,* why not try Alex's earlier books? *Saving Graces* and *The Child at the Edge of the World* are both available from Amazon and Waterstones. *The Carousel of Time,* her first book, is being substantially revised and will be re-published in October 2025.

Visit Alex's website to keep up to date with her life and events: www.alexcharltonbooks.com